FOR THE LADY OF LOWENA

FOR THE
LADY OF
LOWENA

A CORNISH ROMANCE, BOOK TWO

DEBORAH M. HATHAWAY

DRAFT HORSE
PUBLISHING

BOOKS BY DEBORAH M. HATHAWAY

A Cornish Romance Series

On the Shores of Tregalwen, a Prequel Novella

Behind the Light of Golowduyn, Book One

For the Lady of Lowena, Book Two

Near the Ruins of Penharrow, Book Three

In the Waves of Tristwick, Book Four (Pre-Order)

Book Five (Poppy Honeysett's Story), Coming Soon

Belles of Christmas Multi-Author Series

Nine Ladies Dancing, Book Four

On the Second Day of Christmas, Book Four

Seasons of Change Multi-Author Series

The Cottage by Coniston, Book Five

Sons of Somerset Multi-Author Series

Carving for Miss Coventry, Book One

Timeless Regency Collection

The Inns of Devonshire—The Coachman's Choice

For my dear friend,
Arlem Hawks.

Thank you for inspiring me
to be a better writer
and for being there for me every step of the way.

PRONUNCIATION GUIDE

Lowena – low-WHEN-uh
Fynwary – fin-WARE-ee
Gwynna – GWIN-uh
Golowduyn – goal-oh-DEW-in
Tregalwen – treh-GAWL-when
Rudhek – RUE-thek

CHAPTER ONE

ornwall, 1815

    Bright sunshine glinted across the turquoise sea like light on glass. The incoming tide battered the rocks that stood strong near the shoreline, but the rugged pillars remained unmoved. Above, herring gulls and sparrows cried their shrill songs, anxious to have their voices heard, though the ocean's roar didn't acknowledge them, nor did the wind sailing toward the land.

And yet, at the edge of the cliffside, sitting astride his chestnut horse, Mr. Frederick Hawkins did not miss a single sight or sound. His blue eyes swept across the sea as his senses hungrily took in his surroundings—the smell of the salty water and the sound of the wind whispering in his ear.

Can you feel it, Frederick? the wind seemed to say. *That is freedom.*

He drew in a deep breath. Hope swarmed his soul. He could already see the carefree days he would have, the moments of pleasure he was sure to find in Cornwall, all with the mighty sea as his backdrop.

This place…it was nothing like London. There were no towering, brick buildings in sight. No carriage-filled streets. No

glass windows boasting of expensive goods within shops—
goods ladies and their mothers were so anxious to purchase.

No, this wasn't like London.

And he was certainly relieved because of it.

He clicked his tongue and urged his horse forward. "Let us
move farther down. I have an inkling you might fancy a run
on the beach as much as I do."

The horse nickered in response, the wind ruffling his
mane.

They moved toward the beach and the soothing movement of the water. It had been a long while since he'd seen the
sea. A year, to be exact. Last time, his visit had only lasted a
single day.

Now he wasn't visiting. He was staying. He had purchased
an estate and would remain in Cornwall for the foreseeable
future. Longer, if he had the fortune of seeing this view
every day.

Of course, Mother had not understood his desire to be
near the sea, nor to purchase a second home, particularly in
Cornwall.

"You are already so busy with Dawnridge, Freddy," she'd
said, referring to the family estate in Bedfordshire. "You
hardly ever visit me in London any longer, so when will you
find a spare moment for your poor mother when you have *two*
estates to run?"

"I will manage fine, Mother," he'd responded. "And you
could always come to Cornwall if you wish to see more
of me."

She'd muttered some excuse then rapidly changed the
subject. Unlike Frederick, she did not enjoy the idea of living
in seclusion and peace, away from the noise and bustle of
London. In truth, he'd chosen Cornwall for that very reason,
because Mother would "never step foot in such an isolated
county."

He loved her, of course. But every so often, a son needed

time away, distance. Enough space to think for himself and make his own decisions without his mother breathing her own wishes into his ear.

Frederick rolled his neck to dispel the tension rising up his shoulders. He didn't travel over three hundred miles to have Mother's very-opiniated desires *still* give him a headache. In fact, he'd come to Cornwall for a very different reason. And after he signed for his new estate, he would set out to accomplish his next task. The task of finding a wife.

Not any female would do. After all, Mother had thrust him into the arms of many a fine woman, both in Bedfordshire and London. He didn't want to marry just a "fine" woman who cared more about her clothing than the thoughts and feelings of others. He was looking for someone different, someone real. A woman who was not afraid to be herself, especially with Society watching her. A woman who was brave enough to take her boots off and feel the sand in her toes and the wind in her hair.

A woman...quite like that one.

His head tilted to the side, his lips curving as he eyed the woman on the beach nearby. She lay on a purple blanket stretched out across the sand. Only her skirts were visible—a parasol blocking his view of her torso up—but her bare feet basked in the sunshine. Her stockings and footwear rested at the edge of the blanket nearby.

Was she asleep? She had to be. Otherwise she would be more bothered about the water inching closer and closer to her heels poking off the edge of her blanket.

He glanced beyond her to the far end of the sand. The beach was only accessible from his side, due to steep cliffs on the other. The waves had already reached the small formation of rocks that separated him from the woman. If she didn't move soon, the path would be completely taken by the waves.

There was nothing for it. He would have to wake her, if only to warn her of the potential danger approaching.

He rode down the rest of the sloping pathway to the beach before dismounting and looping his horse's reins around a thin rock. Then he headed toward the woman, crossing over the rocks and sand.

As he approached, he regarded her, curious. She lay on her back with an unopened book on her stomach. One bare hand rested on the book while the other stretched out beside her, holding two blue gloves.

Her bonnet was placed at her side, the ribbon wrapped securely around her wrist, and the handle of her dark blue parasol was stuck deep into the sand. The fringe along the edges fluttered in the light breeze.

The woman had intended to sleep, as was evident by the precautions she had taken to not have her belongings blow away with the wind. With her footwear removed, she appeared to be very much at her leisure.

He hesitated to wake her, not wishing to disturb her obvious slumber. As the next wave reached the tip of her blanket, however, turning it a shade darker, he knew he could not prolong the inevitable.

"Miss?" She didn't budge. He spoke louder. "Excuse me, miss?"

Her body twitched. Then a gasp sounded from beneath the parasol, and she sat up right, bumping her head against the shade. "Oh!"

He fought off an amused grin. "My apologies, miss."

Still seated, she pressed dainty fingers against her brow and turned toward him in surprise. His heart tripped. She was even prettier than he'd imagined. Smooth black ringlets decorated her temples and enhanced her light, flawless skin. She squinted as she looked up at him, preventing him from noting the color of her eyes framed with thick, dark lashes.

She gasped again, this time scrambling to her feet. The soft blush on her cheeks matched the color of her parted lips.

She was beautiful, the kind of woman that gentlemen

enjoyed discussing over port around the dinner table. But in his experience, if a woman was this beautiful, she was guaranteed to be trouble.

He hadn't come to Cornwall looking for trouble. He'd come for peace and quiet. And, of course, a wife untouched by London.

He took a step away from her, his voice level despite the sudden wariness coming over him. "Forgive me for startling you, miss. I would have left you undisturbed, but the tide is coming in." He motioned to the water lapping at her blanket.

"Oh dear," she murmured, tugging the blanket out of the waves' reach before facing him again. "I must thank you, sir. My mother would have been terribly displeased to see me returning home with wet skirts again."

Her voice was smooth, like a soft breeze blowing through tall grass, and her smile, charming. Too charming. Why was he staring long enough to even *know* it was too charming?

He looked behind him to the rocks. A wave splashed high into the air, spraying water farther up the sand. "I'm afraid you may be celebrating prematurely. I suspect you may not be able to leave the beach without coming into contact with a few waves first."

"Goodness." The worry in her tone brought his eyes back to her. Her lips pulled to one side. "I suppose I deserve a bit of scolding. I should not have fallen asleep in such a silly place."

She appeared genuinely distressed. But what could he do without involving himself in ways he was not sure he wished to? "I would offer you the service of my horse, but he would not cross safely over the rocks."

"Oh, no, I wouldn't wish for you to risk his well-being for my sake. After all, what is a man without his horse?" Her eyes twinkled. They were blue. Light blue. "No, I will be brave and endure another lecture. But thank you again, sir, for preventing me from becoming stranded here altogether."

She picked up her belongings from the blanket. Frederick

chewed the inside of his cheek. He had been taught from a very young age to do anything he could to help a woman in distress. Even if that meant going against his better judgment and helping in ways he knew, somehow, would lead to trouble.

Was she trouble though? The women he'd known in London had not hesitated to use their feminine charms to trick gentlemen—himself included—into doing their every bidding. But he was in Cornwall, not London. Women had to be different here.

He pushed aside his reservations and took a step toward her. "Why do I not bring your belongings across the rocks for you first? Then I will return and carry you across myself. That way your mother will have no knowledge of your time of leisure on the beach."

CHAPTER TWO

rederick's heart hastened as a smile lit the woman's face. Why was he having such a reaction to her? He'd seen beautiful women before. Of course, no one with such lovely eyes and dark hair.

"Oh, would you?" she asked. "I would forever be in your debt."

He picked up her blanket and shook it free of sand. "It is no trouble, I assure you."

He draped the blanket over his arm and retrieved the rest of her items from her hands—book, gloves, parasol, and boots. Where had her stockings gone? He gave his head a little shake. He didn't need to know that.

When his arms were full, he took a step back. "I'll return in just a moment."

He climbed over the rocks, careful not to stumble with her eyes upon him, then deposited her belongings near his horse and returned to her side.

"Shall we?" he asked, watching the imminent waves draw closer. He didn't need to look at the woman to remind him how attractive she was.

"Yes, sir."

He closed the distance between them in two steps and deftly scooped her up from the sand. She let out a soft squeak, sliding her arms around his neck. Her bonnet, the ribbons still looped round her wrist, rested against his back.

This would be a rather easy rescue. She was even lighter than he'd expected. Though he could do without her arms cutting off his breathing.

He cleared his throat. "When you are settled, would you mind loosening your grip around my neck?"

"Oh, I'm terribly sorry." She relaxed her hold of him. "Will that do?"

He nodded. "Yes, thank…you."

Blast. He'd looked at her again, and now he was far closer to her than before. With their eyes level, he could see the blue more distinctly. Blue, like the clear, shallow water of the sea in the morning light.

"Are you comfortable?" His voice broke. Was he fourteen years old instead of his four and twenty?

She nodded. "Very comfortable, sir. Thank you."

Finally, he tore his gaze away, securing his arms around her once more, his right arm holding her legs and his left encircling her back, then he ventured forth. He walked as smoothly as possible, though even her slight weight made him sink deeper into the wet sand. His gait slowed and her bonnet tapped against his back with each step.

He needed to think of something else to say before he stole another glance at her. Knowing his foolishness, he'd probably fall if he got lost in her eyes again.

"I should have introduced myself earlier," he said. "Mr. Frederick Hawkins, at your service. I do hope you will forgive me for not bowing, as it would be a shame to drop you."

"That it would be," she returned. "I am quite pleased to make your acquaintance, sir, and not only because of your rescuing me. I should like to tell you my own name, as well,

8

but I hardly think it proper, under the circumstances. We ought to wait for another to introduce the two of us."

Was she in earnest? Frederick stared at her profile, the slightest curve to the tip of her nose, the corners of her eyes creased. So she *was* teasing. "My apologies, miss. I should not have divulged my own name then. However, in my defense, I thought we had already dispensed with propriety. After all, I am carrying you across the beach rather intimately without another person or boot"—with a toss of his head, he motioned to her bare feet poking out from the end of her skirts—"in sight."

He saw her smile from the corner of his eye. "I was hoping you had not noticed the irony," she said, "but I see you are too observant, sir. Observant and rather strong. Tell me, do you often rescue women in such a way as this?"

Her voice was light, lilting. It was a tone he'd heard in London before. Heaven help him, but her words were actually proving to capture him.

"Not women," he answered. "But dogs, yes. Some of my hounds have an unnatural fear of water and require me to carry them across rivers, which is decidedly unhelpful during a fox hunt."

Her laughter rang out, reminding him of church bells chiming forth in celebration. He wouldn't mind hearing it again.

"I certainly prefer carrying *you*, though," he continued, "as you whine—and wiggle—far less."

"How relieved I am to hear I am easier to manage than a hound."

His eyes met hers. He could feel himself slipping. Not his footing, but his strength to keep away from this intriguing woman.

He reached the rocks, but rather than risking dropping the woman on the slick, jagged ends, he moved around to where the edges trailed out into the deeper waves. With the water mid-calf, he stepped carefully to avoid any splashes upon the lady's dress.

A wave rushed in, pulling the sand from beneath his boots, but he remained steady. "May I ask you a question, miss?"

"Of course, Mr. Hawkins."

"Did you come out here with the intention to read or to sleep?"

Her eyes jumped to his. She seemed to search for an answer before responding. "You are far too observant for your own good, sir. I'm afraid you have caught me out again. The book, I admit, was a guise so my mother would allow me to go out of doors. Reading in general proves very dull for me, but *The Female Instructor* is by far the worst thing I have ever read. I only allow Mother to believe that I appreciate the horrendous words so I am allowed a moment away from stitching or practicing that dreadful pianoforte."

She stopped with a deep sigh before her eyes widened.

Frederick stared in surprise. Most ladies flaunted their talents, never daring to admit they disliked popular pastimes, for fear of being seen as unaccomplished. This woman had simply blurted her confession without hesitation. How refreshing. Though, the blush gracing her cheeks revealed her discomfiture over her confession.

He ought to speak again to ease her embarrassment. "So your mother. She allows you to read on the beach so long as she believes you are reading material that will prove to better yourself?"

She brought her bottom lip between her teeth before speaking. "Well, in actuality, she still believes me to be reading in the gardens."

"Ah, so that is why you must return home with dry skirts."

"Precisely."

"And do you do this often, nap on the beach?"

"As often as I can, but only ever when my parents are occupied with other matters. If it were my choice, I would be out here every day. I far prefer spending my leisure time here on the sand."

"Especially when your other option is to play the *dreadful* pianoforte."

She pulled her lips together in an attempt to hide her smile, but her eyes were as bright as the sunshine above them.

They reached the dry sand on the other side of the rocks, but Frederick continued carrying her. "So why do you prefer napping here, instead of in your gardens, perhaps under the shade of a tree, or near a bed of flowers?"

Her arms were draped loosely around his shoulders now. "Napping outside is always enjoyable, to be sure. And those *would* be fine spots in which to rest. But I have yet to discover anywhere as peaceful as the beach with its soothing waves, warm sand, and cool breeze."

She closed her eyes and craned her neck, the sun gracing her cheeks. The scent of roses wafted toward him as she moved. She was far too appealing for her own good. And *his* own good.

When they reached his horse, Frederick finally lowered the woman's feet down into the warm sand.

She smoothed down her skirts. "Well, thank you, Mr. Hawkins. I really could not abide another lecture from Mother. I do not know how I can ever repay you."

He picked up her belongings and helped balance them in her arms. "If you are looking for a way to settle the debt, I would not be opposed to you sharing your name with me."

Her eyes sparkled as she took a step back. "One day I will, sir, as I have a feeling this will not be the last time we will see one another."

"How can you know such a thing, miss?"

She continued to walk backwards, her skirts flapping softly against her legs in the wind. "Because you seem to be just the type of gentleman who always finds a woman in distress."

"Are you in distress?" he asked, raising his voice above the waves as she moved farther away.

"No, sir. But if ever I am, I'm certain you will find me." She took another step, but her foot caught in the sand. She stumbled back a few paces. Frederick moved forward to help her, but she managed to right herself without falling.

"Perhaps I will be in distress sooner than either of us realize," she said with a laugh.

He grinned in response.

With a small curtsy, the woman turned and walked away. Her boots in her hand swung from side to side, the stockings poking out from the tops of them.

As he untied and mounted his horse, Frederick's attention continually wavered toward the woman until she disappeared from his view.

He turned back to the spot on the beach where he'd first found her asleep. The waves' long arms had already swept over the sand, and the water sparkled blue, like the woman's eyes.

His lip twitched. He had a good feeling about Cornwall. A very good feeling, indeed.

CHAPTER THREE

"*M*iss Rosewall, what a treasure you are."

"Indeed. The brightest treasure of all!"

Sophia Rosewall lowered her eyes to feign embarrassment. "Oh, gentlemen, you certainly do know how to make a woman blush."

She smiled coyly. As Mother said, feigning modesty was always becoming. Though, remaining humble was difficult when two gentlemen such as these fawned over Sophia, even *with* rehearsed praises. Dinner had not even begun, and they'd already started to thickly coat her with their sweetness.

She was deserving of their attention, though, for how she looked that evening. Every dark lock of her hair was curled to perfection, not a single wrinkle blemished the blue silk of her gown, and her white gloves were pristine, free of any catches in the fabric. She looked just as she should as the daughter of the wealthy host and hostess of that evening's dinner party at Fynwary Hall. No wonder the gentlemen couldn't keep their eyes off of her.

She fluttered the fan beneath her chin, her ringlets dancing about her temples in a way Mother always said looked appealing, though it tickled Sophia's skin mercilessly.

"Honestly, gentlemen," she continued, "you must cease your delightful compliments, or I shall swoon. Or you must at least direct them elsewhere for a time so I may cool my cheeks."

"I shall never stop then," Mr. Singleton said. He was the taller of the two gentlemen standing at either side of her. He possessed a head full of thick hair darker than even hers. "I enjoy that pretty pink on your cheeks far too greatly to see it fade away so soon."

"I won't stop either," Mr. Chester piped in, nearly eye-level with Sophia, "for I would like to catch you, should you swoon."

She placed a hand on both his and Mr. Singleton's arms. "Then I will continue blushing and swooning so both of your wishes shall be granted. Mr. Singleton, you may admire my rosy cheeks, and Mr. Chester, you may catch me as I swoon."

Sophia responded to their laughter with a look of amusement. She'd first met the two friends a few months ago in London, before the gentlemen had come to visit Mr. Singleton's poorly grandmother in St. Just. They were handsome and agreeable, and she enjoyed their doting as much as the next woman, though she didn't consider either of them serious suitors. Mother, on the other hand, did.

Sophia glanced across the room to where her mother watched her with an approving smile, rubies glinting at her throat. Mother obviously hoped for one of these gentlemen to be Sophia's future husband, but without love, Sophia could not be convinced. Fortunately, her parents and their wealth would allow her to make her own decision of whom to marry. And she would marry for love, just as her mother and father had.

Father. Where was he? Sophia looked about the room, but he was nowhere in sight. Come to think of it, she hadn't seen him at all that day.

Before she could deliberate his whereabouts, Mr. Singleton's voice drew her attention back to her admirers.

"Do tell us, Miss Rosewall, what form of entertainment we shall be blessed to have this evening."

"Surely dancing," Mr. Chester said in his unusually high voice.

Mr. Singleton waved a hand in the air. "Dancing is fine enough, but we can do that at any ball. I should like to hear Miss Rosewall pleasure us with her talent at the pianoforte."

"Oh, yes, Singleton." Mr. Chester nodded, pushing out his chest to appear larger than he was, standing next to his friend. "Or perhaps we could hear her recite a lovely poem?"

Sophia bit back a groan and placed another modest smile on her lips. "I would love to do both, gentlemen, but I certainly cannot do everything in one evening."

"Oh, surely you *can* do everything, Miss Rosewall."

"Yes, surely."

Sophia let out a hollow laugh. This was what she had been dreading. She'd begged Mother to forgo a performance from Sophia that evening, whether at the pianoforte or reading aloud, but Mother had been hesitant. She enjoyed basking in Sophia's accomplishments. Sophia typically reveled in the attention, as well, but having to perform talents she despised was always unbearable.

Her parents would hardly appreciate her admitting to such a thing, though, and she couldn't risk the censorious looks and rejection she would receive from the rest of Society. If her mother expected her to perform, then she would do her duty, no matter how exhausting it may be.

"Your playing, Miss Rosewall, is simply divine," Mr. Singleton continued.

"Truly, a talent that was given to you straight from Heaven," Mr. Chester agreed. "I will surely push to hear a performance of any type."

Sophia nearly winced. "Really, gentlemen, you are both too kind."

They *were* kind, and courteous, and attentive. But with her spirits rapidly deflating, she wished she could be anywhere but in that drawing room. The beach, perhaps. Where she could be free for a moment to walk barefooted across the sand, to feel the wind in her hair. To happen upon Mr. Hawkins again.

Mr. Hawkins.

The very name made her lips beg to release their smile. She knew she ought to be concentrating on Mr. Singleton and Mr. Chester, but as they argued about who valued her pianoforte playing better, she allowed her mind to wander to the stranger's gallant rescue of her that morning.

Of course, it was more of a service than a rescue, as she was perfectly capable of climbing over the rocks herself. His offer to carry her had been so generous, she could hardly deny his help.

She warmed at the memory of his arms around her. He'd held her with such care, and he had not seemed to mind a drop about her state of undress. Perhaps that was why she had not hesitated to speak so candidly with him. That, and she was already at ease, due to the absence of her parents and the rest of Society.

Her cheeks warmed as she recalled what she'd shared with him, her dislike of pastimes that women were expected to enjoy. Mother always said if a lady could not improve her imperfections, then she must hide them, for a gentleman sought excellence in his future wife.

Yet, at Sophia's admission, Mr. Hawkins had appeared rather pleased, his eyes shining brightly. Those warm, blue eyes. They were quite like the color of her parasol she had bumped into when he'd awoken her.

"Miss Rosewall?"

Torn from her reverie, Sophia blinked. "Yes, Mr. Chester?"

"I asked what form of entertainment you might prefer this evening."

"Oh, I could do with a little dancing, I think." Dancing, gaming, watching a candle slowly burn—anything would do compared to playing that wretched instrument.

Mr. Chester beamed. His brown hair stood in rigid curls, not a strand out of place. "If we do dance, you must remember that you have promised a first with me, since you were occupied for every single dance this last assembly."

Mr. Singleton chortled. "Our Miss Rosewall is always in high demand."

Sophia's mood improved at the thought of having saved herself from another performance. She made to voice another modest protest of the gentleman's words but paused when she caught sight of the only other single woman in attendance at the party that evening, Miss Claire Kinsey.

Miss Kinsey, who was visiting her aunt and uncle for the summer in Cornwall, stood with her eyes fixed on the ground, her hands clasped in front of her. She hovered behind her aunt, Mrs. Maddern, and didn't say a word, nor had she all evening.

Sophia had an inkling that Miss Kinsey was sent to live with the Madderns so she might find a husband. She wasn't unattractive by any means, but her painfully shy behavior was sure to be the reason gentlemen flocked away from her, and toward Sophia.

Some women did not have the fortune of being brought up by parents who instructed them in the ways of captive conversation. As Sophia had, it was her duty to include Miss Kinsey whenever possible.

"Well, gentlemen," Sophia began, her eyes centered on the girl across the room, "you mustn't despair if one of you does not receive the opportunity to dance with me as your partner, for there is another amiable woman here who shall save you." She motioned across the room, and the gentlemen turned in unison. "Miss Kinsey, do join us."

Miss Kinsey's eyes moved warily to her aunt's before she walked toward Sophia. Her shoulders slumped forward, like she was trying to retreat into a nonexistent shell.

"We were just discussing what a pleasure it would be to dance this evening," Sophia said. "What say you?"

Miss Kinsey's eyes rounded. "Oh, I am not a very fine dancer, I'm afraid."

"Nonsense," Mr. Singleton said, with an amused glance at Mr. Chester, "I'm sure you are a wonderful dancer."

Miss Kinsey shook her head without looking at him.

Mr. Chester nodded. "Yes, indeed. However, as much as I look forward to dancing with you, Miss Kinsey, I must dance the first with Miss Rosewall."

"Then I shall dance the first with Miss Kinsey and the *last* with Miss Rosewall," Mr. Singleton countered.

Mr. Chester furrowed his brow. "Oh, would you not consider swapping, Singleton?"

"No, I would not."

Sophia listened to their back-and-forth with delight. She turned to Miss Kinsey. "Honestly, these gentlemen are quite absurd. I cannot understand them."

Miss Kinsey didn't return her smile. What was the matter with the girl? If she couldn't manage a simple conversation with a *female*, however would she marry?

Sophia straightened her shoulders. The girl's insipid behavior was none of her concern, and Sophia would not allow her to put a damper on the dinner party.

"Now, Singleton, see here," Mr. Chester said, "Miss Rosewall promised me a dance, so I ought to decide when to receive it."

Mr. Singleton smirked. "Yes, but you already decided to have the first."

Sophia glanced between them, settling on Mr. Chester's

reddened face. She would need to end their mostly good-natured argument before it turned into actual animosity.

"Gentlemen, please," she began, "there is a simple way to solve this, of course."

The door opened, and her words ended as she fixated on her father entering the drawing room. There he was. She narrowed her eyes at his dipped chin, his stance missing its usual air of confidence.

"Do go on, Miss Rosewall."

"Yes, you would not be so unkind as to have us wait a moment longer to hear your solution."

She looked again to the gentlemen. "Oh, yes. You see, all we must do is see who is…"

Sophia's attention pulled away again as Mr. Page, the butler, entered the room next. He held his back far straighter than Father had. What was he doing, announcing another guest? She glanced around the room. Now that Father had arrived, all were present.

She didn't have to wait long before the butler's voice carried throughout the room. "Mr. Frederick Hawkins."

CHAPTER FOUR

*S*hock struck Sophia's limbs. Mr. Hawkins? At Fynwary Hall?

She faced the doorway just as the gentleman—the very one who had carried her across the approaching tide, who had brought her to safety, who had yet to flee from her thoughts— stood in her drawing room.

With a growing smile, she observed his features. Strong jaw, masculine lips, a brow that expressed friendliness. His hair was fairer than she remembered, though it held dark undertones. Typically she preferred darker locks like Mr. Singleton's. But Mr. Hawkins might be just the gentleman to persuade her otherwise.

"Miss Rosewall, did you hear us? Since you have kept your plan to yourself, Mr. Chester and I have come to an agreement."

Sophia nodded, though Mr. Singleton's words hardly registered.

"Mr. Chester shall dance the last with you tonight, and I—"

"Excellent," she interrupted, backing away from the

group. "So happy you have resolved the issue. Do excuse me for a moment."

She left without another thought, gliding across the room toward Mr. Hawkins. He still stood near the doorway, speaking with Father. Did they know each other?

Any guess she might have given to her own question vanished as Mr. Hawkins finally glanced at her. He looked away without hesitation, but when his eyes flew back to hers, surprise swiftly gave way to pleasure.

Sophia had received that same look of admiration from many a gentleman, but she'd never been so affected as when Mr. Hawkins watched her. Her heart felt lighter than a muslin skirt blowing in a soft breeze.

Perhaps it was the difference in his stare. Most men tended to scale her from head to toe. But Mr. Hawkins's blue eyes had yet to waver from her own.

"Sophia," Father greeted as she stopped before them. "Allow me to introduce you to my…my new business acquaintance." Sophia would have stared at him for his uncharacteristic stumbling over words, had she not been so taken with the gentleman beside him. "This is Mr. Hawkins. Mr. Hawkins, my lovely daughter, Miss Sophia Rosewall."

She bobbed a quick curtsy, anxious to begin their official acquaintance.

Mr. Hawkins lowered his brow. "Your daughter?" he asked with a glance in her father's direction.

A look passed between the gentlemen. Sophia narrowed her eyes, but Mr. Hawkins's hesitance vanished in an instant, replaced by another smile.

"It is a pleasure to make your acquaintance, *Miss Rosewall*."

All worrying thoughts fled from her mind at his use of her name. "And yours as well, Mr. Hawkins. Are you to join us for dinner this evening?"

"I am. Your father was kind enough to extend the invitation when our matter of business lasted longer than expected. As is evident in my lack of proper dress."

She glanced at his clothing, noting for the first time he hadn't changed since that morning—black jacket, blue waist-coat, knee-high boots. Sand still clung to the edges of them, bringing to mind their time at the beach.

"That is no trouble, of course, sir."

She glanced to Father, who jerked his head discreetly toward Mr. Hawkins. She nodded her understanding at once. She had been given the same look and motion before, when-ever she was to pay special attention to one of Father's acquaintances, usually balding, middle-aged men. *This* acquaintance, however, she would not mind tending to.

"I'm sure we will be delighted to have you join us, Mr. Hawkins," she said. "Now tell me, how long have you known my father?"

Mr. Hawkins's odd reluctance returned, and Father shifted away from them both.

"Excuse me," Father said. "I must see to Mrs. Rosewall."

Sophia stared after him as he strode away. Was he displeased with something? Had he been told of her unsanc-tioned time at the beach?

She pushed the thought aside. Only Mr. Hawkins was aware of that, and he would not have given her up. Besides, he hadn't known she and Father were related until that moment.

With an internal shrug, she returned her attention to Mr. Hawkins, whose eyes roved about the room.

Lowering her voice, she leaned toward him. "Mr. Hawkins, truly, I am shocked to see you here. I knew our paths would cross again, but I never dared hope it would be the very day you rescued me."

Confusion crinkled his brow. "Forgive me. Rescued? To what are you referring?"

Her face fell. "The beach this morning. You helped me

cross the water as the tide was coming in." His blank stare continued, her spirits sinking lower. "I was the woman you found sleeping on the sand?"

"I'm sorry, but you must have me mistaken for someone else. I was on no beach this morning."

Heat rushed to her cheeks. For a single moment, her embarrassment tricked her mind into thinking perhaps she truly had made a mistake. That he wasn't the man on the beach, that he only shared his name and a striking resemblance to him.

But as Mr. Hawkins's lip twitched and his eyes creased at the edges, her mouth dropped. "Why, Mr. Hawkins, you tease."

His lips stretched wide. "My humblest of apologies, Miss Rosewall. I simply could not help myself."

The man had snatched her poise quicker than her maid could help her undress for bed, and that was fast, indeed. She held a hand to her chest. "Goodness, but you were convincing, sir."

He leaned forward, his hands clasped behind his back. "Just as you were convincing with your father, hiding the fact that we have met before now."

She peered up at him. Heavens, was he tall. The top of her head barely reached his chin. "I see I shall have to watch myself near you, Mr. Hawkins." His eyes gleamed. "I must thank you for not exposing my behavior to Father, though. He disapproves of my napping on the beach as greatly as Mother does."

"Well, that was not entirely selfless of me. I hardly think your father would have appreciated me carrying you across the water like one of my dogs."

She placed a gloved hand to her lips, and they shared a soft laugh. Their eyes met, and butterflies took flight in her stomach. "How long have you worked alongside my father? I assume that you own shares in his mine, Wheal Favour?"

"Oh, I…"

"Mr. Hawkins?"

Sophia turned as the Summerfields, elderly neighbors of the Rosewalls, approached from across the room.

"Mr. Summerfield, Mrs. Summerfield," Mr. Hawkins greeted with delight. "A pleasure to see you both again."

Sophia watched the exchange with mild intrigue. How did they know each other?

"What a wonderful surprise it is to have you back in Cornwall," Mrs. Summerfield said, her wrinkles deepening as she smiled. "We didn't see you long enough during your visit last year. Does our granddaughter and her husband know you are here?"

"No, I did not have time to write them. Everything fell into place rather quickly. I only arrived last night."

Mrs. Summerfield leaned forward, her voice low. "Did you inform your mother you were coming?"

"My dear, that is none of our business." Mr. Summerfield said.

Sophia cleared her throat, but she remained unnoticed. How long would they leave her out of the conversation?

"You needn't worry, ma'am," Mr. Hawkins replied. "I told my mother my plans before I came."

Mr. Summerfield patted his wife's arm. "We wouldn't have doubted it. For how long are you here, Mr. Hawkins?"

"For as long as I wish, sir. I'm at my leisure." Mr. Hawkins's eyes finally found Sophia's. "Do forgive us, Miss Rosewall. You must be wondering how we know each other."

"I admit, I am rather curious," she said.

"I was acquainted with the Summerfields' granddaughter in London before she married. I assume you know the Causeys?"

"Oh, of course." Sophia knew practically everyone in St. Just. Mrs. Hannah Causey, the Summerfield's granddaughter, was only a year younger than Sophia's twenty. The Causeys were a charming couple, though they weren't terribly concerned with societal graces.

Mr. Hawkins turned again to the Summerfields. "I trust the Causeys are both in good health?"

"Oh, the very best," Mrs. Summerfield responded. "As happy as two people can be. They are due to return from London in a week or two. I'm sure they will be pleased to see you." She paused, glancing at Sophia. "But I feel it is now our turn to receive an explanation. How do you know the Rosewalls?"

Mr. Hawkins hesitated. "Oh, Mr. Rosewall and I, he… That is to say, we are…"

Sophia didn't understand his discomfort, nor his inability to form a response, but Father expected her to ensure a pleasant evening for the gentleman. She could no longer allow him to suffer.

With a gentle hand on his arm, she answered for him. "Mr. Hawkins and my father are business acquaintances. Are you not, sir?"

"Yes. That we are."

Mother cleared her throat from the other side of the room, ending their conversation and drawing the attention of the guests. "Dinner is served," she announced.

Fabrics rustled and soft footsteps tapped against the floor as the party moved to exit the drawing room.

Mrs. Summerfield turned to Mr. Hawkins with bright eyes. "Mr. Hawkins, you are in for a treat. The dinners at Fynwary Hall are always the finest. No expense spared."

Mr. Hawkins's smile faded. Was he uncomfortable in her home, or had someone simply forgotten to take a spare pin out of his tailored breeches?

"Sophia," Mother whispered in her ear. Sophia paused to listen. "Fortunately, Mr. Maddern could not make it this evening, so we are still at an even number, even with Mr. Hawkins's sudden attendance. But our party has shifted now to favor the single gentlemen. You mustn't allow yourself to forget that Mr. Hawkins is not the only man in want of your affection this evening. Remember, why enjoy one dessert when multiple dishes are offered?"

She walked away with a reassuring nod in Sophia's direction, joining the guests as they left the drawing room.

Sophia took a moment to find the composure Mother's words had stripped from her. Sophia had quite forgotten herself when she was with Mr. Hawkins, and Mother had obviously taken notice.

Typically, Sophia wouldn't be opposed to Mother telling her to dote on multiple men. But in that moment, she did not understand why she needed to pander to two gentlemen fawning over her when she lacked interest in both of them and expressed clear interest in another. Was everything to be a game while courting?

After another moment, she brushed aside her musings and replaced her pleasant look. She knew her place was to ensure all their guests were tended to, so with the eyes of Society and her parents on her, she would do as she was told.

Paying attention equally to Mr. Singleton, Mr. Chester, and Mr. Hawkins would prove quite the task. But what else could be expected of the most amiable—and the only vocal— single female at a dinner party?

CHAPTER FIVE

*F*rederick couldn't believe his luck. Not only had he found the mysterious woman from the beach, but he was seated right next to her at her dinner table. Someone up above was certainly looking out for him.

He'd been uneasy at first when he'd discovered that she was Mr. Rosewall's daughter. He should have known, of course, what with finding her asleep on her father's land. Still, his surprise had quickly turned to joy, as he had yet to stop thinking of her since that morning.

"How fortunate I am to be seated next to you, sir," Miss Rosewall spoke softly beside him.

Frederick had to agree. "I was only just now thinking the—"

"Next to *him*? What of me, Miss Rosewall? Are you not just as pleased to be near me?"

Frederick leaned forward to eye the gentleman seated at Miss Rosewall's left.

"Oh, Mr. Singleton," she said, "you already know I am pleased to be with you, like always."

At Mr. Singleton's smirk, Frederick's mouth dried. Miss Rosewall certainly knew what to say to please a gentleman.

He set the disconcerting thought aside as the meal began, glancing around the open room. It wasn't as large as the dining room at Dawnridge, but it was spacious enough for the ten of them to sit comfortably around the table. A great number of candles brightened the tableware and food, shining on the red walls framed in goldwork. It was unquestionably beautiful.

Like Miss Rosewall.

She leaned toward Mr. Singleton again. Frederick took a spoonful of his artichoke soup to avoid listening to their conversation, but Mrs. Rosewall soon provided distraction enough.

"Mr. Hawkins," she said, speaking from the head of the table at his right, "I do hope you will enjoy the meal this evening. We always strive to make dining at Fynwary Hall a fine affair." She raised her chin proudly.

"I am already enjoying it, ma'am, I assure you. And I must thank you for accommodating me at such short notice and dressed in a manner hardly appropriate for such a fine room and occasion."

"Of course. We are always happy to welcome Mr. Rose-wall's acquaintances in our home."

Frederick glanced to Mr. Rosewall at the other end of the table. He stared at his drink instead of eating, his face pale. Apparently, Mrs. Rosewall hadn't taken notice of her husband's ill health, as she continued conversing with Frederick.

"From where do you hail, Mr. Hawkins?"

Frederick swallowed another spoonful of soup. "Bedford-shire, ma'am. I run my family's estate there, Dawnridge."

Her eyebrows arched with pleasure. With dark hair and light skin, she looked similar to Miss Rosewall, who, evidently, was still engaged in conversation with Mr. Singleton. But Mrs. Rosewall's features were more severe, her nose and chin rigidly pointed.

"Is there a lady of Dawnridge?" she asked.

"Yes, there is."

Mrs. Rosewall's face fell, but he was more interested in Miss Rosewall swinging her head around to look at him. So she was listening to him after all.

"That lady is my mother, Mrs. Hawkins," he finished. "She rarely spends time in Bedfordshire, however. She prefers life in London, so she rents a townhome in the city."

"Living in London must be rather exciting," Miss Rosewall said. Frederick tried not to be too pleased to have maintained her attention. Mr. Singleton would no doubt be pouting. "We have only just arrived from London this month. My dear father allows us to go every Season. Father always does what is best for his daughter."

She turned warm eyes on Mr. Rosewall, whose smile appeared as more of a wince.

The few hours Frederick had spent with Mr. Rosewall would suggest that the gentleman was always silent. Perhaps his lack of conversation was merely due to the negotiations they had made.

Frederick wondered again why the man had insisted they keep their business to themselves. Such talk would hardly be welcome around the dinner table, especially if his neighbors were unaware of what had taken place between them. Though, his wife and daughter would know. Wouldn't they?

His mind reverted to Miss Rosewall asking after their business, and an unsettling weariness crept nearby, like storm clouds inching toward the sun.

"Do you have siblings, Mr. Hawkins?" Mrs. Rosewall asked.

"No, I did not have that fortune."

"Something you have in common with my daughter then."

Frederick glanced to Miss Rosewall. "Indeed?"

She nodded, a soft curve to her lips. "I do not consider it a misfortune though. I quite enjoy benefiting from the full attention of both of my parents."

Frederick spoke so only she could hear. "Though, you must admit, that can at times be a misfortune."

She sipped at her soup to hide her smile.

"Where are you staying, Mr. Hawkins?" Mr. Summerfield asked across from him, his wrinkled face as kind as Frederick remembered.

"At the illustrious Golden Arms Inn," he joked.

"Oh, that will not do," Mrs. Summerfield said, farther down the table. "No, you must stay with us at Rudhek Manor for the remainder of your visit."

"Indeed," her husband agreed. "You'd be most welcome."

Frederick had always liked the Summerfields. How pleasantly surprised he'd been to have discovered them there that evening. "Thank you both. But I will not be staying at the inn for much longer."

A cough sounded from Mr. Rosewall. His forehead glistened with sweat that no one but Frederick seemed to notice.

"Does your father live in London with your mother, Mr. Hawkins?" Mrs. Rosewall enquired.

Frederick struggled to switch his mind from the Summerfields, Mr. Rosewall, and Mrs. Rosewall. "No, my father died when I was fourteen."

"Oh, what a tragedy."

Frederick debated on telling her what a tragedy it really was. How he and his mother were relieved, happy even, when the man had finally died. But his troubled history with his father was the last thing he wished to discuss that evening. Instead, he simply nodded.

Miss Rosewall studied him. Had she noticed the shroud that had come over him? Thankfully, the conversation shifted, and the meal progressed.

The guests helped themselves to the various foods laid out in polished bowls and trays around the table. Fish, beef-steaks, roasted potatoes, pickled vegetables. It was an impressive spread.

How had they managed such a fine setting? If what Mr. Rosewall had said to Frederick was true, then this must have set them back a great deal.

"Do you spend much time in London with your mother, Mr. Hawkins?" Mrs. Rosewall asked.

Frederick had barely managed two bites of his roasted potato before she had resumed her questioning. "I make it a point to visit her at least twice a year."

"Mrs. Maddern, you and your husband enjoy London, do you not?" Mrs. Rosewall asked.

The woman at the far end of the table, seated to the left of the somber Mr. Rosewall, rested her fork and knife over her plate. "Oh, yes. We would have remained there longer this year, but Mr. Maddern's health did not permit. We enjoy it nearly as much as the Stedmans."

Miss Rosewall leaned toward Frederick with a soft voice. "The Stedmans are neighbors of ours," she explained.

The scent of roses tickled his nose. "I see."

"When are the Stedmans to return from London?" Mrs. Rosewall asked.

A knowing half-smile spread across Mrs. Maddern's lips. "Why, Mrs. Stedman has never said. Apparently, Miss Stedman was spurned by a gentleman not so very long ago, so I suspect they are to remain in London for as long as the rumors take to fade away."

Frederick was grateful his chewing stifled his yawn. Gossip, the one thing he wished he could extricate from dinner parties.

"You know, my niece has never been to London before," Mrs. Maddern continued. "Have you, Claire? My dear sister, Claire's mother, does not have the resources."

The young woman sitting directly across from Frederick shook her head. She was a pretty girl, though her blonde hair and pale skin caused her to appear as if she might faint at any given moment.

"Oh, Miss Kinsey, what a shame," Miss Rosewall said. Her smooth tone reminded Frederick of butter being spread across warm bread.

"Mr. Hawkins," Mrs. Maddern said, "you must have visited London more than any of us, which makes you the expert. Might you share with my niece what Town is like so she is prepared should she ever have the fortune of having a Season there?"

Frederick wasn't blind, nor was he oblivious. He knew the workings of a caretaker attempting to bring attention to her ward. But any fool could see that Miss Kinsey was painfully uncomfortable with the attention.

He smiled kindly at the girl, hoping to alleviate her discomfort. "I am certain you would enjoy yourself. Though, I ought not be the one to tell you what to expect, as I'm afraid I have never been partial to the city."

She didn't respond. Her head hovered so low her ringlets nearly touched her plate.

"Oh, I love the city." The gentleman across from Miss Rosewall pumped his head up and down, his curls remaining unmoved. "You'll never find more excellent entertainment than in London."

"To be sure, Mr. Chester," Miss Rosewall agreed. She paused for a moment, as if waiting for everyone's attention before continuing. "But you were born in London, sir, so of course you would enjoy it there."

Mr. Chester radiated pure joy. "You know me well, Miss Rosewall."

The man's eyes lingered on her, and a bothersome ache twisted Frederick's stomach.

"Do tell us, Mr. Hawkins," Mr. Chester said, "why do you not find that same delight in Town?"

Along with his father's life and his mother's desire for him to wed, this was yet another conversation Frederick did not wish to have. He couldn't very well behave like Miss Kinsey, though, ducking his head to avoid saying a word.

"I simply discovered that there are far more lovely women elsewhere to capture my attention," he replied, far short of the truth. "To remain in London would surely be a disservice to myself."

That should settle their questions for a moment. Never mind that he had once enjoyed London. He was no longer going to dwell on the place and the people it produced. Not while he was in Cornwall and his future stretched before him as bright and endless as the sea.

"I do find myself agreeing with Mr. Hawkins," Mr. Singleton said, "for the prettiest women in all of Society reside in Cornwall, if not at this very table."

Mr. Singleton's false praises were as obvious as a cravat that had been tied too tightly round one's neck.

Speaking of which, why *was* Frederick's cravat so tight? He fought the urge to tug at the white fabric, a habit Mother had tried to rid him of since he'd worn his first.

"Oh, Mr. Singleton, you do flatter us," Miss Rosewall said with a twittering laugh. "I'm sure I shan't eat another bite until my smile lessens. Don't you agree, Miss Kinsey?"

Miss Kinsey merely nodded, straight-faced. She seemed to be enjoying the flirting between Mr. Singleton and Miss Rosewall as much as Frederick was.

Miss Rosewall's eyes swept around the table. "I must say then how favorable my circumstances are, surrounded by the most handsome gentlemen in all of Cornwall."

Her comment resulted in a number of chuckles, but Frederick's polite laugh stuck in his throat as he caught sight of her hand resting on Mr. Singleton's arm.

CHAPTER SIX

*A*n icy thread weaved its way through Frederick's heart. Miss Rosewall couldn't be attached to Mr. Singleton, not with how she had been flirting with Mr. Chester only moments ago. Not with how she'd touched Frederick's own arm in the same intimate manner in the drawing room. Could she be interested in all three gentlemen?

Frederick struggled to swallow the meat that turned dry in his mouth. Had he been wrong about her? He thought, what with her behavior on the beach, that she was different than most women. Could he have been so distracted with his hopeful views of Cornwall that he had not noticed her performance?

Miss Rosewall laughed at another of Mr. Singleton's prepared compliments. This time, the sound, those lilting bells, reverberated in Frederick's ears and scratched at his soul.

He longed to leave but forced himself to remain seated, though the meal stretched out, and Miss Rosewall proved herself incapable of being silent for a single moment.

"Have you seen Mr. Chester's new horse?" she asked anyone who would listen. "He is so elegant with his white coat. Of course, such a marvelous horse deserves a marvelous rider, and he certainly has one in Mr. Chester."

Mr. Chester straightened in his seat and glanced around to ensure everyone had heard the compliment. "You exaggerate, Miss Rosewall. I do enjoy the exercise, but you are a far better rider than I could ever be."

"No, I assure you. You are as superior a rider as I have ever seen. You have so many talents, sir."

"And what of me, Miss Rosewall?" Mr. Singleton asked. "What talents do I possess?"

Frederick nearly groaned. Was this man truly anxious for attention from a woman who extended compliments cheaper than a two-pence sweet?

He tried to chew another bite of his food, but it rolled about his mouth, tasteless, as Miss Rosewall leaned toward Mr. Singleton.

"You, sir, have just as many talents as your friend, I assure you," she said. "Your dancing, for one thing, exceeds the abilities of half the gentlemen in Cornwall. Indeed, I know at least a dozen women who look forward to having you as their partner for every ball, for they know you would never deign to tread on their slippers."

Frederick shook his head at the laughter that followed. How could he have been so stupid as to think she might have only had eyes for Frederick when they had only just met?

She turned to him next, flashing a charming grin. He'd warned himself about that smile. Fortunately he had realized the truth before he'd fallen too far.

"Now, Mr. Hawkins," she said, "do not think I have forgotten about you. Indeed, I have saved the best for last. But I fear I am not acquainted with you well enough to know what your talents are. Though, if I didn't know any better, I would assume that you are an excellent hunter. Especially with your *hounds*."

Her twinkling eyes hinted at their time together on the

beach, and confusion tormented his mind. Which was the real Miss Rosewall? The one who slept on a beach without stockings or gloves and laughed at herself for tripping in the sand? Or the attention-seeking woman who spouted flirtatious remarks, believing she could win any gentleman she wished?

He bounced his knee unobtrusively beneath the table. He was not going to get caught up in all of this. If she partook in games like the women in London, expressing interest in a man only until a wealthier gentleman came along, he refused to play. She was not the only woman in Cornwall, nor was she the only woman in the room.

She *was* in need of a little humbling, and if the arrangement he'd just made with her father had not done the job, he knew what would.

"Yes, Miss Rosewall," he responded. "I do enjoy hunting. Though I assure you, I do not excel so very much as to warrant any praise from you." Her confident look faded, and he faced forward before she could say another word. "Miss Kinsey, how long have you been staying with your aunt?"

Sophia blinked mutely at Mr. Hawkins. Had she said something offensive to warrant his brushing her aside? Miss Kinsey mumbled a response to his question, but Sophia hardly heard it, too concerned with the change that had come over the gentleman.

She had done her best to make him feel welcomed, but still his spirits had seemed to decline throughout the meal. His and Father's.

She looked to the end of the table where Father sat staring at his drink, his plate of food untouched. He'd hardly said a word all night. Had his business matter with Mr. Hawkins turned sour? Was that why Mr. Hawkins was upset, as well?

Her brow lowered for only a moment. It would not do her

any good to simply dwell on the problems. She would solve them instead. She'd done a fine job being attentive to Mr. Singleton and Mr. Chester, as was evident by her mother's proud glances, but Mr. Hawkins appeared to be in need of more attention.

What a shame to have to spend more time with him.

She smiled to herself, leaning toward the gentleman. "Sir, I—"

"Miss Kinsey, I trust you are staying well, what with your uncle in poor health."

Sophia pulled back, blinking in surprise. Had Mr. Hawkins interrupted her on purpose? What was with his sudden interest in Miss Kinsey?

Miss Kinsey, of all people.

After a dessert of peach compote and almond cake, the women made for the drawing room. Sophia attempted to speak with Miss Kinsey, but after half an hour of trying to pry more than one-word responses from the woman, she was relieved to have the gentlemen join them.

She had intended on seeking out Mr. Hawkins straight-away, but Mr. Singleton sidled up to her in an instant.

"Typically, I enjoy a glass of port," he said, dimples deep, "but knowing you were in here while I, in there, was simply too much for me to bear."

She looked over his shoulder to where Mr. Hawkins was already in conversation with Miss Kinsey. That was strange. He hadn't sought out Sophia first. "I missed you, as well, Mr. Singleton," she said distractedly.

"Have you deduced our entertainment yet?" Mr. Singleton asked.

She stifled a sigh. Would it be rude of her to ask him to be silent for a single moment so she might think in peace? "I am certain we shall find out soon enough."

She glanced to Mr. Hawkins in time to see his eyes pull away from her. Her lip curled. Now she understood. Mr.

Hawkins was not at Sophia's side because Mr. Singleton *was*. The poor man was jealous.

Sophia couldn't help that other men vied for her attention. But she *could* help Mr. Hawkins see that she was more interested in him than the others.

"Do excuse me for a moment, Mr. Singleton," she said, and she headed across the room without waiting for his response.

In an instant, she reached Mr. Hawkins and Miss Kinsey. "I must say, I saw the two of you deep in conversation, and I simply had to know of what you were speaking."

Miss Kinsey, if it were possible, dropped her head even more. Mr. Hawkins simply stared at Sophia impassively. "I was merely speaking with the lovely Miss Kinsey about my home in Bedfordshire."

Sophia stared. The *lovely* Miss Kinsey? This had to be Mr. Hawkins being polite.

"I see," she said. She turned to Miss Kinsey, struggling to deduce what Mr. Hawkins saw in her that was 'lovely.' She supposed she had nice green eyes. "I was sorry to hear of your uncle's health this evening, Miss Kinsey. You must tell him we missed him at our party."

Miss Kinsey nodded.

"Are you enjoying your stay with them?" Sophia pressed.

"I am, thank you."

Sophia had to lean in to hear her words. The girl was insufferable. Was she really so shy, or did she merely dislike everyone around her? Everyone but Mr. Hawkins.

Sophia turned to face him, struck again with how handsome he was, even with his blank expression. It would appear Miss Kinsey's lack of conversation was draining him, as well.

"And you, Mr. Hawkins, are you enjoying your time in Cornwall?"

"I am."

Now his answers were sounding like Miss Kinsey's. Sophia

needed to get this man away from the dull woman. "Did you enjoy the port my father chose? He only uses his finest for special company, which means you must be superior indeed."

"Yes, I was grateful for it." He looked to Miss Kinsey. "If you will excuse me, ladies, I should like to thank him for it right now."

As he walked past her, the scent of leather lingered, no doubt still clinging to his breeches from his ride that morning. Her heart stirred, but she stared after him with dismay. He'd taken the escape she'd provided him, but now Sophia was caught in Miss Kinsey's dreary web of silence.

"Did you enjoy dinner, Miss Kinsey?" she asked.

Miss Kinsey shifted her feet. "It was delicious, thank you."

Sophia waited for her to say more.

She didn't.

"The sunshine has been exceptional of late," Sophia said next. Oh, dear. She was now resorting to talk of the weather. "I do hope the rain will not come for a few days yet."

"As do I."

Sophia clicked her teeth together. Mother told her it was a bad habit, especially around gentlemen, but Sophia hardly thought it would matter in the presence of Miss Kinsey.

Anxious for a way out of the conversation—or lack thereof—Sophia looked around her. Mr. Hawkins spoke with Father and the Summerfields, and Mrs. Maddern was with Mother. But Mr. Singleton and Mr. Chester stood together with their eyes already upon her.

They would make the perfect escape. She waved them over, to which they responded with a fair gallop across the room.

"Miss Kinsey and I are in need of entertainment," she said. Miss Kinsey didn't respond, and Sophia fought the urge to groan. "Shall I have Mother decide on what we are to do this evening?"

"Certainly. Though, you know what my vote is for," Mr. Chester said.

Mr. Singleton took a step forward, partially blocking Miss Kinsey from their circle. The girl hardly seemed to notice. "Yes, and mine, as well."

"We shall see, gentlemen," Sophia said.

Of course, she already knew Mother would not choose dancing, what with two ladies and three gentlemen to pair up, but Sophia would leave that disappointing news for her mother to deliver.

Soon enough, when entertainment was called for, and dancing was excluded, the group collectively settled on playing whist.

Two tables were set up, four chairs spaced around each one. Sophia headed straight for Mr. Hawkins as he took a seat at the empty table. His eyes pulled away from hers once he saw her coming, and he turned to face Miss Kinsey instead.

"Miss Kinsey, will you be my partner?" he asked. "With your cleverness, we are sure to win."

CHAPTER SEVEN

$\mathcal{S}$ophia's smile faltered. Mr. Hawkins must have known she was intending to request him to be her partner. What did he mean by asking Miss Kinsey instead?

The girl looked rather horrified as she sat down across from him. She directed her eyes anywhere but Mr. Hawkins.

Sophia, however, directed her eyes *solely* on Mr. Hawkins.

She hadn't been his first choice. She could not remember the last time that had happened to her. She was always every gentleman's first choice.

"Miss Rosewall, do tell me you will be my partner."

She breathed a sigh, half-relieved, half-annoyed. Mr. Singleton. There was one gentleman who would choose her above all others. She looked graciously up at him, but before she could respond, Mr. Chester appeared beside him, seemingly from thin air.

"No, you must be my partner, Miss Rosewall," he said.

The friends looked to one another, a silent battle of wills ensuing before Sophia produced a dry laugh to dispel her own discomfort. A discomfort produced not from their argument, but from coming second to Miss Kinsey. "You are both so silly. There is no need to quarrel." She glanced to Mr. Hawkins, but he continued shuffling the deck of cards with his head down. "We can settle this easily. Whoever does not play as my partner this evening will receive my first dance at the Maddern's ball next week."

"But I—"

"Yes, Mr. Chester, I know I have already promised you the first, but if you forgo your chair to Mr. Singleton this evening, I shall then save you two dances instead of just the one."

Mr. Chester looked down his nose at Mr. Singleton, as much as he could being a full head shorter. "In that case, Singleton, you may play as Miss Rosewall's partner this evening."

With his chest pushed out, he joined the other table.

Sophia took her place across from Mr. Singleton, only then noticing her Father standing beside Mr. Summerfield to observe the games. Father's eyes remained on the fire crackling in the hearth rather than on his guests playing whist.

The meal hadn't proved to buoy his spirits, nor had his port, and the weary half-circles carved beneath his eyes had only darkened. Perhaps he'd contracted Mr. Maddern's cold. She would suggest for Mother to send for Dr. Rennalls that evening.

"I am pleased Mr. Chester has allowed me to partner with you, Miss Rosewall," Mr. Singleton said, breaking through her thoughts. "I trust playing whist is one of your many talents?"

Sophia could not share how truly exceptional she was at the game. Instead, she smiled furtively as she removed her gloves. "That is for you to discover yourself, sir."

Mr. Singleton exuded pleasure. He and Mr. Chester were enjoying themselves that evening. Mother would be pleased. Mr. Hawkins, however…

She glanced toward him, but he was busy extending the shuffled deck to Mr. Singleton. Mr. Singleton then proceeded to deal thirteen cards to each player before revealing the trump suit with a flourish.

Diamonds. That was unfortunate. Sophia had only six of them, all lower-numbered. She would need to keep track of which cards had been played, just as Father had taught her. Victory would come easily, though, as it always did for her. Providing Mr. Singleton did his part, of course.

She leaned toward Mr. Hawkins, arranging her cards in numeric order as she did so. "I hope *you* do not have a talent for whist, sir, as I truly despise losing."

His eyes lacked the luster of a smile. "I doubt I possess any talent greater than yours, Miss Rosewall."

His words did not sound like the compliment they should have been. Sophia glanced around the table. No one appeared to have noticed the slight but her.

Mr. Hawkins played first, laying down a two of spades.

Sophia could not decide if he was attempting to rid himself of pointless cards, or if he was simply rubbish at the game. Either way, she was sure he could use some encouragement.

"Excellent start, sir," she said. "And now you have me pondering what strategy you undoubtedly have hidden up your sleeve."

Mr. Hawkins pulled in his lips and nodded.

With no spade to follow suit, Sophia played her lowest diamond. Miss Kinsey laid down another spade, and Sophia smiled at her own victory.

Then Mr. Singleton took his turn. Instead of laying a sensible card, he put down another diamond.

"Wait a moment, no..." But it was too late, the card having already been played. She clamped her mouth shut.

Mr. Singleton looked up at her with a quirked brow, pulling the trick he'd won toward him. "We won that round, Miss Rosewall."

"Yes, I know, but..." She shook her head. Never mind that he'd wasted a trump card when they'd already won that round together. It was only a game, after all. "Yes, well done, sir."

She thought she heard a snort come from Mr. Hawkins, but when she looked to him, his mouth was hidden behind his cards.

Mr. Singleton led the next round, but Miss Kinsey took the trick with a two of diamonds.

"I knew I chose the right partner," Mr. Hawkins said.

Sophia frowned, every bit as uncomfortable with his words as the shy Miss Kinsey.

"Very good play, Miss Kinsey," she said, attempting to swallow her pride.

"Do you play whist often?" Mr. Hawkins asked.

"Yes, as often as I can manage," Sophia replied as the cards were dealt.

He stared. "Oh, I was asking Miss Kinsey."

"Ah." Sophia stared down at her new cards, her cheeks feeling as if she'd spent far too long in the sunshine. "My apologies."

"My sisters and I used to play often when we were children," Miss Kinsey finally responded.

Sophia had never heard the woman say so much. Of course Mr. Hawkins would be the one to draw her out of her shell.

Miss Kinsey won another round, then Sophia the next.

"Just the beginning of our victory," Mr. Singleton boasted.

Sophia glanced to Mr. Hawkins. The muscles in his jaw twitched.

The game continued, and Mr. Hawkins won his first trick before playing the ace of diamonds, another instant win. Sophia and Miss Kinsey played lower cards, but Mr. Singleton placed his king of diamonds, though there was no chance of his winning.

Had the man never played before in his life? What was he thinking? She should have partnered with Mr. Chester. Surely he could not be this bad.

Unable to bear another wasted trump card, she raised a finger. "Oh, you might not wish to—"

"The card has been played, Miss Rosewall," Mr. Hawkins interrupted, setting his winning trick at his side of the table.

Sophia clamped her mouth shut with dismay. Mr. Singleton proceeded to win another round, again taking it from Sophia.

"Another win for us," he said.

Sophia blinked at him. "You do know, Mr. Singleton, in order to win a trick, only one in a partnership needs to play a high diamond?"

"Of course," he responded with a casual lift of his brow.

She bit back a groan, catching Mr. Hawkins's eye. Why did he appear so entertained? Was it because he was winning, or because she had a ninny for a partner?

With each passing round, the discourse around the table suffered, as did Sophia's patience with Mr. Singleton. When the final rounds commenced with no chance of her winning the game, she attempted to brush aside her frustrations by striking up a conversation between her and Mr. Hawkins.

"Tell me, where did you learn to play so well? Was it the time you spent in London?"

His eyes remained on the cards he dealt into four piles. "No, I made it a point to never adopt any habit from London that I did not value."

"You do not value the victory in a game?"

He pushed the hands he'd dealt across the table toward Mr. Singleton, Miss Kinsey, then Sophia. She reached for her cards too early, and the tips of her fingers brushed against the top of his hand.

Their eyes met for a single moment, a connection made as strong as the fierce beating of her heart.

Mr. Hawkins pulled back. "No, I do not. Especially not games that are played in London."

Sophia focused on her cards rather than on her fingers still tingling where they had touched. "I really cannot imagine why you do not enjoy London, sir. It is so lively and exciting, with such wonderful entertainment and people."

"Yes, if one can take pleasure in such company."

Perhaps this man was *not* the one who'd rescued her that morning. He was so sullen, she couldn't make any sense of it. "What is there not to like of the company there?"

"Plenty."

His voice was gruff, final. He wished to end their conversation, but why? Why did he dislike London, and why was he continually snubbing her kindness?

Her mind was already in disarray when the final round began. She could not win with her last card, and she was fairly certain Mr. Singleton would find some way to ruin their chance of success.

She scolded herself half-heartedly. Her mood had grown too dark to feel true remorse for her uncharitable thoughts.

Sure enough, after Miss Kinsey played her final diamond, she and Mr. Hawkins took the round and the game.

"It appears we have been bested, Miss Rosewall," Mr. Singleton said. "Well done, Mr. Hawkins, Miss Kinsey. A noble victory, indeed."

Miss Kinsey stood from the table. "Excuse me," she squeaked out before scurrying away.

Mr. Hawkins stood, as well. "Allow me to join you, Miss Kinsey."

As he made to leave, something snapped within Sophia. Confusion, impatience, indignation. Everything she shouldn't be feeling. Such emotion had not been caused by losing the game, by Miss Kinsey's silence, or even by having a silly partner. They were caused by Mr. Hawkins's sudden and inexplicable indifference toward her.

She stood abruptly, holding her hand up to stop him from following Miss Kinsey. "Just a moment, sir. I asked you a question. You could at least show me the courtesy of responding with more than a single word."

He stared at her impassively.

Sophia was only vaguely aware of Mr. Singleton stepping away from the table to join Miss Kinsey by the hearth, a look of discomfort on both of their faces.

"What is there not to like about the company one finds in London?" she repeated.

"Do you truly wish to know?" Mr. Hawkins asked.

"I do."

He raised a careless brow, his words coming low and deep, so quickly she barely had time to process them. "I do not enjoy the people who are more concerned with their own looks and accomplishments than the feelings of others. It is a hunting ground. A place for them to play their game. The game of who can catch the richest husband."

Sophia's eyes widened, shock striking her dumb.

He took a step toward her, speaking so only she could hear. "I had hoped Cornwall would be exempt, but to my great dismay, *you* have shown me that these games also exist here."

His pointed look was unmistakable, his accusatory words penetrating her defenses.

Her nostrils flared, and the veins in her neck pulsed as she struggled to maintain decorum. His words were distasteful, ungentlemanlike in the truest manner. How dare he, a perfect stranger, come into her home and accuse her of such things after only a few moments with her? He took issue with her flirtatious words, but what female didn't flirt? And what gentleman, for that matter?

She clenched her teeth. "Mr. Hawkins, how dare you—"

"Good evening, Miss Rosewall," he interrupted, then with a curt bow, he left her side.

CHAPTER EIGHT

*S*ophia stared after Mr. Hawkins. So he wasn't jealous.
He was simply a horrible, ungenerous, judgmental
man. She ought to march right up to him and demand he
retract his unfeeling words. But that would create a scene
Mother would have to clean up later, and Sophia couldn't do
that to her.

Instead, she smoothed her skirts, brushed back her
ringlets, and raised her chin. She would show them how a
proper member of Society ought to behave. She would rise
above Mr. Hawkins's comments and act poised and regal,
something he could never do. Let Miss Kinsey have him all to
herself. The two deserved each other.

Besides, Sophia would rather enjoy her time with the *true*
gentlemen in her home that evening.

And enjoy them she did. She giggled and flirted to her
heart's content, though Mr. Hawkins's judgmental eyes were
upon her more often than not until the night ended and the
party finally dispersed.

She and Mother bade goodbye to their guests at the door
with gracious words and curtsies. Sophia had lost sight of Mr.
Hawkins as the group filed through the entryway and left

Fynwary Hall, but she didn't mind. She would not have said goodbye to him anyway.

When the tall, double doors closed behind the last of the guests, Mother sighed. "Goodness, what an evening!" She linked her arm through Sophia's and led them back to the drawing room. "You did well tonight, my dear. As charming as I have ever seen you, to be sure. Mr. Chester and Mr. Singleton both appear to be quite taken with you. Tell me, has your opinion of them changed? Might you consider either of them as a suitor?"

After discovering that Mr. Singleton proved a poor whist partner—and no doubt Mr. Chester, as well—Sophia was bound and determined to never marry either of them. "I do not know, to be truthful. I fear they both lack...something." A personality, perhaps? Intelligence? "But I will continue befriending them, of course."

Mother patted her hand. "You may as well, if only to help you discover what it is you wish for in a husband." The swishing of their silk gowns filled the air as they walked down the corridor. "What did you think of Mr. Hawkins?"

Sophia hesitated. "Well, he is handsome, I suppose. But I fear he is not as amiable as he appears to be."

"I did notice after whist that he hardly spoke. Did something occur between the two of you?"

Sophia bit her tongue to prevent herself from clicking her teeth. "I'm afraid so, yes. He spoke rather bluntly and accused me of, well, never mind. He was simply not as gentlemanly as I hoped. Especially after he saved me from—" She froze. Mother's eyes were upon her. Sophia scrambled for an answer that did not reveal the time she had spent with him on the beach. "Saved me from-from speaking with Miss Kinsey all evening."

Mother watched her for a moment before looking away. "Yes, I suppose that is fortunate then. She is a fine enough girl but far too silent to be amiable. At any rate, I am sorry to hear about Mr. Hawkins. Perhaps he may turn out to be a fine gentleman yet."

Sophia nodded, though she highly doubted her words. Mr. Hawkins was deplorable.

She had every intention of saying as much to Father that very night, but as she followed her mother into the drawing room, her feet planted to the floor, tongue curbed.

"Mr. Hawkins?" Mother said.

Sure enough, the gentleman was still standing by the hearth, his tall figure commanding the attention of the room far more than Father's slouched stance nearby.

"We didn't know you were still here," Mother continued. She exchanged glances with Sophia. Had he heard their conversation outside the room? "If you were waiting for your horse, I'm sure he is ready by now."

Mr. Hawkins glanced to Father. "Thank you, Mrs. Rosewall, but your husband…"

"I have asked Mr. Hawkins to stay behind for a moment." Father's voice was ragged, matching the weary crease of his brow. "Please, Mrs. Rosewall, Sophia. Do sit down."

Mother settled on the settee near the fire, but Sophia chose the seat farthest from Mr. Hawkins. He stood with his hands behind his back, holding as still as Sophia when she was being measured for a new gown.

His calm demeanor caused a wariness to come over her, especially when she compared it with her father's uncharacteristic fidgeting. "Is everything all right, Father?"

"There is something I wish to discuss that concerns us, all of us."

Sophia's stomach swayed, unsettled. What on earth could Father have to say that involved all of them? Something business related, perhaps? Father owned the majority of the shares in his mine, Wheal Favour. Had Mr. Hawkins bullied his way into purchasing a few himself? That would certainly explain Father's low spirits.

Her blood boiled. She couldn't stand for it, especially not after what Mr. Hawkins had said to her earlier. "Father, I must speak with you."

"In a moment, Sophia." Father's chest lifted as he drew in a breath. He faced them directly to show his composure, though his lined brow exposed his discontent. "Now, we know that the Rosewalls, like many landed gentry, have suffered our fair share of gossip in relation to our wealth and circumstances, as well as our standing with Wheal Favour."

Sophia nodded. She was well aware of the envious members of her own class starting rumors—rumors of their mine failing, scandals between family members, loss of wealth —purely to make themselves appear higher than the Rosewalls. In the end, the gossip always died out. Why would Father mention them now?

He lowered his head as he continued. "The rumors in relation to the mine now, however, are true. You remember this last flooding incident. Well, the gentlemen with shares in Wheal Favour have collectively decided to cease funding the mine. So I have no other option but to sell."

Sophia gasped, holding a hand to her neck as her throat constricted. Wheal Favour had been in their family's possession for generations. How could he sell such a legacy?

She turned to Mother, whose skin glowed as white as Sophia's newly ordered ball gown.

"They have ended their support because of a simple accident?" Mother asked, her voice high-pitched.

Father winced. "They have not been pleased with my decision to go against their advisements in regard to…" He rubbed the back of his neck. "In regard to a number of things. They warned me that they would either sell shares or pull their finances, should another accident occur, but—"

"How is any of that in your control?" Mother asked, her nostrils flaring, a sure sign of her attempt to rein in her emotions.

Father's eyes shifted, guilt contorting his features, but he remained silent.

"Could you not have purchased their shares? Found other investors?" Mother asked next.

"No. That is what I must explain to you now."

Sophia hardly heard their words, her mind still attempting to sift through the information. Father had sold the mine, but to whom?

Her eyes slowly trailed across the red, decorated carpet her slippers rested upon until her eyes landed on a pair of sand-stricken, knee-length boots.

Of course it would be him.

"I fear that——"

"Have you sold it to Mr. Hawkins, Father?" she interrupted.

Father's jaw tensed. "How did you know?"

His eyes shot to Mr. Hawkins, who instantly shook his head. Did Father truly think she was so daft as to not have deduced the answer herself? Why else would the man be standing there if he had not purchased their family's mine?

"Of course it is Mr. Hawkins," she blurted out. "That is why he is here, is it not? To flaunt his new possession in front of us who suffer."

She raised a daring brow at Mr. Hawkins. His eyes narrowed, but he remained silent.

"That is not why he is here, Sophia." Father's voice was firm, a tone he did not normally take with his only daughter. "I invited him to join us so you and your mother might see how amiable a gentleman he is. He would not triumph over our losses. He will take good care of Fynwary Hall, of that I am sure."

"What?" Mother blurted.

"Fynwary Hall?" Sophia questioned at the same time. "Don't you mean Wheal Favour?"

Father's mouth parted, his whole face flaming red. "Forgive me, I had hoped to share the news more gently, but I thought you had guessed that he had purchased..." He broke off with a sigh. "You misunderstood. Mr. Trevethan is the one who will be purchasing the mine. Mr. Hawkins will be purchasing, *has* purchased, our home."

CHAPTER NINE

*S*ophia frowned, shaking her head. Father was teasing, that was all. She laughed dryly. "What a terrible joke, Father."

She looked to Mother for support, but her gaunt countenance did nothing for Sophia's apprehension.

"You must understand, Mrs. Rosewall," Father began in a soft voice, his blue eyes haunted and stricken with grief, "I have done everything I possibly can to keep Fynwary Hall. There is nothing left to be done. I kept my financial failures to myself so you might both enjoy life for as long as possible in the way you are accustomed. But now things must change, and not for the better."

Sophia pulled back in a daze. Father was speaking the truth. He had actually sold their mine *and* their house. What were they to do for money? Where were they to live? The air continued to be pressed from her lungs. "How has this happened, Father?"

He crossed the room to stand behind Mother's settee, resting a hand on her shoulder. Mother visibly stiffened, still ghostly white.

"When Wheal Favour was not fetching a profit a few years

before," Father explained, "I was forced to take out a number of loans, not only to fund the mine, but to pay for our extravagant living." He swallowed. "When the mine was profitable again, I was able to repay one of the loans. But after the recent internal damage the mine has suffered due to the flooding, I have been unable to make payments. The bank has decided to call in the loans immediately, otherwise we could have leased the property. I haven't the money to repay them, so short of my going to debtor's prison and the bank seizing our property, I find our only option is to sell Wheal Favour and Fynwary Hall and use the money to satisfy the debts."

A knot tied in Sophia's stomach, the blood fleeing from her face. Father had sold their house, and now Mr. Hawkins, the man who'd insulted her in her own home, would own Fynwary Hall.

Her toes curled in her slippers. She could only imagine his impassive expression, the same look he'd carried most of the night, but she did not have the strength to look up at him. Not when her life had been stripped bare right before his eyes.

"When must we leave, Mr. Rosewall?" Mother asked, staring at the wall behind Sophia, her voice void of emotion.

Father hesitated, softly squeezing his wife's shoulder. "In two days' time."

Another pain pinched at Sophia's heart. Two days. Two days were all they had left in the home she had been born and raised in, that Father had been born and raised in, and his father before. It was too much. The knot in her stomach contracted.

Mother sniffed, closing her eyes. A single tear escaped her eyelashes and curved down her cheek. Father didn't see, standing behind her, but Mr. Hawkins reached forth, extending his handkerchief.

Mother accepted it with a simple nod, but Sophia still refused to look at him. Why was he there? Never mind that he was asked to be. Could neither he nor Father see that their world, their future, was hanging precariously in the balance? Veritably ending?

Their future. Sophia's future. Her heart sank. "Father, my dowry?"

Slowly, his eyes met hers. One look was enough. She knew the answer.

Gone.

She pressed a hand to her mouth. Her way of life, her future, everything she had in terms of securing a husband vanished from her sight. She could not blame Father, whose shame was so apparent, who had done his best to give his family a good life.

But she would blame who *was* responsible.

With all embarrassment gone, anger billowed inside her. She turned to Mr. Hawkins, anticipating his heartless eyes. She would respond to them with a scowl that would leave him unmistaken as to how she felt about him.

But when their eyes met, she halted. He was not indifferent, nor was he proud. If Sophia didn't know any better, she would have thought he looked pained. His brow was drawn high, his lips rigidly straight. His eyes reflected the despair felt so tangibly in the room.

Why was *he* pained? Why should he be in despair? He must have been told the state of Father's finances, yet he'd still been cruel to her that evening. He was not losing his home. He was gaining one. *Another* one.

Sophia, on the other hand, was losing everything. For what sane gentleman would ever choose to marry a woman without the promise of a single shilling?

Clarity rushed through her like a blast of wind pushing open an unlatched window. Mr. Hawkins's behavior, his sudden change from that morning, now made sense. He had been the perfect example of generosity and kindness when he'd thought her to be a wealthy lady. But nearly the very moment he'd realized who she was—the daughter of a man who had lost everything—he'd shifted his attention from her to someone more deserving, a woman who was now more eligible than Sophia. Miss Kinsey.

How dare the man? His discomfort was no doubt nothing more than a simple act.

With a piercing glare, she stood to face him. "How could you, Mr. Hawkins?" His eyes met hers, hardening as she spoke. "How could you sit at our dinner table, impose on our party, stake your claim on our house before we have even left the premises?"

"Sophia..."

She hardly registered Father's warning tone. "My father has not worked hard each and every day of his life to—"

"Sophia."

"—have some self-proclaimed gentleman flaunt his wealth and position by throwing an honest family out of their rightful home. It is not fair. I will not stand for this. I will not—"

"Sophia!"

She turned wide eyes on her father. Never had he raised his voice so loudly. "But, Father, how can he expect us to leave in two days? The man—"

"*Mr. Hawkins,*" Father interrupted, emphasizing his name, "has offered us every opportunity to remain here for as long as we need. It is I who has decided when to leave Fynwary Hall. I did so weeks ago."

Weeks? Father had known what was to happen for weeks? She struggled to maintain hold of her anger as the questions, the numbness, pulled a thick fog over her mind. Mother kept her eyes closed, as if opening them would force her to see how her life was now plummeting to the ground.

Father continued. "Mr. Hawkins has been more than patient, and—"

"Sir?" Mr. Hawkins's deep tone filled the room.

Sophia spun toward him. Why was he speaking? He didn't have the right.

"I know you wished for me to remain here," he said, "but I think it will be best for all concerned if I take my leave. Please, do excuse me."

"Of course, of course." Father led him toward the door, speaking under his breath, but the silence in the room sent his voice echoing about the walls. "I'm terribly sorry to have put you through all of this, Mr. Hawkins. I perfectly understand your desire to leave."

Sophia's glare followed Mr. Hawkins until he paused at the door, nodding at Father. "Thank you, sir. I will see myself out."

Then his eyes found Sophia's. He studied her for a single, unreadable moment. His mouth parted as if he wished to say something, but in the end, he simply dipped his head and left the room without another word.

Father closed the door. Sophia blew out a breath, her cheeks puffing with the air. "Thank goodness he has left. I'm sure I never wish to see that awful man again."

Father's fierce eyes darted toward her. "Sophia, that was unfair of you to treat him in such a way."

She pulled back, her eyes wide. Why was he upset with her? She had not seen such anger from him since she'd rather willfully painted down the entire banister when she was nine years old. Granted, his frustration was warranted then. What had she done to incur his wrath now, short of speaking the truth to one despicable gentleman?

"Father, Mr. Hawkins hardly deserves your support. Do you know what he said to me after—"

Father's hand cut through the air. "Stop, Sophia. That gentleman is now our landlord."

"Landlord?" She glanced to Mother. Her eyes remained focused on her hands laced together in her lap.

"Mr. Hawkins has very graciously offered to lease Lowena Cottage to us. And I have accepted."

"Lowena Cottage?" She pulled back with repulsion. They,

the Rosewalls, would be staying at Lowena Cottage? The shabby little house perched on the cliffside at the very edge of their property?

She cringed. Mr. Hawkins's property.

"Yes," Father said. "And we will be grateful to him for allowing us to live there when he could just as easily find anyone else. He even went so far as to offer the first few months to us free of charge." His eyes trailed off, as if he was not aware that he still spoke aloud. "Of course I declined. I may have lost everything else, but my pride stays intact." His eyes returned to Sophia. "You would do well to not offend the man. We should not give him reason to turn us out. That is precisely why I invited him to join us for dinner this evening."

Sophia pressed a hand to her churning stomach. She was dreaming. A horrible, terrifying dream. She would not live at Lowena Cottage. Father would not allow her and Mother to fall so low.

Yet, as each moment passed by, the reality of her future life weighed heavier and heavier on her mind.

"Mr. Hawkins will be keeping on most of the servants," Father continued, "and I have agreed that Fynwary Hall will come fully-furnished and equipped, as we will hardly have any use for such finery at the cottage." He seemed to brace himself before sitting next to Mother, placing his hand over hers. "My dear, it is not all bad, I assure you. I will find something in the way of work so we may continue with a somewhat comfortable living."

Father, work as if he were a member of the lower class? They, live comfortably at Lowena Cottage? Sophia scoffed. Father was mad.

"Truly," he continued, ignoring Sophia and leaning forward in an attempt to meet Mother's eye. "Mr. Hawkins is a good man. The best of men. He will treat our home with the dignity it deserves." He paused. "*His* home, I should say."

Hearing those words aloud was the knife that severed the

rope holding Sophia back. Her hands fisted. "This is not his home, Father. This is *our* home, and I refuse to live in such a place as Lowena Cottage."

Father's stern brow turned to her. "This is his home, Sophia. You have already made things insufferably uncomfortable for him. I will not allow you to worsen the matter by stubbornly refusing to leave his house."

She huffed out an indignant breath, only vaguely aware of the hysterics bubbling within her. "I have made things uncomfortable for him? What about what he has done to us? No, Father. I will not leave here. You cannot force me to do so. I refuse to live in a home unfit for even servants, and I refuse to leave Fynwary Hall." She plopped down onto the sofa, folding her arms. "I will not allow my home to fall into the hands of an ungrateful, insolent man who can only—"

"Sophia," Mother hissed, "enough!"

Sophia's eyes widened, cowering as her mother continued. "Your father has spoken. We shall do as he says."

Her words were final. There was no reason for Sophia to speak any longer. She looked between her parents, their unhappy faces fixed on her. They had not even peered at Mr. Hawkins with such disappointment.

The knowledge stung. With a quivering chin, Sophia stood and fled from the room, waiting until she was far enough away from the drawing room to finally allow her sobs passage through her lips.

CHAPTER TEN

*F*rederick pushed the letter from his steward aside and leaned his elbows on the small desk, his interlaced fingers pressed against his lips.

His eyes followed the people walking below his window as they passed by the Golden Arms Inn. They walked in a slower manner here, relaxed as they greeted friends and smiled at one another. Their world seemed far happier than how he felt in his room.

Two nights had passed since his dinner at the Rosewalls. Three since he'd been sleeping at the dreadful inn. Before the dinner party, Mr. Rosewall had offered him a room at Fynwary Hall. Fortunately, Frederick had possessed the foresight to decline his offer.

As tired as he was of the Golden Arms—its prickly, woolen blankets, the constant bustle coming from below his room, and the horrendous food—the deplorable living conditions were far better than the awkwardness of staying at Fynwary Hall as the Rosewalls packed away their few belongings and made ready for their move to the cottage.

Why Mr. Rosewall had thought it wise to tell his family in front of Frederick that they no longer had a source of income or a home was beyond him. The tension was palpable, and he had taken his first opportunity to escape.

Mr. Rosewall may have done so out of fear, hoping Frederick's presence would allow his wife and daughter to remain calm. Or perhaps so their anger would glance off Mr. Rosewall and hit Frederick instead. Mrs. Rosewall had certainly maintained decorum, but the same could not be said about her daughter.

Frederick concentrated more intently out the window. He'd promised himself he'd no longer think of the Rosewalls. Mr. Rosewall reminded him too greatly of Frederick's coward father. And Miss Rosewall, well, she had been the greatest disappointment of them all. Not only had she turned out to be the type of woman he'd tried to avoid in London, she'd then proceeded to blame Frederick for her own father's inability to keep their home.

Of course he had compassion for them. He would be heartless if he didn't also suffer with a great deal of culpability. When he'd first arrived at Fynwary Hall, he was under the impression, because Mr. Rosewall had told him such, that he would take possession directly. Seeing that the Rosewalls were not yet ready to leave, Frederick had offered to return in a few weeks. Mr. Rosewall had declined, however, ensuring Frederick that they would be gone in two days.

Such a revelation had shocked Mrs. Rosewall, and her sorrow had pressed keenly on Frederick's mind, as did Miss Rosewall's dismay. He'd even felt remorse for his unkind words to her after their game of whist, though that had quickly vanished when she'd accused him of ruining her life.

Frederick sniffed with derision. He may be the one pushing them from their home, but he was essentially saving her father from debtor's prison. He had very little patience for a man who could keep such secrets from his family, like his own father had.

He combed his fingers through his hair and stood from his

desk, approaching the window for a better view, though he couldn't see the ocean from the inn. Perhaps he ought to take another ride. He'd ventured to the sea multiple times a day since he'd arrived in Cornwall. The waves did much to soothe his nerves.

Nerves that should not even be present.

Blast that woman and her family. He had not come to Cornwall to get himself wrapped up in the center of a scene from some theatrical drama. He'd come for peace, a pleasant time, and, Heaven-willing, a potential wife.

Since Miss Rosewall was anything but a potential wife, he would instead consider Miss Kinsey. He couldn't carry on a conversation with her, but at least she wasn't pretending to be someone she wasn't. If his true intent in coming to Cornwall was to find a proper spouse, then he would be wise to no longer dwell on Miss Rosewall.

The sooner he forgot about her, the better.

Sophia shivered, the movement causing her to wake from her slumber. Why was it so cold in her room? And why did those birds chirp so closely to her window? They had never been that loud before.

She rolled onto her back with a groan. As the sun fell across her face, she pulled out of the way, squeezing her eyes tightly closed.

It could not be any later than eight in the morning. Mills knew Sophia didn't wish to be awoken before ten o'clock, so why on earth had the lady's maid opened the curtains already?

Sophia stretched her arms over her head as she drew in a deep breath. But as a strange scent accosted her senses, she abruptly stopped.

Damp wood. Wet straw.

She opened her eyes just a fraction, allowing them to

adjust to the light. When she found the spring green bed hangings missing from her four-poster bed, and her large, brightly lit fireplace gone, she sat upright with a gasp. This was not her room at Fynwary Hall.

This was Lowena Cottage.

Her head spun, though whether from the quick movements or the memories pouring over her, she could not be sure.

She cast her eyes about the room, *her* room, and her lip curled in disgust. Cobwebs littered every corner, ceiling to floor, and the walls were bare, decorated solely by the cracks running up and down the grey paint. The only pieces of furniture within the room were a small wardrobe, a desk, and her bed that now trembled dangerously with each movement she made.

It was just as well that there was no further furniture. Nothing else would have fit, apart from the smallest hearth she had ever seen situated near the foot of her bed. Surely it was unfit for warming a room even half the size of her new, miniscule living quarters.

By the looks of it, the fire had gone out hours ago, which had undoubtedly contributed to the frigid temperature of her room. That, and the very chilly and very steady draft sliding past her shoulders.

She burrowed farther into her thin blanket and looked to the window. The curtains hadn't been opened, after all. They were merely too small to cover the entire pane, which was not a difficult feat, as the window was nearly a fourth of the size of hers at Fynwary.

From the crack in the curtains, she could see a distinctly crooked gap between the wooden ledge of the window and the frame, evidence that the window hadn't been installed properly.

Wonderful. That explained the draft and why the birds were so loud. And the waves. Goodness, the cottage must be right on top of the sea. If the crack in the window allowed the sound of the outdoors in, she could only imagine what other creatures besides the spiders could enter her room. She rubbed her crawling skin at the thought.

With her room in such a terrible state, Sophia wondered how the rest of the cottage appeared. She had arrived so late last night, well after dark, that she could hardly recall a single sight.

They had initially planned to leave Fynwary Hall early the morning before, but with Sophia refusing to leave her room, they missed their aim by nearly an entire day. Truthfully, she would be there still, had it not been for Mother speaking sense to her.

"Sophia," she had said, "if we do not leave this very moment, Mr. Hawkins will arrive, and you shall have to face him again. Is that what you wish to do? Because I would prefer never seeing that gentleman again."

After her words, Sophia had promptly quit the house, and Mother had continued on in her silence. Sophia did not blame her for not wishing to speak. After all, what could any of them say that hadn't already been thought by each one of them?

Another cool wind sailed past her, and she looked to the empty hearth again. Why had Edith not maintained the fire last night? The cottage was a far cry smaller than Fynwary Hall. The girl should have no difficulty in the upkeep of the rooms.

If hiring the servants had been up to Sophia, she would never have chosen to bring along Edith, their scullery maid turned housemaid. Nor would Sophia have hired Mrs. Cuff, the woman who would now act as their housekeeper, though her duties would also extend to playing the part of lady's maid, as they couldn't afford Mills to be brought with them.

Mrs. Cuff had come highly recommended by their previous housekeeper, but Sophia wondered how good she could be if her only option was to take work at a poorly cottage.

Time would tell if the servants would do their work admirably. Though, perhaps she could give their efforts a test right now.

Still lying in her bed, she glanced around the room for a servants' bell. Her brow crinkled when her search came up empty, and she realized the house was probably too small to have one.

She released a great sigh. This cottage was becoming more cumbersome by the minute. How was Mrs. Cuff to know when to come to her room with breakfast? Sophia could hardly shout out her desires through the house, no matter how small it was. That was far too undignified for a Rosewall.

Her stomach growled. She pressed a hand over her abdomen to suppress it. Typically, she would never consider eating breakfast so early, but having refused nearly all her meals for two days, she could do with proper nourishment.

Especially considering what she had planned for her day, solving the problem dear Father had unwittingly created for them. She'd concocted her plan only the day before as she'd watched the servants pack away half her dresses—"Not all of them will fit in the cottage, miss"—and only a handful of her belongings.

The gowns she didn't bring along, most of them old and out of fashion, would be sold for scraps to help pay for rent in the coming months before Father found a job.

Sophia knew he was already busy attempting to better their circumstances, either by finding work with reputable gentlemen or looking into future investments. One day, she hoped to see him take back Fynwary Hall from the gentleman whom she would never speak of again. But that would be a long time from now.

Sophia's forthcoming plan, however, would provide her a way to leave Lowena Cottage far sooner. With any luck, she would not even spend a single night longer attempting to sleep on this lumpy, damp mattress. She may have been distraught the night Father had told her the news, but now she was filled with hope.

Her stomach growled again. She really could not allow such an unladylike sound to continue, no matter how cold she was.

Quickly, she slid from her bed and crossed the brisk floor to the small wardrobe. Thumbing through the clothing Mrs. Cuff had managed to put away tidily, Sophia spotted her dressing gown.

The comfortable cover and her slippers provided better warmth before she finally left her room, opening the door with a loud creak that pierced the air.

She peered down the corridor. The walls were the same drab grey that her bedroom suffered with, but a window spilled golden light across the floor, specks of dust shimmering in the air.

Two doors were situated side-by-side across from Sophia's room. She stopped in front of the first, listening as muted voices sounded behind the door. Mother and Father were no doubt discussing ways in which to leave Lowena behind.

She sighed with relief. She could always rely on her sweet parents. They all deserved so much better than this cottage.

The voices quieted as she tapped softly against the door. Footsteps sounded, then the door opened.

To her surprise, the housekeeper stood before her. "Mrs. Cuff, I was just on my way to find you."

"What can I do for ye, miss?" She stepped outside of the room, pulling the door behind her.

Sophia failed to catch a single glimpse of Mother before the door closed. "I typically don't take breakfast this early, but I require such this morning, if you would be so kind."

"Yes, miss."

"I will dress shortly after. And do have Edith tend to my fire. It is unbearably cold in my room."

"My apologies, miss. I'll have her see to it right away."

"Thank you. Oh, and at your earliest convenience, I should like you to purchase bells so I do not have to go in search of you each time I am in need of something. I should think my mother would agree to this, as well."

"Yes, miss."

Sophia peered over the woman's shoulder at Mother's door. "Is my mother in there now?"

"Yes, miss, but she asked to remain undisturbed for the rest of the day. She didn't sleep well."

"Did any of us?" Sophia mumbled. She wiped away her contempt and began again. "When she is feeling better, do tell her that I am to call on the Madderns this morning. If she finds the strength, I would enjoy her company, but if not, I must go alone."

Sophia knew calling without a companion would hardly be proper, but she had no choice. Her plan needed to go into effect that very day.

"I'll tell her, miss."

Sophia nodded her thanks and returned to her room. She refused to allow the shabby interior to darken her mood. Not while she had hope yet. All she needed to do was wait for the hours to pass by, then she could go to the Madderns and carry out her strategy.

With any luck, her life and her future would be changed forever, and this time for the better.

CHAPTER ELEVEN

$\mathcal{F}$rederick shifted his feet, fighting the urge to glance at the clock at the far side of the Maddern's drawing room. He supposed he didn't really need to check the time. He'd only just arrived, yet he couldn't wait for when he could leave without causing offense.

He stifled a yawn as the silence ticked by. He'd received a wonderful night's sleep at Fynwary Hall the night before, and still, he struggled to remain alert.

Perhaps that was simply due to his company. Miss Kinsey was kind, appeared intelligent, and was very pretty with her soft, blonde hair. But if she wasn't the most painfully shy woman he'd ever come across. It was nearly impossible for him to carry on a conversation with her.

"So you are from Kent?" he asked.

"Yes, sir."

"Do you miss it there?"

She nodded.

"And your sisters, how are they faring without you?"

A flicker of anguish crossed her face. "They are well, sir. But they miss me, as I miss them."

Her voice broke. He glanced to Mrs. Maddern in discomfort, but the middle-aged woman merely watched her niece with compassionate eyes.

Wonderful. Not only was he failing in his attempt to encourage Miss Kinsey to speak, he was now causing her pain by the topics he chose. This visit was getting worse by the minute.

"Kent is a beautiful county," he said, changing the subject before both women could burst into tears. "I had the pleasure of visiting there a few years ago on business."

Miss Kinsey nodded.

Mrs. Maddern sent Frederick an apologetic look. He smiled to ensure the woman that all was well.

In truth, it was. He could be patient. He had all the time in the world to get to know Miss Kinsey better, to see if they matched well enough to wed. Of course, at this rate, it would take a lifetime to get to know Miss Kinsey's true feelings, but he could be patient for a woman who was inherently good. A woman who didn't flirt with every gentleman within her arm's reach.

"And how are your parents?" he asked in a rush. The silence had allowed his mind to stray to a place, to a woman, of whom he would no longer think.

"They are well."

He continued in a soft voice, fearing she might run away like a skittish deer if he spoke any louder. "I do not know if they are anything like my own mother, but if they are, it must be a welcome relief to be away for a time. Parents can be difficult to maneuver."

Her eyes met his for one brief moment before dropping again to her hands. "I have never taken issue with my parents."

He swallowed his sigh. Yet another thing the two didn't have in common.

"Have you told Mr. Hawkins about your love of poetry?"

Mrs. Maddern asked, attempting to draw her niece out, as well.

Miss Kinsey shook her head. "No, but I do have a certain fondness for it."

Frederick's smile weakened. Good heavens. He enjoyed reading as much as the next person, but poetry? He could not abide it. The writing was far too cryptic. He much preferred straight-forward, no-nonsense speech.

"My niece is quite skilled in rehearsing certain poems. She has even written a few verses herself."

"Oh?" He could like poetry. He would just have to try a little harder to do so. "And how often do you write them?"

"Often."

He nodded, wracking his brain for something further to say. Relief came in a different form when the Madderns' footman entered the drawing room, pulling their attention away from the uncomfortable conversation.

"Yes, what is it, Peterson?" Mrs. Maddern asked.

"Miss Rosewall to see you, ma'am."

Frederick's stomach dropped. Blast. What was the woman doing there? He far preferred speaking, or not speaking, with Miss Kinsey than being with Miss Rosewall again.

He glanced to Mrs. Maddern. She was looking at him with widened eyes, no doubt wondering how the interaction between him and Miss Rosewall would be. After all, the whole of St. Just now knew that he owned Fynwary Hall.

The footman stepped aside, and Miss Rosewall entered the room. He would never have thought this woman was capable of tripping in the sand, so gracefully she curtsied to them.

Her lips curved, her eyebrows drawn high on her fore-head, giving her a pleasant aura. She did not appear for the worse, living at the cottage. Perhaps the move had done her good, even eased the hatred she felt toward Frederick.

But as her eyes fell on him, they hardened to an icy blue,

and a coldness seeped through his person, slithering down his spine.

"Miss Rosewall, do come in," Mrs. Maddern said. Her eyes moved to Frederick's once more. "We had no idea we'd have the pleasure of seeing you this morning."

Miss Rosewall moved farther into the room. "You must forgive me for calling without notice, Mrs. Maddern, Miss Kinsey. I simply did not have the opportunity to visit with the both of you enough at our dinner party, so I thought to make amends this morning." She looked at Frederick. "Mr. Hawkins," she greeted coolly.

He responded with a stiff bow.

She sat down on the only seat available—the sofa right next to where he stood—and raised her chin, her neck long and slender. She really was lovely.

No. No, Miss Kinsey was lovely.

"I trust you are both well," Miss Rosewall asked the aunt and niece. "And Mr. Maddern?"

"He is feeling much better, thank you," Mrs. Maddern responded. "He is out riding this morning."

"Thank goodness you and Miss Kinsey have not suffered with the same cold."

"Indeed." Mrs. Maddern skirted her eyes. "And how is your own family, Miss Rosewall?" Her question was laden with curiosity and hesitation.

"We are doing very well, thank you."

Miss Rosewall had spoken so convincingly, Frederick would have believed her, had he thought she could ever be happy in reduced circumstances.

"And your mother?" Mrs. Maddern pressed.

Miss Rosewall sighed. "I see. You must have heard what has happened to my family." She stared down at her folded hands. "We are doing better than one might suppose. Mother is tired, but that is to be expected after such an upheaval to our lives."

Sorrow thickly laced her voice, but as she glanced sidelong at Frederick, fury still lit her eyes.

Frederick couldn't believe it. She was actually playing the victim, no doubt hoping that he would appear as the one responsible for her new, pitiful existence.

He would not allow that lie to spread, nor the woman to manipulate others to benefit herself.

He clasped his hands behind his back, his nails digging into his palms. "Miss Kinsey, before we were interrupted, you mentioned liking poetry. Do you enjoy Shakespeare then?"

Miss Rosewall glared up at him. She obviously did not wish the conversation steered to anyone but herself.

"Yes, sir," Miss Kinsey responded.

"And do you prefer his sonnets or his plays?"

"I haven't a preference."

Miss Rosewall jumped in, her smooth tone grating at Frederick's patience. "I myself adore Shakespeare's plays. Miss Kinsey, have you had the opportunity to see one of them performed at the theatre?"

"No, I haven't."

"Oh, you really ought to make that a priority. I'm certain you would enjoy it. There are times when I prefer the theatre to even a ball."

Frederick's fists clenched tighter. He glanced toward her just as she moved her eyes away from him. How could he have ever thought those hollow, blue chasms were warm?

He forced his attention on Miss Kinsey. What color of eyes did she have? He couldn't tell with how low she hung her head.

"Speaking of a ball," Miss Rosewall continued, "I can hardly wait for yours. It has only been a few weeks since the assembly in St. Just, but it seems a lifetime ago since I've danced. Yours will be here before we know it."

Mrs. Maddern readjusted her skirts over her knees. "So you still wish to attend?"

Miss Rosewall pulled in her brows. "Why, of course I do. I assume I am still invited?"

"Of course you are, my dear, of course. I only thought that, what with the strain of you moving to Lowena Cottage, you would not have the energy to attend."

A small vein pulsed in Miss Rosewall's otherwise unmoving neck. "Well, as we are all still enthusiastic, even after such a move, I can hardly think of a reason *not* to attend. Can you?"

She looked to each person in the room, ending on Frederick. Her eyebrow raised daringly.

Frederick itched to challenge her, as she challenged him, but Mrs. Maddern's flustered response came first.

"Oh, no, Miss Rosewall. Of course we are most pleased to have you attend. It will be a pleasure to have you be one of our primary dancers, along with my lovely niece, of course."

A satisfied expression unveiled on Miss Rosewall's face. Mrs. Maddern, however, shifted uncomfortably in her seat.

Frederick was certain the woman had not wished for Miss Rosewall to attend. The aunt was no doubt hoping that her niece might be allowed to blossom then.

Miss Rosewall, however, did not care for anyone's desires but her own. Such was evident as she continued speaking, entirely unaware of the growing restlessness in the room.

"Oh, Mrs. Maddern, you have such a lovely home." Her eyes trailed around the drawing room.

The walls were a Saxon green and covered with images of ancestors and golden sconces. It *was* lovely. But Frederick kept his eyes on Miss Rosewall. She was up to something else now, though he wasn't sure what.

"I always feel so happy when I call here," Miss Rosewall continued. "There is something about Benlett House that feels, well, that feels like home. Miss Kinsey is so very fortunate that you have taken her in with welcome arms and given her such a lovely place to call her own."

Frederick's lips pressed flat. Miss Kinsey made no reaction, but Mrs. Maddern nodded her gratitude.

Miss Rosewall's head pivoted as she eyed the crown molding bordering the room. "So clean and tidy. And so spacious! You must have a great deal of spare rooms just collecting dust." An airy laugh blew past her lips. "Oh, to have such space again. I fear Lowena Cottage is surely lacking in that regard. Of course, the cottage *is* lovely, if not a little dirty. And small. So small I hardly have room for any of my belongings." She forced an exaggerated wince to her eye. "It is a struggle. But I am managing as best I can."

Frederick clenched his jaw, his muscles twitching. There it was, the true reasoning behind her call. He could hardly believe her audacity.

A look of discomfort crossed Mrs. Maddern's features. She was no doubt aware of Miss Rosewall's workings. "Under the circumstances, we're certainly glad you're doing as well as you are, Miss Rosewall."

"Yes, we are doing remarkably well." Miss Rosewall looked past Frederick to the hearth, rubbing her upper arms and raising her shoulders. "How very warm it is in here. No doubt due to that lovely fire. The cottage has very little heat, I'm afraid. I do hope I will not catch a cold while living there. Miss Kinsey, you must enjoy the warmth here, as well."

Miss Kinsey's eyes traveled up, then fell straight back down, her voice softer than usual. "Indeed, I do."

"Though you must get lonely, at times, do you not?" Miss Rosewall pressed.

Frederick longed to groan at her blatant hinting.

"Aunt and Uncle are very fine company," Miss Kinsey said. "I could not wish for more than that."

A gracious response from a gracious woman. Unlike Miss Rosewall, who continued to speak only for her benefit.

"Oh yes, your aunt is of the highest quality. But you really ought to have a companion your age. Don't you agree, Mrs.

Maddern? Would your niece not benefit with someone to guide her through the norms of social graces? Someone who could be near her, why, even live at Benlett House if you wished it."

CHAPTER TWELVE

*U*nbelievable. Frederick could hardly keep his temper checked. Miss Rosewall was playing another game, a game to get out of Lowena Cottage and into Benlett House by using Miss Kinsey's innocence and Mrs. Maddern's kindness.

Frederick had seen the cottage from afar that very morning on his way to visit the Madderns. It was small, and the roof and a few of the windows were badly in need of repair—repairs he, as landlord, had every intention of seeing to. But it was the largest house that Fynwary Hall leased to others, not to mention more than sufficient for a family of three whose father had no more income than a small share in a weakened mine.

Did Miss Rosewall not realize how fortunate she was to not be living in the poor house? Was she so ungrateful to not even appreciate the fact that she had a roof over her head?

No, she was oblivious to it all and was now willing to leave her parents behind so that she alone might enjoy a life of leisure.

The silence in the drawing room was palpable. Unbearable. Mrs. Maddern avoided Miss Rosewall's penetrating gaze, obviously unsure of how to proceed.

From his viewpoint, Frederick could see Miss Kinsey's rounded eyes as she stared at the carpet. She looked ready to run from the room, as skittish as any fawn he'd ever seen.

If Miss Kinsey was a fawn…Miss Rosewall was the fox.

The wily, conniving fox.

As a child, Frederick hadn't been able to stand up to his father's manipulation. But he was no longer a child, and he would not allow Miss Rosewall's games to proceed.

His voice shattered the silence. "Well I, for one, believe Miss Kinsey has a fine companion in Mrs. Maddern. After all, who better to share one's home and time with than a loving member of one's own family?" He turned to Miss Rosewall, whose eyes flashed heatedly up at him. "And you must agree, Miss Rosewall. How grateful you must be to have your mother as your companion, and you as hers. She would certainly be miserable without both her husband and her daughter with her at Lowena Cottage."

Miss Rosewall's chin jutted forth, her brow lowering menacingly over her eyes.

"Oh, goodness, yes," Mrs. Maddern said, sighing with obvious relief. "Just imagine your poor mother without you by her side. Your father, too. You know how they dote on you. Just as I dote on my niece. Claire, you have noticed the very same, that the Rosewalls love their daughter wholeheartedly, have you not?"

Frederick was surprised with how quickly Miss Kinsey nodded. "Indeed, they do." Her voice was loud. Well, louder than usual.

"I have noticed the very same," Frederick agreed, if only to place more kindling onto Mrs. Maddern's fire of resolve. "They would miss you a dreadful amount."

Miss Rosewall pursed her lips, unamused with what had just occurred. Frederick, on the other hand, could not be more pleased. He sent a smile in her direction, a smile that was not returned, which only pushed him to continue his own game.

"In fact, I'm certain your mother is missing you this very moment, Miss Rosewall. Why do you not allow me to escort you home?"

"I hardly think that is necessary," she replied, venom thick in her voice.

Mrs. Maddern stood, Miss Kinsey following suit. "Oh, what a lovely idea, Mr. Hawkins," Mrs. Maddern said. "So generous. You must accept his offer, Miss Rosewall. After all, you really ought not be walking around unaccompanied."

"But I only just arrived," Miss Rosewall said. "And I have something else I wish to discuss with—"

"Come, come, Miss Rosewall," Frederick said, extending his hand to where she was still seated. "I insist."

Now it was Miss Rosewall who could not find a way to protest, what with three people clearly wishing for her to take her leave. With flared nostrils, she stood, brushing past his outstretched hand.

Frederick hid his gratified smirk.

"Good day, Mrs. Maddern, Miss Kinsey," she said. She paused at the door only long enough to curtsy, barely suffering a glance at Frederick before mumbling for him to make haste. Without awaiting a response, she marched from the room.

Finally satisfied that Miss Rosewall would not confront Mrs. Maddern and her niece with any more unreasonable requests, Frederick bade farewell to them both, making his way from the drawing room and through the house.

Miss Rosewall was nowhere in sight. It was no surprise that she would leave without him. Truth be told, he was relieved. A walk home with Miss Rosewall was not how he wished to spend his morning.

He quit the house and retrieved his horse from the groom, greeting the chestnut gelding with a rub to his forelock.

"That was not amusing, Mr. Hawkins."

Frederick whirled around at the voice, coming face-to-face with Miss Rosewall, who had seemingly appeared out of nowhere. She stood with her arms folded, lips pursed, and nose in the air.

She'd undoubtedly decided to wait for him simply to scold him for foiling her plan. "Oh, are you still here?"

He tugged on his gloves. He could hear the impatient tapping of her boot on the gravel, though her foot was hidden beneath her skirts.

"Of course I am still here," she said. "Though I would still be in there"—she waved her arm toward the house—"had you not rudely pulled me away from my friends, causing me the greatest of impositions."

He scoffed, stroking his horse's neck. He'd made up his mind long ago to never be goaded into an argument, but this woman had a spectacular ability to break down the walls of his determination.

"And what of the imposition you would have caused the Madderns," he said, "had I allowed your selfish plan to—"

"Selfish?"

Finally he met her eyes. There was more fire in them than he'd imagined. Blast, if she didn't look just as alluring when she was angry as when she was happy. Her full lips pouted, and her frowning, dark eyebrows caused her eyes to become even more pronounced.

What the devil was he doing, noticing her beauty? Especially when she'd revealed, once more, that it only ran skin-deep.

"Yes, *selfish*," he repeated. "There is no other word for your behavior toward them and your own family."

With her chin jutting forth, she took a step forward. She was a head shorter than him, but her ferocity made her seem a foot taller. "My father was wrong to sell Fynwary Hall to you. You, who are in no way a gentleman."

Frederick shook his head. Why had he been quelling his

frustration, checking his temper and his words, when Miss Rosewall refused to extend the same courtesy?

Forgetting his desire to be the ever-in-control gentleman he'd taught himself to be, he leaned toward her, speaking through bared teeth. "I am more a gentleman than you could ever be a lady."

She gasped, pressing a hand to her chest in rehearsed revulsion, a reaction that only added to his desire to tear her pride straight from her elevated chin.

"How could you have even considered leaving your family behind so you might live a wealthier life without them? Have you no care for either of your parents?"

She sputtered, attempting to retaliate, but his words could not be stopped.

"And what did you mean by positioning yourself to benefit from poor Mrs. Maddern's charity? Surely you noted her discomfort? Her clear desire to say no?"

To his surprise, and to her credit, a flicker of discomfort crossed her features. But it was gone in an instant when she scoffed. "*Poor* Mrs. Maddern? Does she look poor to you with her newly redecorated drawing room, and her fashionable gowns, and Miss Kinsey receiving everything she wishes? I hardly think so. At any rate, the Madderns and my parents have been friends for years. You would not know such a thing, as you are a stranger here, but she would have gladly accepted me into her home because that is just the sort of woman she is."

His jaw twitched at her obstinance. "You claim to know her better, and that may be so. But why..." He glanced around them to ensure they would not be overheard, continuing in a lower register. "Why was *I* the one coming to her defense? Helping her excuse herself from becoming a guardian over *two* young women? Can you not imagine how Miss Kinsey's presence here might already have affected the couple's lives? To add another woman indefinitely living in their home would be an unthinkable burden on them all."

She looked away. "They would be glad to have me," she muttered, scrambling for a defense. "And I am not selfish, *you* are."

He barked out a laugh. "Oh, yes. *I* am selfish."

"You are," she repeated with vehemence. "You are the one who has pushed my poor family—my *truly* poor family—into a cottage unfit for habitation. You forced us out of our rightful home, caused my father to feel shame before his family, my mother to be unwell. You caused it all. Yes, sir, you are the selfish one."

She was crazed. That's all there was to it. Mad, entirely without sense. "I had nothing to do with your father's poor choices, Miss Rosewall. He is to blame for all of this, not I."

They stood staring at one another, both breathing heavily with unrestrained animosity. But when tears sprung to her eyes, shock rattled Frederick's body. Blast it all. He knew he'd gone too far with those final words. Still, he clenched his teeth, fighting off the guilt he felt for allowing his tongue to run loose.

Miss Rosewall quickly blinked away the moisture. As she spoke, her tone was level, void of all emotion. "You do not know my father, Mr. Hawkins. And you do not know me. So don't pretend that you do."

Frederick struggled with his desire to contradict her words and the knowledge that he'd allowed himself to become wrapped up in his emotions.

With a deep sigh, he rubbed at the back of his neck. "You are right, Miss Rosewall. I do not know you. I should not have spoken so unkindly."

Their stares locked, and for the briefest of moments, Frederick thought he saw vulnerability in her eyes, a flicker of worry, and a tremor shook his heart. She looked helpless, afraid...real.

In the next instant, it was gone, replaced once more by her haughty demeanor. "No," she said in response to his words, "you shouldn't have."

With a brusque curtsy, she swept past him without a glance back.

Frederick watched her leave, securing his hat atop his head as he fought off an exasperated groan. He felt for the woman and her newly changed circumstances. He sincerely did. But her treatment of Mrs. Maddern and Miss Kinsey, and her unwillingness to admit to the truth in matters, was insufferable.

How grateful he was that she obviously did not wish for him to accompany her home. He did not think he could do so without once again trying to force some sense into the woman.

He knew it would do them both little good.

CHAPTER THIRTEEN

"*T*hank you for hiring the carriage tonight, Father," Sophia said as they bounced up and down across the uneven road.

She avoided staring at the peeling leather on the empty seat next to her and the stains on the dirty floor beneath them. It was a great deal smaller and a great deal untidier than the carriages they had kept at Fynwary Hall, but this would certainly be more appropriate to arrive in for the Maddern's ball than on foot.

Father nodded, staring out of the smudged window. "I was happy to do so for you."

Sophia wondered what was so arresting to keep his attention away from her. He'd hardly said a word the entire ride, and they were nearly at Benlett House.

"I'm certain we will one day be able to afford to keep our own carriage and horses again," she offered next. "Hopefully sooner rather than later."

He tossed his head in a half-hearted nod. Sophia pulled her lips to one side. She knew Father was still coming to terms with their reduced circumstances, as was Mother. They'd both kept to their rooms a fair amount since losing Fynwary Hall a little over a week ago, but Sophia couldn't understand why they appeared to have already given up.

She, herself, was more than weary of staying at Lowena Cottage, especially after being confined indoors due to rain nearly every day since they'd arrived. She greatly enjoyed no longer playing the pianoforte, as there was no room for the instrument, but the insufferably long and lonely days had begun to grate on her spirits.

There was still hope to be had, though. They wouldn't remain at Lowena forever. Father would find work to improve their income. Until then, Sophia would continue seeking out old friends and neighbors, beyond the Madderns, who would be willing to help the Rosewalls, whether by lending money, homes, or advice. All she had to do was ask. And, of course, ensure the meddling Mr. Hawkins kept out of her way.

Thunder rumbled in the distance, thankfully preventing her mind from dwelling on the gentleman and their heated argument the week before. She cagily eyed the heavy clouds blocking out the waning July sun. She had hoped it wouldn't start raining until they'd at least arrived at Benlett House. Now her hair and dress risked becoming ruined, despite the umbrellas the servants would surely be holding up for the guests.

Father sighed, and she again aimed her attention at him. "Are you looking forward to this evening, Father?"

He'd always enjoyed balls before. They all had. But he merely nodded.

"I'm sorry Mother couldn't be with us," she continued.

His eyes moved to the floor of the carriage. "As am I. But I'm relieved she chose to remain at home. She has not yet recovered from the move and needs her rest."

Had any of them truly recovered yet? "Well, I'm certainly glad you have chosen to join me."

"Indeed."

Convincing her father to come to the ball had taken a fair

amount of charming words and careful pleading on Sophia's part. She still couldn't understand why he was so hesitant to attend.

"Do you like my gown?" she asked, smoothing down the white silk of her dress. "I think it is rather becoming."

His eyes snapped toward her gown, as if he only just now noticed what she wore. "When did you purchase that?"

She blinked. "Mother and I ordered it a few weeks ago."

"Oh, then yes, it is lovely. As all your gowns are."

She tipped her head to one side, curls bouncing lightly against her brow. Had he thought she'd spent money they didn't have?

Just then, the carriage rolled to a stop in front of Benlett House. A familiar exhilaration bubbled within her, replacing her worry over her father's behavior. She'd been looking forward to this evening for weeks, especially after moving to the cottage.

The prospect of returning to the world where she belonged, where she could dance, and flaunt, and flirt to her heart's content—where she could receive the attention she so deserved—was all too wonderful. She was in such a wonderful mood, in fact, that she could even be convinced to play the pianoforte. Though, if she thought that was an actual possibility, she would still find a way out of a musical performance.

She allowed Father to help her down from the carriage. With an anticipatory, hopeful sigh, she took in the sight of the Madderns' home.

Benlett House was half the size of Fynwary, but still grand in its own nature. The house had two, red-brick stories with dozens of stone-framed windows and pointed roofing. Lights glowed from within each of the windows, and the gardens had been immaculately tended to in preparation for the evening's ball.

The last time Sophia had stood outside these grand doors had been a less than pleasant experience. But she would not allow the memory of her argument with Mr. Hawkins to taint the excitement she held for that evening. She would enjoy her time dancing with Mr. Chester and Mr. Singleton, as well as the other gentlemen she would meet. She would taste the refreshments, speak with whomever she wished, and, weather permitting, might even enjoy the gardens firsthand with the gentleman of her choice. This was what Sophia wanted to do. This was what her parents wanted her to do.

A trickle of hesitation trailed down her conscience as Mr. Hawkins's words from the dinner party echoed in her mind.

You have shown me that these games also exist here.

She grimaced. The game of catching a wealthy husband. That was hardly what she was doing this evening. She was merely out to enjoy herself for the first time in over a week, so enjoy herself she would.

With Father leading her forward, they joined the line of guests entering the Madderns' home. A few couples looked in their direction. Father turned away, but Sophia politely nodded, accustomed to such stares of admiration. She had been pleasantly surprised with Mrs. Cuff's ability to make her hair presentable enough for the ball. Her dark locks were twisted high in a chignon, and small, white flowers speckled the twist. Her curls weren't flawless by any means, but they certainly would suffice for a country ball.

They entered the house, and after their names were announced, Father released her hand. "Will you be all right on your own for a moment, my dear?"

She nodded. "Of course."

"Then I shall be in the card room if you need anything."

Mother would hardly approve of Sophia's father and chaperone swapping her for the card room, but Sophia could hardly ask him to remain by her side the whole evening.

Besides, she didn't have time to worry over him and whether or not he had the funds to enjoy a game of cards— did he?—for she had plans to carry out.

She followed the waves of people into the ballroom, taking care not to bump shoulders in the entryway. The large room was decorated with fresh, purple flowers and greenery. The chandeliers and sconces shone brightly against the shining wooden floor, and the cream curtains were pulled back to allow in what was left of the summer evening light. The room held a buzz of excitement, an anticipation for the coming first dance, and Sophia could not wait to be a part of it.

This was the world in which she belonged. Not the one filled with dusty walls and creaking doors.

She meandered across the dance floor, a decorous lift to the corner of her lips. Her hands were folded lightly in front of her as her fan dangled from one wrist. She passed by more looks. Her brow twitched with the slightest of frowns as she wondered if they stared for other reasons. She quickly brushed the bothersome thought aside. They must simply be surprised that she looked so well, despite coming from the slovenly cottage.

She paused near the center of the room, a perfect vantage point to see and be seen. Holding her neck in a way she knew looked appealing, she scanned her eyes across the crowd, in search of any gentleman's attention she might capture.

To her dismay, the first person she found was Mr. Hawkins. Now how had she gone and found him so quickly? She was about to look away, but her eyes were drawn to the group around him, four other ladies and gentlemen, Miss Kinsey included.

The young woman looked rather fetching that evening. Her gown wasn't as white as Sophia's, nor anywhere near as fine, but it at least complimented her fair hair and pale skin.

She stood with the others, who were all enraptured as Mr. Hawkins spoke. Sophia couldn't make out what he said, but in the next moment, the group laughed. Even Miss Kinsey broke her signature solemn look and nearly grinned.

Sophia's stomach leapt at the sight of Mr. Hawkins's confident smile. She'd forgotten how much she enjoyed it. His care-free nature began to spread its light-heartedness to her, and… and now it distracted her from her tasks.

She scolded her wayward mind. She was there to enjoy herself, to find someone to help her escape Lowena.

She wasn't there to admire Mr. Hawkins's perfectly symmetrical face, nor his lean frame in his green, high-collared waistcoat and black jacket.

CHAPTER FOURTEEN

rederick had spotted Miss Rosewall the moment she'd entered the ballroom, though he'd quickly returned his attention to the small party around him. These people were delightful, no pretenses or illusions of grandeur, simply at the ball to enjoy themselves. They were kind and welcoming, like nearly every person he'd met thus far in Cornwall.

It was just his luck that he had happened on the only ostentatious woman his first day in the county.

As the conversation shifted to one of the young women and her new pug, Frederick finally allowed his eyes to stray for the briefest of moments to Miss Rosewall, who was situated near the center of the room.

He'd be lying if he said he wasn't attracted to her. Her features were perfectly appealing to any eye. Her white gown that night appeared new, and her hair was done up in a way that accentuated her long neck and shining, black locks. She was beautiful, and the smirk on her lips revealed that she believed the very same.

He would have never thought that this woman had lost her

fortune and her future. How he despised her ability to lie. It was the same talent his father had.

Frederick blinked, breaking his stare. There were many women there tonight beyond Miss Rosewall, and he would enjoy getting to know each one of them better, beginning with Miss Kinsey.

He faced the quiet girl more directly, turning his back on Miss Rosewall in the process. "Might I have the pleasure of dancing the first with you, Miss Kinsey?"

"I would be delighted, sir," she responded, though she looked as if she'd just swallowed a piece of molded bread.

Frederick credited her expression to a simple shyness rather than any aversion to him, then pasted a smile on his face.

Now that he had his first dance sorted, he could begin to enjoy his evening. And under no circumstances would he look over his shoulder to catch another glimpse of the alluring Miss Rosewall.

Sophia stepped to the side, peering around a few guests to see what Mr. Hawkins was saying to Miss Kinsey. Had he asked her to dance the first? If so, why had Miss Kinsey not fled from the room in fright?

Sophia simpered, pleased with her wit, but her amusement vanished as Mr. Hawkins glanced over his shoulder, and their eyes met.

Immediately, she pulled away, coming face-to-face with another guest. "Miss Ward?" she said in surprise. "I didn't know you'd returned from London already."

The woman her age skirted her eyes about the ballroom, as if she wished to be anywhere but right there, speaking with Sophia. "Yes, only yesterday," she responded in her customary self-important tone.

Sophia fought a grimace. She had never really liked Miss Ward. The woman thought a great deal too much of herself, despite her mousey brown hair and plain features, and the fact that her family earned half as much money as the Rosewalls had. In truth, both girls had only ever tolerated each other, friends solely when it benefited them both. Now that the Wards had returned to Cornwall, though, Sophia could finally reap the rewards from befriending the woman again.

"Well, I am glad to see you have returned home at long last," Sophia said. "We have certainly missed your company at our parties."

Miss Ward narrowed her eyes so slightly, Sophia was sure she'd imagined it. "Thank you, Miss Rosewall. I was going to call at Fynwary Hall, but I heard that you've been required to move to Lowena Cottage."

Sophia checked her embarrassment. A Rosewall ought not feel ashamed about anything. "Ah, yes. I thought you might have heard. I suppose there is no use denying it then. Yes, we have moved into the cottage. But I assure you, it is only temporary. I suspect my father will find other means so we might live somewhere a little finer."

"I do hope so, for your sake," Miss Ward said, wincing with exaggerated pity.

Excellent. Sophia needed that pity, feigned as it was, to work to her advantage. Although, swallowing her pride would prove to be a struggle.

"How is life at the cottage?" Miss Ward asked, her indifferent tone unable to mask the intrigue piqued in her eyes.

Sophia pulled on a sorrowful expression, just as she had done with Mrs. Maddern, though she hoped to be more convincing this time. "Well, it is rather small for the three of us and our servants, but I just so happened to—"

"You have servants?"

Sophia paused. Did Miss Ward truly think them so destitute, so set apart from Society, that they would no longer house servants? "Of course we do."

"But not many, I gather."

"We have more than enough servants to suit our needs, I assure you."

Of course, that wasn't exactly true. But why should Sophia have to admit how often she rang out her new bell, only to receive no response from either Edith or Mrs. Cuff? The number of servants the Rosewalls kept was none of Miss Ward's concern.

Sophia tapped her slipper against the smooth, wooden floor. Miss Ward was irritating her already. Did Sophia really wish to ask if she could temporarily stay with her and her family?

If the choice was between staying with them or Lowena Cottage, Sophia already knew her answer.

She began again. "At any rate, I happened to mention that we struggle for space at Lowena to Mrs. Maddern, and she graciously extended the offer for me to remain here with her. At least until my family is back on their feet."

Miss Ward's eyes widened. "She did?"

"Indeed. I was nearly ready to accept, but I'm afraid Miss Kinsey does not wish to share her aunt's attention with anyone but herself."

Miss Ward gasped, whispering, "She said such a thing?"

Sophia simply raised her shoulders. She'd have to remember to say an extra prayer for repentance come this Sunday.

"I can't believe it," Miss Ward breathed.

"I couldn't either. But I can hardly stay where I am unwelcome, as much as I appreciated the offer. Now I shall have to remain at the cottage. Unless, of course, I can find somewhere else to stay…"

Sophia knew her hinting was obvious, but Miss Ward had always proved simple, so heavily hint she must.

Miss Ward rubbed her gloved forearm. "Oh, Miss Rose-wall, I—"

"Ah, Miss Ward!" Another voice interrupted. "You have returned to us at last. I thought you might remain in London forever."

Sophia bit her cheek, forcing back a frustrated sigh as Mr. Chester joined them. Was it just her, or did he appear taller than usual?

"Good evening, Mr. Chester," she greeted, bestowing the man with her best smile in order to keep herself from eying his feet.

Mr. Chester turned toward her. "Miss Rosewall? I did not expect to see you this evening."

Sophia thought perhaps the man was jesting, but when he toyed uncomfortably with the sleeves of his jacket, she paused. "Why would I not be here?"

He and Miss Ward exchanged a glance. "Because of your removal from Fynwary Hall, of course," he replied. "One would think you would be overcome with exhaustion after such an ordeal."

Sophia tapped his arm playfully with her fan. "Mr. Chester, I would have thought you knew me well enough to know that I would never miss an opportunity to dance, no matter how exhausted I may be."

He bared his teeth in what she assumed was an attempt at a grin. "Yes, of course."

A deafening silence arose between the three of them, even with the hum of the other guests around them. Sophia couldn't understand their behavior. But why was she dwelling on their awkwardness when her time could better be spent in laughter and enjoyment?

Sophia faced Mr. Chester more fully. "I—"

"Tell me, how have you been, Mr. Chester?" Miss Ward didn't seem aware that she'd cut off Sophia's words with her question.

Sophia pursed her lips with disapproval, but they continued their conversation, taking no notice of her.

"Well enough," he replied. "Better now that you are here with us."

Miss Ward modestly tucked in her chin.

Sophia narrowed her eyes as she watched their interaction. Had they formed an attachment when all of them were in London together last month? Sophia hadn't taken notice before.

"I must say, I have greatly missed being your dance partner, Miss Ward," Mr. Chester continued. "Do tell me you are not occupied for the first. If so, I should dearly love the pleasure."

Sophia's eyebrows drew together. He'd practically fought Mr. Singleton to obtain the first dance with Sophia. Had he already forgotten? "But, Mr. Chester, I thought that—"

"The pleasure would certainly be mine," Miss Ward interrupted again. She took his outstretched arm then finally turned to Sophia. "Do excuse us, Miss Rosewall."

CHAPTER FIFTEEN

*S*ophia watched them walk away, her mouth hanging open. When she noticed a stern look from an elderly couple, she snapped her lips closed and gave them a pleasant nod.

The moment their disapproving eyes departed, her frown returned. Mr. Chester had been flirting with her, showing express interest in her, during the Rosewall's dinner party. Had his affection shifted from Sophia to Miss Ward in a single evening?

It is all a game.

Sophia shook Mr. Hawkins's words from her mind. If Mr. Chester truly forgot the dances she had promised him, then he really must be in love with Miss Ward. His flirting with Sophia would have been a simple lapse in judgment.

With a potential engagement on the horizon, Sophia hardly wished to stand in their way. Besides, there were plenty of other gentlemen here who would be happy to show Sophia the attention she deserved. Of course, Mr. Hawkins would not be one of them.

She clicked her tongue at herself. How had her mind

reverted to him, and her eyes to the spot where he had previously stood? He wasn't there now, nor was Miss Kinsey.

Her eyes swept across the crowd until falling on raven black hair hovering near the refreshment table.

Mr. Singleton. He would make a fine partner.

Like a hound to a rabbit—no, not one of Mr. Hawkins's hounds—she weaved in and out of the couples with dexterity. When she finally reached him, she tapped his shoulder with her forefinger. "Good evening, Mr. Singleton. I have wonderful news for you."

Mr. Singleton whirled around, his brow jumping in surprise. "Miss Rosewall?"

Sophia's patience thinned. Why was everyone so surprised to see her? Did they truly think her so weak that she would become indisposed by simply moving to a different house? Or were they surprised for different reasons, because her circumstances had changed, and they now thought her unworthy to…

She closed her eyes for a brief moment to shut out the thought. She wouldn't allow her mind to stray to such a place. She was still the same person as she was before, only temporarily poorer.

Raising her chin, she continued. "Did you hear me before, sir? I said I had wonderful news."

His eyes flicked over her shoulder. "Oh?"

Where was that accompanying smile of his that he had whenever he was with her?

"Mr. Chester has made himself occupied for the first set, so you and I may dance together now."

His eyes darted about the room. Why did he appear so skittish, as if he were hiding from something, or from someone?

"Forgive me, Miss Rosewall, but I already have a partner for this dance. Miss Ward has agreed to dance with me, you see."

Sophia cocked her head. "Miss Ward? But she has just promised herself to Mr. Chester."

Mr. Singleton averted his eyes. "Did I say Miss Ward? I must have seen her passing by. No, I meant Miss…Miss Roberts."

Sophia followed his line of sight to see the young Miss Roberts standing next to her mother. "Oh, well, I trust you will enjoy her company."

Mr. Singleton gave a stiff bow and walked away without so much as a glance in her direction. She watched him depart, attempting to swallow the dryness that suddenly coated her throat. It had to be a coincidence that both he and Mr. Chester were occupied for the first dance. Hadn't it?

"Are you in line, miss?"

Sophia nearly jumped at the sound of a gentleman behind her. She looked to see a line forming near the refreshment table, a line she was holding up.

"Oh, forgive me," she muttered, stepping aside.

She was flustered, a feeling she was not accustomed to, a feeling caused by others' inattentiveness.

She could still blossom, she could still attract a partner, like a bee to a flower. She simply needed to show just how sweet of a flower she was.

Moving to the center of the room again, she straightened her back until it ached and placed a pleasant expression on her face.

No gentleman approached. Perhaps the room was too crowded for her to be seen?

She made her way to an open doorway that led to the gardens. Cool air sailed into the warm room. From there she could see a number of gentlemen standing and speaking with other guests. Did they all have partners? Had they seen that she was in need of one?

She tried not to become too discouraged. After all, it was only the first dance of the evening, and if she did not have a partner, it was not the worst thing that could happen. Then again, she had never attended a ball where she was not occupied for every single set. In truth, if she sat out, she was not quite sure what to do with herself.

A strange panic flapped in her chest, suppressing her desire to be seen. What if people noticed she was alone and judged her for it? More importantly, what was so terribly wrong with her to have no one wish to dance with her?

She backed up closer to the open door, crossing an arm over her stomach. What was this feeling, insecurity? It was foreign. Unwelcome. She knew not how to be rid of it.

"But Miss Rosewall would have been surprised, too. How could she not have been?"

Sophia's ears perked up. She raised her head toward the open door. The wind rustled the curls on her brow, bringing Mr. Chester's distinctly high-pitched voice past her ear.

A second voice spoke. "Oh, indeed. My family and I were, as well, when we heard the news."

Miss Ward. Her conspiratorial tone could not be mistaken. Sophia held her breath to better hear their hushed words.

"You know," Mr. Chester said, "I believe it occurred the very night of the dinner party that I attended at Fynwary Hall."

Sophia's heart sagged like a saturated silk bonnet. The ball had been meant to distract her from her troubles. Overhearing such gossip would hardly help. Yet, she could not move away. She leaned in closer, hidden behind the open door, drawn to their conversation like a moth to the flame.

"Did you notice any sign of what was about to occur?" Miss Ward asked. Her voice was hungry, eager. Like a feral cat eying a beached pilchard.

"Only Mr. Hawkins's presence might have given us some suspicion. But he and Mr. Rosewall, and indeed, all of Mr. Rosewall's investors, kept quiet about his waning funds."

"I'm certain even if Mr. Rosewall *had* told his wife and daughter earlier, they would not have listened to him."

"You are right in that regard, Miss Ward."

Sophia clutched her fan with both hands.

"I really do not like to speak ill of her," Miss Ward continued, "but Miss Rosewall and I have always had a somewhat strained relationship. Honestly, though, she could do with a little humbling."

Sophia could just imagine the woman's annoyingly thin eyebrows raised. Miss Ward could do with a dousing of humility herself.

"She is far too fixated on herself," Miss Ward continued. "No wonder she didn't see her poor father struggling. I'm sure *I* would have, had my own father been under such strain."

Sophia pulled back, the bitter sting of the words striking at her spirit. What a cruel accusation. Sophia loved her father. It was not her fault that he had so aptly hidden his secret.

Images flashed through her mind. Father's weary eyes, his strained look when she'd first mentioned purchasing a new ballgown, his constant finger to his temple as if to quell an unending headache.

The memories continued, and a tension settled around her ribs, as if her stays had tightened on their own.

"I really do commend her for coming this evening, though," Miss Ward said. "I would not have had her same confidence had *my* family lost everything. I'm sure I would never appear in Society again."

"Yes, but does she even realize her circumstances have changed?" Mr. Chester asked.

He no doubt stood on the tips of his toes to appear taller than Miss Ward, though Sophia knew it would do him little good.

"Well, she is certain to know after this evening, I'm afraid." Miss Ward sighed. "A pretty dress may do wonders for a fatigued appearance, but with no dowry, she will hardly have men flocking after her as her pride is accustomed to."

Sophia's frown grew. Fatigued appearance? Pride?

"Indeed. I will still dance with her myself, as I am a gentleman, but I will not be surprised should others choose not to do so. Mr. Singleton, for one."

Miss Ward hummed in agreement. "Though, according to Miss Rosewall, she believes she will rise above her circumstances yet."

"She must be in denial. From what I understand, her father has lost everything. Even if he were to find work—though, who would hire him, I know not—his wages would be so lacking, they would still struggle to keep even the small cottage afloat."

Sophia's mind spun. Their words weren't true. They *couldn't* be true. Father would find a way. She knew he would.

"Perhaps she does realize this," Miss Ward said, "and that is why she has been throwing herself at the mercy of others." Her voice quieted further, but Sophia, foolishly, listened on. "Miss Rosewall was supposed to stay with the Madderns, but Miss Kinsey wouldn't allow it. I, of course, do not blame Miss Kinsey in the slightest. Why, just before you came upon us, I believe Miss Rosewall was in the very act of asking if she could stay with *my* family! Can you believe it?"

Mr. Chester barked out a dismal laugh. "The nerve she must have to request such a thing, and for so long. She was no doubt expecting to be provided with a dowry, as well."

Sophia shook her head as if they could see her. She did not wish to stay with her neighbors forever. Only until Father could earn enough money to…

Her breathing shallowed. The musicians tuned their instruments, and the dancers moved toward the center of the floor. Quickly, she pressed up against the wall as Mr. Chester and Miss Ward moved past her.

"Are you ready to dance now, Miss Ward?"

"Indeed, Mr. Chester. I have been longing to do so for over a month now."

They laughed then disappeared into the crowds.

Sophia remained where she was. She was not selfish. She was not in denial. Someone *would* dance with her that evening because…because Father would find a way to provide her with a dowry again.

She ignored the emptiness of her words and looked to the crowds before her, forcing herself to remain positive. But when she caught sight of Mr. Singleton dancing with not the young Miss Roberts he'd mentioned before, but a different woman entirely, the weight on her shoulders became unbearable.

It was true. He had not wished to dance with her. And the others?

She looked around. A few couples skirted their glances away when she caught them staring, and her stomach stiffened.

How stupid she was to have thought that they had admired her earlier, when their eyes merely revealed their shock at her being there. They were no doubt wondering the same as Mr. Chester and Miss Ward. How did the daughter of a diminished gentleman have the audacity to show her face at a ball?

No one would wish to dance with her. She was a poor choice in partner, and an even poorer choice in wife.

Tears pricked her eyes. She bit her lip, refusing to allow her emotions to show. These people, they were correct. She shouldn't be there. Not in her current financial state. Not until Father could provide for her again.

If he ever could.

An urgency quickened her heartbeat. She needed to speak with him. She needed him to calm her worries, just as he had when she was a child, frightened of riding a horse for her first time. Just as he had when she had expressed her concerns with marrying someone out of duty rather than love.

He had always helped her before. He would help her now.

She whirled on her heel, but before taking a single step forward, she collided with a green waistcoat. She yelped in surprise and teetered backward, but strong hands clasped her upper arms, preventing her from a fall.

"Miss Rosewall, are you all right?"

CHAPTER SIXTEEN

*S*ophia squeezed her eyes closed. Why was it him? Of all gentlemen there that evening, why Mr. Hawkins?

"Excuse me," she mumbled, attempting to back away.

Mr. Hawkins maintained his hold of her, his strong hands causing her head to spin. No, the heat of the room and the gossip she'd overheard was what caused her head to spin.

"Are you unwell?" he asked.

"No," she lied. She finally managed to break away, and his hands fell to his side. "Please, excuse me."

"Do you have a partner for the second dance?"

She paused, wincing. Had he been watching her, or was he asking her himself?

She could laugh at her own stupidity. He would not dance with her. No one would. "No, sir. I need to speak with my father."

"Of course. Miss Rosewall, I…"

He hesitated, and Sophia dared a glance at him. The sincere concern she witnessed was far worse than any look of pity or censure she'd expected.

Tears threatened to slip past her eyelashes. Her breathing

came in hitched tremors. She knew she could not say a word without revealing more than she wished to.

With a quick curtsy, she flew past him, feeling his eyes upon her as she bumped against shoulders left and right. The music began, signaling the start of the first dance. The first dance for which Sophia did not have partner.

That hardly mattered now. She needed to find Father. Her advancement did not stop until she rounded the corner and reached the outside of the card room. She allowed herself a moment to regain composure, then peered through the doorway.

She spotted her father in an instant. He sat behind a table, swirling his drink around in his glass, dark grey circles beneath his eyes. He was the only one not surrounded by conversation and laughter. He was the only one not playing a game.

Sophia's heart plummeted, the sinking sensation pulling her breath down with it. She shouldn't have asked him to come. He must have known how she would be treated, how they *both* would be treated. Yet he had done so for her, his daughter.

She was selfish. Just like Miss Ward and Mr. Chester said. Just like Mr. Hawkins had said. She was selfish, unwanted. Unfit to be around such fine company and at an even finer ball.

She took a step back, intent on quitting Benlett House without Father's notice, but her movement caught his attention.

Their eyes met. He stood directly, making his way toward her. "Sophia, whatever is the matter? You look pale. Come, sit for a moment."

She remained where she stood, pain blinding her awareness of others. She fought the urge to speak, to ask him his reasoning, but her soul begged for answers. "Father, why did you agree to come tonight, when you knew…"

His features pulled down. "Sophia, I did not have the heart to tell you."

"What else have you not told me?" Her voice raised. "Have you found work? Enough to provide me with a dowry?"

A couple walked by with curious glances. He took her arm and pulled her near a darkened corridor. Once they were securely out of earshot from any passerby, he responded. "Sophia, I have told you everything. We have lost *everything*. And finding work has been difficult."

Difficult? Had he even left the house? Or had he been in hiding, just like Mother, just like Sophia ought to have done tonight?

"Even if I do find work, it will be hard enough to make ends meet." He scratched at the back of his head. "I do not think it probable that I will be able to save any amount of money worthy of a gentleman."

Somehow, Sophia had expected the words. Hearing them aloud did nothing but cause the knowledge of her ruined future to become paved in her brain. She was ruined. Forever. And she was a fool to have ever believed otherwise.

"But we will be all right, Sophia," Father said, taking her hand in his. "I have written to my aunt and expect to hear word from her soon."

"Your aunt?" Sophia stared at Father in disbelief.

She had never met her Great Aunt June, had only ever heard stories of the woman who disapproved of everyone and everything, especially her nephew.

Before Sophia was born, Father was given the estate by his father—June's brother—despite a promised arrangement for June to receive it upon her brother's death. Because of that, Great Aunt June had moved to Yorkshire and had not communicated with the Rosewalls since.

Sophia could not blame Father for reaching out to the now-wealthy widow. Sophia had done the same, in essence, begging others to rescue them from their circumstances to avoid living with the consequences of Father's mistakes.

But his aunt would not help him. Just like their neighbors would not help her. They were alone in the world. Utterly, entirely alone.

"She will not respond, Father. You and I both know it."

He raised his arms out to his side, palms up. "What else would you have me do, Sophia?"

What would she have him do? She would have him take back his senseless decisions, find some way to reobtain their fortune.

Instead, she took a step away from him. "Nothing, Father. Forgive me for forcing you to come tonight. I can see now it was a mistake."

"Let us return home together then."

Home? She did not have a home. Fynwary Hall was no longer theirs, and Lowena Cottage would never be hers. "No, I-I think I shall walk."

"Walk? But it will surely rain, Sophia. And I rented the carriage for you. Besides, you wouldn't wish to ruin your lovely dress."

She didn't hear his words. She didn't hear anything. "I will return to the cottage now, Father. Good evening."

"Sophia?"

She turned and walked away from him, moving in a daze, no longer aware of the looks from others, the music from the ballroom, or the dancers' laughter.

She was alone as she walked through the crowds, as she donned her wrap given to her by a footman with a curious eye, as she left Benlett House behind and walked down the gravel road in the opposite direction of the guests arriving late.

Soon, she left the grounds and the road, crossing the long grass of the countryside. Her slippers would certainly be ruined if she continued, but she didn't stop, nor did she know where her feet took her.

The clouds had darkened due to the setting sun, the land cloaked in a cool, grey blanket. A brisk wind nipped at her cheeks and attempted to pull her hair from her pins one ringlet at a time.

The first drops of rain began to fall from the sky, speckling her gown. The water splashed on her cheek, nose, brow. She didn't know how long she walked, nor how far from the cottage she strayed, but when the sound of the ocean reached her ears, she continued until the dark expanse stretched out before her.

She stood at the edge of the cliff, the wind tearing at her skirts, arms folded as the rain stung her face and slid down her back. The horizon was indistinguishable, rain muddling the line between clouds and water. The angry waves thrashed upon the rocky shoreline below. Their roar was deafening.

As a child, she had been afraid of the sea during storms. She had been convinced that a great wave would snatch her from the tops of the cliffs and drag her down into the water's depths. Father had been the one to ease her fear, reassuring her that he would keep her safe.

As she grew, the sea no longer frightened her. But her life…her life was now terrifying. And Father could not ease her worries.

No one could.

She tried to stand strong, but her knees buckled. She collapsed into the wet grass as she thought of all that was now lost. Her home, her future, her faith in her father.

This was her new reality, being alone and forgotten. Being nothing.

"Miss?"

CHAPTER SEVENTEEN

Sophia gasped, swinging around at the sound of a woman's voice.

"Miss, are ye well?"

When had it gotten so dark? Sophia could hardly see the young woman standing right behind her. Her approach must have been silenced by the storming sea.

Sophia nodded. "Yes, I am well."

"Are ye sure, miss?" Her accent was thick, belonging to the working class.

Sophia sniffed, swiping the wet hair from her brow. "Yes, thank you."

She tried to stand, but her foot slipped on the wet grass. She stumbled forward, the woman reaching out to steady her.

"You're shakin' like a hairless dog, miss. We best get ye warm 'fore ye catch cold."

Sophia hadn't noticed her shaking before, nor how cold she was. Her gown was soaked through, and the grass pressed against her foot through a hole in her slipper.

"Where's home for ye, miss?"

Sophia wiped the moisture from her eyes and looked to the woman who released her hold of her. She appeared to be the same age as Sophia, her hair held back by a scanty piece of cloth. Their eyes met, and the woman's brow rose.

"Miss Rosewall?"

Sophia stared. "Yes, how…"

"Sorry to startle ye, miss. I'm Gwynna. Gwynna Merrick, miss. My father works at Wheal Favour. We're tenants of your father's. *Were* tenants, rather."

"Oh, I see." Of course the young woman would know Sophia and not the other way around. Was her name Gwen? No, Gwynna. "Well, thank you, Gwynna, for asking after me. I suppose I had better return home—return to the cottage now."

"Lowena Cottage? 'Tis too far, Miss Rosewall. We must get ye warm quick. Come with me to my house. 'Tisn't so far from here. Then we can borrow a wagon and take ye home after."

Sophia pulled her shawl tighter around her shoulders, which only proved to soak her further. "Oh, no, that won't be necessary, thank you. I'll walk from here."

A great shiver wracked her body, and Gwynna shook her head. "No, ye won't, Miss Rosewall. Come along." She placed her arm around her and urged her forward. "My home is but five minutes away. Yours is near twenty."

Sophia could do little else but allow Gwynna to lead her forward. At least the young woman's logic was sound. Sophia really had no idea how to find her way to the cottage in the dark and during a storm. She'd also become increasingly weak from the cold, and from the strain of the evening.

Her steps faltered. For one brief, blissful moment, she had managed to forget about her time at the ball.

"What are ye doin' out here, miss, all alone and at dark?"

Sophia chewed her lip. "Simply enjoying a walk?"

"In that dress? If I didn't know any better, I'd have thought ye were attendin' a party or a ball."

Sophia shrugged. "Perhaps I was. But it's of little conse-quence now."

She ignored Gwynna's searching look. Sophia had never much desired silence. She enjoyed speaking, usually about herself, but now she wished to speak about anything *but* herself.

"And what are you doing out here, Gwynna, all alone and at dark?"

Gwynna was the one to look away now. "Visitin' family."

They both had their secrets, and neither of them wished to divulge much more of them to strangers.

They carried on in silence. Away from the cliffside, the rain no longer pierced her skin, though it still fell down in droves upon them. The land had grown dark, and with no light from the moon or stars, she could hardly see a thing.

"How do you know which way to go?" Sophia asked, her voice jerking as she shivered again. She'd never traveled in such darkness. The carriages always had lights to guide them.

Gwynna pointed straight ahead. "There. Papa always leaves a lantern out on nights such as these to help wayward folk."

Sophia strained her eyes to see into the distance, finally spotting a small light hovering before them. Thank goodness for *Gwynna's* father, a man with sense.

By the time the shadow of the small home appeared, Sophia was shivering all over. She was grateful for her wrap, if only for the modesty it provided her, now that her white gown was transparent.

She had behaved stupidly that evening, not only for attending the ball in the first place, but also for not accepting the carriage ride. Why had she charged forth into the rain? It certainly hadn't done anything to improve her mood. Not to mention it had entirely ruined her dress and slippers.

"Here we are, Miss Rosewall," Gwynna said as they

walked around the small home. The light of the lantern glowed against the wooden door. "Let's get ye warm now."

She pushed the door open, then stepped aside for Sophia to enter next. The house was half the size of Lowena, with its kitchen, dining table, and sitting area all rolled into one small room.

Despite the size, Sophia was instantly enveloped with warmth. Not only from the fire crackling at the side of the room, casting its orange glow across the floor, but also because of the smell of meat and bread wafting past her nose. The rain on the roof echoed throughout the room, the sound soothing, now that it was not pouring down on them.

Sophia stood awkwardly behind as Gwynna closed the door then stood in front of her. "Mama? Papa?"

"Gwynna! Oh, she be home, Travers!" A woman with an apron entered the room, her hair pulled back in a soft bun. "Where have ye been, ye naughty girl. Your father was about to ride out to find…" Her words trailed off as Gwynna stepped to the side, revealing Sophia's presence. The woman, Mrs. Merrick, rounded her eyes. "Miss Rosewall? 'Tis a surprise to see ye here."

"Mama," Gwynna said, "Miss Rosewall got caught in a bit of bad weather. I brought her here to warm up and said we'd find a way to get her home safe."

Mrs. Merrick blinked, still staring at Sophia with an unreadable expression. Unreadable, apart from the clear unease she felt.

Sophia looked to the puddle she created on the floor. She'd truly taken leave of her senses. How else could she have allowed a stranger to bring her to her home?

"I'm terribly sorry to intrude," she mumbled.

"'Tis not an intrusion at all, miss," Gwynna interrupted. "Is it, Mama?"

The words seemed to jar Mrs. Merrick from her thoughts. Her face brightened. "Oh, not at all, Miss Rosewall." She crossed the small room and urged Sophia to the chair nearest the fire, the warmth instantly soothing Sophia's aching limbs. "Sit here, and we'll warm ye up in no time. Gwynna, fetch an extra cover from Jago's room, will ye?"

After Gwynna left, a man, no doubt Gwynna's father, entered the main room. His long hair hung away from his brow but down to his chin, and a patchy beard stretched across his jaw. His dark eyes fell on Sophia, his tanned face shaded white.

Sophia clutched her shawl, praying for invisibility to escape his penetrating stare.

"Here be the blanket, Mama."

Gwynna's footsteps slowed as she entered the room, staring at her father's unflinching eyes on Sophia.

"Papa," she said softly, "Miss Rosewall lost her way in the storm. I offered to help her back to Lowena Cottage once she be warm."

Mr. Merrick nodded, his eyes still on Sophia's, hard and constant. "I'll be about findin' a wagon, then," he said gruffly.

He left the house without another word.

Mrs. Merrick and Gwynna fussed over Sophia without mention of Mr. Merrick's clear displeasure with having Sophia in his home. Gwynna removed Sophia's shawl and placed it before the fire to dry as Mrs. Merrick draped the blanket around Sophia.

Sophia flinched. She felt like a burden, and she never felt like a burden. She was behaving selfishly yet again, imposing on this family in the worst way.

"I'm terribly sorry for all of this," she said. "If you will but allow me to, I am certain I will be able to find my way to the cottage from here."

Mrs. Merrick waved a dismissive hand in the air. "Not a problem, miss. We're happy to help. Now, tell me, what were ye thinkin' bein' outside in nothin' but this dress and slippers?"

Sophia glanced to Gwynna. Would Mrs. Merrick demand an answer?

"The ball she was attendin' didn't suit, so she came home early," Gwynna replied for her.

Mrs. Merrick quirked a brow at her daughter but said nothing else as she moved toward the kitchen.

"Thank you," Sophia mouthed out.

Gwynna gave her an encouraging nod.

Mrs. Merrick returned to her side in an instant with a bowl of stew that made Sophia's stomach rumble. She hadn't smelled anything so appetizing since coming to Lowena. Mrs. Cuff was better at working with hair than with food.

"Now ye eat this, miss. I'd insist ye remove that dress of yours and wear one of my Gwynny's, but I'd be afraid of you drownin' in it. You're as thin as a blade of grass."

Gwynna chortled, and Sophia weakly smiled. She was sure she'd never been spoken to in such a way in all her life. Yet somehow, she didn't mind it.

Over the next half hour, Sophia felt as if she were no longer in her body, instead watching from above as these strangers took such great care of her, she would've thought she was a queen. They took turns wringing out her drooping locks, stoking the fire, and refilling her bowl of stew, the best Sophia had ever eaten.

She couldn't understand their kindness. They were no longer tenants of Father's, so they owed her nothing, and yet, their generosity continued.

Before long, Mr. Merrick returned, and he and Mrs. Merrick disappeared down the side corridor, to where Sophia assumed the bedrooms were situated. She and Gwynna sat in silence until her parents returned.

"My husband has secured a wagon, so he can take ye home when you're ready, miss," Mrs. Merrick said.

In truth, Sophia didn't know if she would ever be ready to leave. Something about their home spoke warmth and love to her. She had felt far better there in that half hour than she had for a week at Lowena, excepting Mrs. Merrick's initial reaction to seeing her and Mr. Merrick's obvious discomfort with her presence.

But she couldn't impose on their kindness any longer.

"I'm ready now," she said, standing with a grateful nod.

Before Sophia could don her still-damp shawl, Mrs. Merrick swung a cloak around Sophia's shoulders. "Here, miss. Take mine. 'Tisn't as fine as what you may be used to, but it'll keep ye out of the rain 'til ye arrive home."

Sophia expressed her gratitude, then followed Gwynna and Mr. Merrick outside where she clambered into the wagon after the father and daughter.

The wagon lurched forward, and Sophia grasped onto the small ledge, the only thing preventing her from falling to the ground. She much preferred a carriage with walls, and a roof, but the wagon was a far cry better than finding her way home alone in the dark on foot.

With Gwynna there, she almost didn't mind Mr. Merrick's deliberate silence. Almost.

The rain had lessened to a mere sprinkling, but Sophia could not wait to peel herself from her wet clothing, and to alert her parents that she had arrived at the cottage. Of course they would still be awake, worrying over her safety.

But when the wagon pulled to a stop in front of Lowena, there was no lantern to greet her, nor a single light shining in any of the windows.

"Will your parents still be at the ball, miss?" Gwynna asked as Mr. Merrick handed her the reins, jumping down from his side of the wagon.

"No, Mother stayed home this evening. She is probably sleeping." She shifted awkwardly on the wagon's seat to face Gwynna. "Thank you for your help this evening. If you hadn't, I would still be stuck on that ridge."

"Happy to help, miss," she said.

"Miss Rosewall?"

Sophia turned to Mr. Merrick standing beside her, extending his hand toward her.

She accepted his assistance and rather ungracefully leapt from the wagon. "Thank you, Mr. Merrick."

He tipped his cap to her then resumed his place beside Gwynna.

Sophia gave one last departing wave then walked to the front door. She closed it behind her as the wagon pulled away, the horse's tack jingling in the distance.

She glanced around the dark, empty entryway. No fire greeted her, no smell of warm food. Only silence.

Father would be home by now. Should he not have ensured himself of Sophia's safety before retiring, as Gwynna's father would have done?

She trudged up the steps, unfastening the cloak around her neck. Mrs. Merrick's cloak. She'd forgotten to give it back to Gwynna before they left. As she slid the threadbare fabric from around her shoulders, the scent of the Merrick's home— fire, stew, and old wood—lingered around her.

A strange ache pierced her heart. She brought the cloak to her nose as she made her way to her room, willing herself to remember the warmth she'd felt as she entered her cold, dark chambers.

She didn't bother to ring the bell for Mrs. Cuff to help her dress, nor for Edith to light a fire. She pulled her gown off herself, leaving it on the floor as she donned a dry night dress and slipped into bed. Her mattress sloped to one side as she laid her head against her flat pillow.

The rain plinked against her window. The ocean's waves splashed on the rocks beneath the cottage. As the strain from the evening pressed down upon her, the loneliness of her quiet room echoing in her ears, she clasped the cloak to her chest and wept.

CHAPTER EIGHTEEN

"*M*adderns. Miss Kinsey. Rennalls. Summerfields. That should do it."

Frederick raised his quill from the paper, finishing off his list aloud. This picnic he was planning would be a small affair. Small and simple. That would give him ample opportunity to finally draw Miss Kinsey from her shell and get to know her better. Heaven knew he had no success in that regard at the ball last night.

The ball.

Frederick tapped the tip of the pen up and down on the paper, the drops of ink creating a blot that slowly grew, spreading through the thin veins of the parchment.

He'd enjoyed himself as best he could at Benlett House the night before, dancing, eating, and conversing until the early hours of the morning. But a pall had been cast over his time there after seeing Miss Rosewall overcome with…grief? Disbelief? Fear?

He rubbed his chin with his left hand. Whatever emotion he had seen, it had been enough to send Miss Rosewall fleeing from the ball. And it had been enough to actually make him consider asking her for a dance. Thank goodness she'd left before she would have embarrassed him by her sure decline of his offer.

Frederick eyed the large ink circle on the paper, though he barely registered its growing width. The look in Miss Rosewall's eyes had haunted him, and the fact that she had not readily dismissed him as she was known to do.

Had someone been cruel to her? Had she overheard the rumors about her, that she should not be at the ball, that no gentleman would now dance with her? Either way, as a gentleman, he needed to ensure she was well.

Her family's cottage was still in need of repairs. Perhaps he would call on them to see what else needed fixing, and to ascertain for himself if Miss Rosewall was all right. Knowing such would surely allow him to move on.

Then he could finish his plans for the picnic and look forward to getting to know Miss Kinsey without his persistent thoughts of Miss Rosewall insistently getting in his way.

Sophia didn't leave her room the day after the ball. She hardly left her bed. What was the point of doing so when she had nowhere to go, no one to see?

Mrs. Cuff brought her meals throughout the day, but Sophia merely nibbled at each plate. She wasn't sure if the bland food was due to Mrs. Cuff's inability to cook or to Sophia's darkened mood. Either way, her appetite had vanished after eating the Merricks' stew. As did her desire to do anything at all.

She had attempted to read a book but couldn't become engrossed in the storyline. Next, she'd considered stitching but couldn't be bothered to finish the handkerchief she was embroidering for herself. There was no purpose furthering the talent if she couldn't one day showcase her ability in her own household.

Mrs. Cuff had eventually offered to fetch her drawing supplies, but Sophia wasn't sure she'd be able to form any sort of picture, so cold were her fingers in her frigid room, even with the fire lit. She had stuffed an old chemise into the crack in her window to block out the draft, but it did little to drown out the sound of the storming sea.

The sea.

How it mocked her with its freedom, when all she had was her prison at Lowena Cottage.

With a pillow to her ears, she had slept most of the day away. The next morning, however, as the bright sun washed over her through the window, Sophia rolled out of bed with a groan. She had been awake for hours, merely wasting away staring off at nothing in particular. It had to be nearing ten o'clock. She needed to stretch her legs. Did she even know how to use them any longer?

Instead of the cold, wooden floor she'd expected to feel on her toes, her feet landed on a scratchy fabric. She peered down to see Mrs. Merrick's cloak sprawled out across the floor.

Sophia winced. She'd forgotten all about the cloak. It must have tumbled from her bed the night of the ball. She glanced over her shoulder to the window, light glinting against the glass, preventing any view she might have had.

At least the sun had come out. Mrs. Merrick might have needed the cloak in yesterday's storm, but she wouldn't in today's weather. That was fortunate, for Sophia really wasn't up to walking that morning.

But as she stared at the worn, shabby fabric, she shook her head at her selfish idleness. Of course Mrs. Merrick would need her cloak sooner rather than later. She certainly would not have another in her possession.

Though it had been dark inside the Merricks' home, it was clear they were a poverty-stricken family with little money to spare, even for food. Had Sophia usurped one of their meals by devouring so much of their stew? With three mouths to feed—or was it four? They'd mentioned another name that night, Gwynna's brother, perhaps. Had she eaten his helping?

Guilt turned her conscience. How could Sophia have been so thoughtless? If the Merricks couldn't afford more food, they certainly couldn't purchase another cloak, even should they need it. Sophia hadn't the funds to acquire new outerwear either now, but at least the ones she had were thicker than a spare sheet of paper.

The answer was simple. She needed to set aside her indolence and return the cloak. She wasn't entirely certain where Gwynna lived, but most of Father's tenants, previous tenants, were housed north of Fynwary Hall. Sophia would merely cross over the open fields to find her way, and to remain unseen. She couldn't bear the thought of facing anyone from her own class. Her *old* class. That especially included the Merricks' landlord.

Sophia had done well to prevent her mind from dwelling on Mr. Hawkins, but as thoughts of him now infiltrated her mind, her shoulders slouched.

She had recognized the look he had given her the night of the ball, that clear desire to help. It was the same look he had when he'd rescued her from the tide, and it was that same desire that made him speak with Miss Kinsey at the Rosewall's dinner party. It was the pure desire to be a gentleman.

He was more of a gentleman than Mr. Chester and Mr. Singleton, though she couldn't blame the two of them for their avoidance of her. She would have done the very same had she seen someone attempt to be who she no longer was.

Their actions had injured her pride. But Mr. Hawkins's behavior had bruised her conscience. Even her very heart. How could she have ever blamed him for Father's mistakes? She needed to make matters right with him, to apologize. But that would mean admitting to her foolishness, and that was not something she had the courage to do.

She moved to ring her servants' bell, but her hand paused on the handle. Mrs. Cuff would no doubt be sitting with Mother, and Edith, who knew what that girl got up to during the day?

Sophia pulled her hand away, tapping her fingers against her nightdress. She couldn't wait for Mrs. Cuff to help dress her in another hour or two. She needed to be about her task immediately before she had the chance to talk herself out of it.

She would dress herself.

She laid her lavender walking dress, her simplest option, on the bed, then removed her night dress and set about her task. The chemise was easy enough to don, but lacing her stays proved far more difficult. She struggled with tightening the back-laced garment for nearly ten minutes before making do with what she had. They were not as fitted as she preferred and caused her dress to droop slightly across her front, but she hardly thought Gwynna Merrick would take notice or care if Sophia looked a little worse for wear. Besides, her Spencer jacket was sure to hide her upper dress anyway.

Her next task of seeing to her hair proved even more difficult than dressing. She hadn't bothered to have her locks put in curling rags the night before, so her black tresses hung about her face in a wavy mess. She wouldn't risk the chance of singeing her hair with a hot iron—had she even brought hers from Fynwary Hall?—so she did her best twisting up the unruly mane before securing it with pins.

When she finished, she eyed herself in the small mirror on her desk, only able to look at one side of her hair at a time. The twist was lopsided, but her bonnet would cover most of it. The curls hanging near her temples didn't look terrible, either. She'd almost forgotten what her natural curls looked like, having always preferred the ringlets her lady's maid had formed.

She set down her mirror and donned her green Spencer jacket and straw poke bonnet. It didn't really matter how she looked. No one would notice either way. Except, perhaps, Mother.

Draping Mrs. Merrick's cloak over her arm, Sophia left her room and crossed the corridor to her mother's, though she wasn't sure if she should even disturb her. They hadn't spoken since before the ball. Would Mother even notice Sophia's absence from the cottage that morning?

Either way, leaving without alerting someone of her whereabouts seemed ill-advised. With a sigh, she tapped lightly on the door.

To her surprise, Mother responded. "Come in."

Sophia slowly opened the door and poked her head inside. "Mother?"

"Sophia? How are you, my dear?" Her voice sounded wispy, as if making the slightest sound took all of her energy.

Sophia entered the room, closing the door behind her. She caught the strong scent of smelling salts and tea. "I am well. And you?"

She weakly blinked. "Slightly better."

The move had been a struggle far more for Mother than the rest of the family. Sophia couldn't help but wonder if her weakness was due to the exertion of moving, or simply because Mother could not bear the thought of her new way of life.

"Where is Mrs. Cuff?" Sophia asked.

"She has gone to fetch more tea. Thank goodness she is as attentive as she is. I might be more ill, otherwise."

More ill? Mother couldn't be any paler than she was. Her cheeks were sunken in and her lips, dry.

"Are you going out?" she asked, motioning to Sophia's bonnet.

Sophia nodded.

Wariness crossed Mother's muted eyes. "May I ask where you are going?"

Sophia swallowed. "To deliver a basket to the poor."

It wasn't entirely a lie. Gwynna's family *was* poor. Mother simply would not understand why Sophia would wish to visit those who were once their tenants.

Her eyes softened at Sophia's believable lie. "How kind you are, Sophia. Even when we have little for ourselves, you still think of others."

Sophia stared at the cloak over her arm. If that were true, she would've returned the cover yesterday instead of moping about her room. She certainly would not have lied simply to save herself from Mother's disapproval.

"Did you enjoy the ball?" Mother asked.

Sophia folded her arms across her front. "I always do, don't I?

"Your father told me you left early. I do hope that wasn't due to any poor conduct you received."

Sophia's eyes snapped up. Did Mother know? She looked innocent enough, but if Father had suspected ill-treatment, then Mother must have, as well. That was no doubt the reason she had refused to attend the ball herself. Still, Sophia didn't wish to discuss it. She'd much rather forget about the whole affair.

"No," she responded. "I left because I grew too warm and needed a walk in the fresh air."

"I hope you reached home before the rain began."

Sophia smoothed the cloak over her arm. "No, but I was seen to."

Mother didn't hear her response, her attention drawn to Mrs. Cuff bustling in through the door with a tray of tea, her wide girth skirting around Sophia.

"Miss Rosewall, you be needin' anything?" she asked. Her accent was strong, but nowhere near as thick as Gwynna's.

"No, thank you. I was just on my way out. Do feel better, Mother."

"I will, dear."

With a departing nod, Sophia took her leave. That was the

most she had spoken with Mother since leaving Fynwary Hall. Mother had never been much of a conversationalist but speaking with her was certainly better than conversing with the spiders in her bedroom.

Sophia quit the house, closing the old door behind her with a quick tug, anxious to be on her way. But when she faced forward, her feet stopped in their tracks.

CHAPTER NINETEEN

For a solid week, there had been nothing but clouds and rain, excepting Sophia's first day at the cottage, when she'd been distracted with her plan to escape the house.

Now, a blue sky stretched out before her, ending only where it kissed the sapphire sea. Calm waves lapped at the white sand below the cottage, leaving darkened marks on the shore before slinking back to the rest of the water. A small trail curved round the land from Lowena to the beach, pink wild-flowers lining the pathway.

Lowena might be a prison, but at least it allowed her spectacular views. How had she missed such an incredible sight with the sea practically at her doorstep?

Sophia walked up to the stone wall encircling the cottage, but before she could lift the latch on the wooden gate, a sweet scent tickled her nose.

Was that...strawberries? She turned her head, sniffing again until she spotted a small patch growing near the side of the wall. The smell was far too tantalizing to keep away. She made for them, pulling one from the vine and sinking her teeth into the fruit.

The flavor spread throughout her mouth like the waves sliding up the sand below. The sweetness made her jaw smart, her tongue to tingle.

If this wasn't the most delicious thing she'd ever eaten, she didn't know what was. She reached for another, the sun shining on the red fruit brighter than any ruby.

There was more than enough here for Mrs. Cuff to attempt a pie. Or perhaps Sophia ought to take a basket to Gwynna's family. That would take care of one lie Sophia had told Mother.

Edith could pick the strawberries faster than Sophia, but with no idea where the girl had got to, Sophia decided to get started on her own.

She glanced around, her eyes falling on a small basket that held thick gardening gloves and a small spade. She set the items near the house then went back to the vines and knelt in the grass before the strawberries.

After picking enough to fill her basket and continuing to sample far more than she needed to, Sophia stood, brushed off her skirts, then made once more for the gate.

She hesitated. She didn't wish to risk the chance of meeting anyone, but Mrs. Merrick deserved having her cloak returned to her. Sophia would simply have to do it.

With squared shoulders, she walked through the gate. It closed with a loud clack behind her. She blew out a heavy breath. She had done it. She had left the cottage. That was something her own mother couldn't even do.

Sophia's confidence grew with each step she took, especially as the sights around her distracted her from her fears of being seen.

She really could not have chosen a more beautiful day to venture out. The rain had brightened the world around her, despite the excess in mud it caused. Orange butterflies flitted past. Honeybees hummed as they moved from pink sea thrift to yellow gorse. A soft breeze swayed the tall grass, mimicking the movements of the waves. Occasionally, the smell of the strawberries in her basket mixed with the sea's scent. So pleasant had Sophia begun to feel that she unwittingly hummed a tune as she traversed.

However, when she caught sight of a few small homes in the distance, memories of the other night pressed on her mind. Life was different now. She could never go back to the way things were. Her life, her future, her family's future, all of it hung precariously before her, casting a dark shadow over her short-lived hope.

She struggled to keep one foot in front of the other. Why was she there with her basket of strawberries? This would not improve the Merrick's situation any more than it would improve her own at the cottage. It was a silly notion. A choice befitting a fool. She should return to Lowena, behind the safety of the stone wall. At least there she didn't have to worry about what others thought of her.

She reached the small settlements, intent on leaving the cloak on the Merrick's doorstep without a knock. But as she looked around her, she had no idea which home was theirs.

Five houses stood on either side of a small, dirt path, each establishment smaller than the next. It had been so dark the other night, and she had been so weary, that she could not remember if Gwynna's home had been on the left or the right.

She stood in the center of the pathway, glancing at each hovel that possessed no more than two windows, a flat roof, and wooden walls. She had not seen the houses in the daylight since she was a child and Father had taken her to show her their tenants. Mother had brought baskets for the poor only a few times before tasking the servants to do the job instead.

Sophia couldn't imagine living in such a place. Lowena, at least, could claim a view. These only faced each other and a few decaying trees.

A door opened to the left of her, and she started. Her first instinct was to run and hide, cringing at the attention that would come with her standing in such a place.

When a young woman exited her house with a basket in hand, Sophia paused. Was that Gwynna? She looked a great deal different in the daylight. Her simple brown dress was mostly covered with a grey, stained apron, but her hair held back with that same faded scrap of fabric was unmistakable.

Sophia faced the woman with a strained look. "Gwynna?"

Gwynna—it *was* her—looked up with a startled expression. Her features were finer than Sophia remembered. She had high cheekbones and an olive complexion, no doubt from spending too much time in the sun, but the color only accentuated her round, amber eyes.

She was pretty, no mistaking. A great deal more so than even Miss Kinsey and Miss Ward. In truth, if Gwynna wore a fine dress, Sophia was sure the young woman could pass as a lady, even with her freckles.

"Miss Rosewall? What are ye…"

Sophia held up Mrs. Merrick's cloak. "I came back to return this."

Gwynna retrieved the cloak with a grateful nod. "Mama will be pleased."

Sophia held up her basket of strawberries next. "And I brought these."

Gwynna's eyes widened as she accepted the basket, now juggling one in each hand. "So many of them?"

Mortified, Sophia looked away. Why had she brought such a large quantity? Gwynna obviously didn't know what to do with them all. "Lowena Cottage is practically overrun with them. I didn't wish to see them go to waste."

"Well, I be that grateful for them, miss. And how are ye doin', after the other night?"

Sophia looked away. "Much better because of you and your family."

Gwynna nodded. They stood in an awkward silence.

For reasons she could not understand, Sophia wished to linger, but with nothing else to say, and no reason to remain, she took a step back. "I hope you enjoy the strawberries. Do let me know if you ever wish for more. Good day, Gwynna."

"Oh, but, miss," Gwynna said, stopping her departure, "this be a lot of strawberries. I don't think we'd be able to finish them 'fore they rot."

As if on cue, a strawberry tumbled to her feet. Sophia reached down to retrieve it, her cheeks redder than the fruit. "Forgive me, I did not realize."

"No, 'twas generous, miss. I only meant, well, my father is at the mine, and I was to bring the men some food of our own." She raised her basket. "There's not much, mind. But I'd wager he and the other men be yearnin' for somethin' sweet like these strawberries. Would ye like to join me there now?"

Sophia blanched. The mine, Wheal Favour. Father's old mine. "Oh, no. I'm afraid my mother wishes for me to return home straightaway."

Gwynna's face fell. "Are ye certain?"

"Well, I…" Sophia paused.

Going to the mine her family once owned would be too cruel a reminder of all they had lost. Her humiliation would be acute if anyone recognized her, which they were sure to do, as Gwynna's family had.

But it had been quite a while since Sophia had been with someone who wished to be near her, and Gwynna had seemed genuinely upset with Sophia not joining her.

Gwynna readjusted the cloak and the baskets in her hands, and another two strawberries tumbled from the mound. Both baskets would be terribly cumbersome to carry all the way to the mine. Sophia bit her lip. Perhaps if she wore her bonnet low enough, she could remain unnoticed. And if she stayed but a moment…

"Very well," she said, reaching for the basket of strawberries. "Allow me to help."

Gwynna's face brightened, and she handed the bushel to Sophia. "I be glad, miss, to have ye join me."

Sophia stared for a moment, taken aback at the sincerity with which Gwynna spoke. Sophia couldn't understand why the woman wished to be around her and her depressed spirits, but she wasn't about to discard the amity. Not after her only supposed friends had rejected her.

Gwynna put her mother's cloak inside, then returned to Sophia. They moved alongside each other in silence. Sophia fought for something to say, a task she'd never struggled with before.

In the end, it was Gwynna who concluded the silence. "Can I ask ye a question, miss?"

Sophia nodded. "I suppose."

"What really happened that night, the night I found ye all wet and shiverin'?"

Sophia stumbled on a rock. She retrieved the few strawberries that had tumbled to the ground before continuing. She couldn't meet Gwynna's stare. "It's as I said. The ball simply didn't suit me that evening."

"If ever I attended a ball, I'd not leave. Father'd have to pull me out by my hair. I'd love bein' at the center of all that attention."

Sophia sniffed with derision. That was what had caused her humiliation at the ball in the first place, her desire to draw attention to herself by endlessly speaking. All *that* had done was provide fuel for gossip. "It is not as wonderful as you may suppose."

She caught Gwynna's curious look, but Sophia hesitated. The embarrassment of what really happened that evening had nearly buried her. She felt insecure and inferior for the first time in her life. Now she simply wished to hide, to cower away like Mother.

"Ye can keep your secrets, miss, like we all. But I'd not be the one to judge ye, happen you're worried of that."

Sophia nodded. Of course Gwynna would not judge. She seemed more than sincere in her desire to know what was troubling Sophia. But reliving that night by speaking about it would be unbearable. Wouldn't it?

A strange wind of carelessness slipped past the blockade attempting to protect Sophia from discomfiture. What did it matter if Gwynna knew? Sophia's foolishness for attending the ball was sure to be known already throughout all of Society.

She wet her lips. "You have heard what has happened to my family," she began.

Gwynna nodded.

"Well, the truth of the matter is, I left the ball because I am not welcome in my own class. I was foolish enough to ask for help from people I once considered my friends and to join a ball I had no right to attend. Because my family and I have no money, we are no longer seen fit to attend social gatherings. We have nothing to our name, so we are worth nothing to others."

CHAPTER TWENTY

*S*ophia waited for the weight to lift from her shoulders, but the shame of those disapproving eyes at the ball continued to judge her.

Gwynna didn't respond, a solemn expression to her face. She was no doubt upset that such a thing could happen to the Rosewalls. Yet, as Sophia recalled her own words, her throat tightened.

Gwynna could be under no illusion that high society looked upon the working class with condescension. Though, for Sophia to throw such words in her face, to tell Gwynna that she was worth nothing simply due to her financial state, even after all she had done for Sophia, it was unthinkably cruel.

Shame filled her, not only because of her choice in words, but because she was guilty of thinking the same thoughts as the class that no longer wanted her.

She tried to take back her unkindness, but her words refused to cooperate. "I meant, in the eyes of Society, that they believe—they thought that *my* family is nothing." She sighed. Never had she felt so inelegant. "I am sorry, Gwynna. I shouldn't have said such a thing."

Gwynna raised a shoulder. "No need to 'pologize, miss. I'm well aware of what Society thinks of I. And 'tis no matter. I'm happy with my way of life." A weakened, half-smile spread on her lips. "Though, I wouldn't mind dancin' more. We can't afford a subscription to those assemblies in town, but we do a fair bit durin' our gatherin's on the beach, and that more than suffices us simple folk."

Sophia looked away. She couldn't dwell on Gwynna's way of life any longer. It too greatly resembled her own now. Unable to afford simple luxuries, to attend social gatherings. Unable to be truly happy.

Gwynna, at least, had loving parents who were concerned about where she went and with whom she spent her time.

Sophia did not.

They followed the muddy pathway, reaching the view of the shimmering ocean once more, continuing over the curves and hills of the cliffside.

As they arrived at the top of the next incline, Wheal Favour's copper-colored chimney appeared. Grey smoke billowed from its top, lingering only a moment before disappearing into the blue skies.

A jumble of nerves caused Sophia's stomach to lob. "How long has your father worked at the mine?"

"Long since 'fore I was born."

Sophia motioned to Gwynna's basket, a grey cloth draped across the top. "Do you bring him food every day?"

"Lately I have." She stared out to the sea. "I used to be a bal maiden, see, but now I pass the days away by bringin' food for him and the others who ain't got family for a simple fee each month. 'Tisn't much. But every little bit helps me family have food on the table."

Sophia's brows rose. "You were a bal maiden?"

"I was."

When she was a child, Sophia had occasionally joined Father as they rode to the mine. She recalled seeing women breaking apart the stones that the men had brought up earlier. If Gwynna had worked for Father, as well, had Sophia ever seen her?

"How old were you when you started?" she asked.

"Eight or nine, I believe."

Sophia's mouth parted. "So young?" When *she* was nine years old, Father had just purchased her first horse for her. While she was learning to ride, Gwynna was performing manual labor. She pushed the unpleasant image from her mind. "However did you manage?"

"'Twas hard when I was young, but my arms grew strong. I was used to the work 'fore long."

That morning, Sophia had been upset about having to dress herself and pick strawberries on her own. Yet Gwynna did not utter a word of complaint about spending her childhood working at a mine.

"May I ask why you stopped?" Sophia asked next. "Did it not suit you any longer?"

Gwynna's eyes pulled away. Sophia didn't know how, but she had gone too far with her questioning. She would have to be careful when she spoke with her again.

Sophia paused, taken aback. She wished to speak with Gwynna again. The young woman certainly proved a fine distraction for Sophia's troubled life, and her conversation was surprisingly entertaining. More so than Miss Kinsey's and Miss Ward's. Mother would hardly approve of the acquaintance, but she didn't need to know.

Before long, the grey and brown stone structure of the mine came into view, drawing her full attention.

Wheal Favour stood near the edge of the cliff. A pathway and a steep incline of grassy rocks were all that divided the mine from the sheer drop of the cliff that revealed the rushing sea below. The engine house was built against the side of the sloping land, four stone walls shooting straight into the air far overhead.

Sophia had forgotten how tall it was.

"Papa'll be just this way," Gwynna said. "He comes up 'round this time each day."

Sophia followed her along the pathway past the front of the mine. The land around them bustled with miners. Men, women, and children alike transported, broke down, and cleaned the rocks. A few of them glanced toward Sophia with curiosity, so she ducked her head and stared at the pathway.

"There he be," Gwynna said.

They stopped a short distance from the engine house. Sophia spotted Gwynna's father sitting with a few other men near a pile of discarded rocks.

Their clothes were darkened, and their dirty faces glistened with sweat. She didn't remember them being so filthy, or so tired looking.

"Mornin', Papa," Gwynna greeted. "Miss Rosewall here has brought us some fruit from her patch at the cottage. She wanted to share 'em with us all."

Sophia hadn't blushed so much since she was fifteen and her dress had been caught in a doorway at her first ball. Why had Gwynna not taken credit for the strawberries? Then the attention could've been on *her*.

Sophia stepped forward, ignoring the looks of the men as she thrust the basket unceremoniously into Mr. Merrick's hands where he sat. "Here you are."

She shuffled back, standing slightly behind Gwynna before realizing she'd dropped more strawberries, the fruit now resting at Mr. Merrick's feet.

He simply stared at the basket. "Th-thank ye, miss."

Quick footsteps sounded nearby, a few of the younger girls running toward them. Their faces shone red from the sun and exertion. One of them appeared to be no older than seven. They stared at the strawberries with widened eyes and smiling lips.

"How much for one, miss?" asked one of the older girls, her brow wrinkled as she looked up to Sophia.

Sophia blanched. "Oh, no, we brought them to share, free of charge."

Their faces brightened, and they crowded around the basket at once. Sophia moved a few paces back to allow them more room.

Mr. Merrick handed the basket to the girl with the wrinkled brow. "See they're shared, Delen."

She handed them out one-by-one to the children before moving to the gentlemen. Sophia would've enjoyed their eagerness, but as she watched their little smiling faces, heard their giggling and quiet whispers for more, her heart twisted.

They were thrilled over strawberries. Strawberries that were in such abundance at the cottage that they were rotting on the grass beneath the vines.

She looked at their calloused, dirtied fingers and rosy cheeks then turned away. She wanted this feeling gnawing at her heart to leave. But when a loud cough pulled her attention to Mr. Merrick, Gwynna standing at his side, her mouth grew as dry as sand.

The man's whole body shuddered as he coughed into his blackened handkerchief, the noise so loud, Sophia thought for sure he would injure himself. No one else in the group gave him a second glance. Was this a common occurrence, this coughing as if his own lungs were choking him?

She recalled dinner parties that occasionally mentioned miners, their harsh working conditions and hours, but to see it firsthand, she could not pull her eyes away.

Gwynna's hand rested on her father's back until the coughing subsided, then she reached into her basket and extended him a Cornish pasty. Mr. Merrick's haggard breathing leveled as he accepted the food, then he caressed his daughter's cheek with his sullied hand and took a large bite of the pasty.

As he chewed, his dark eyes fell on Sophia. They hardened instantly. She looked away, her cheeks ablaze. For one reason or another, the man disliked her.

Father had mentioned his investors being displeased with some of his decisions with the mine. Did that mean the miners had been upset, as well?

She glanced around, noting more stares like Mr. Merrick's, hardened, accusatory, and her breathing shallowed. They did not want her there. Whether it was because of Father's past decisions or the fact that the Rosewalls' circumstances had changed, they didn't approve of her presence at the mine. She didn't belong at Wheal Favour. Just like she didn't belong at the Madderns' ball.

If she didn't belong in either of those places, just where *did* she belong?

"Merrick!"

She jumped at the sound of a man shouting near the engine house. Mr. Merrick stood, kissing his daughter on the cheek. "The foreman's havin' us meet the new owner and a few of his investors. Tell your mother I'll be home late tonight." He walked past Sophia. "Thank ye for the strawberries, miss."

His voice was hardly warm, but he nodded all the same as he walked away. Gwynna was too busy handing out Cornish pasties to see the exchange. Everyone, Mr. Merrick included, seemed upset about the Rosewalls' history. So why did Gwynna not?

Sophia looked back to the woman's father. But as the crowd parted, her eyes landed on someone else, and a jolt cut through her stomach.

"Mr. Hawkins?"

CHAPTER TWENTY-ONE

*S*ophia's heart stumbled. There was no mistaking Mr. Hawkins's confident stance, his hands clasped behind his back. *He* certainly didn't need to puff out his chest like another gentleman she knew. Or stand on the tips of his toes to be higher. His broad shoulders and tall, cut figure were enough on their own.

Was he one of the mine's new investors? Did he know she was there?

She whirled away before he could see her, wringing her hands. It was only a matter of time before she was noticed. She stood out from the miners and the bal maidens like a wrinkled dress at a private ball.

Dress. Her dress!

She looked down at her skirts. The lavender muslin was covered in grass stains and strawberry drippings she didn't know she'd acquired. With her lack of curls and loose stays, she must look even worse a sight. This was not what she needed in her fragile state, to be seen as the poor woman she was already deemed to be. Her only option was to flee. Quickly.

She moved to Gwynna, whose brow pulled together with a

look of concern as soon as she saw Sophia. "Are ye well, Miss Rosewall?"

Sophia glanced over her shoulder. She didn't have time to explain. She didn't know *what* to explain. "Of course, but I fear Mother needs me at the cottage now." She nodded in departure then walked the opposite direction from which they had come.

"But, miss," Gwynna called out, pointing to the engine house, "if ye go that way, you'll be back at home sooner."

Sophia dared a glance at the pathway where the men still spoke. There was no way she could walk by without Mr. Hawkins and the rest of the miners noticing her.

No, she would go the opposite way, even if it took her an extra hour to return to Lowena. "Thank you, but this way will suffice."

Gwynna gave her an odd look, but Sophia scurried away as quickly and unnoticeably as possible. She forced herself not to run, picking up her skirts slightly to avoid any chance of tripping and slowing down her progress, though the mud already hindered her in that regard.

She moved away from the mine along the pathway, the sea to her right, a small incline to her left. She didn't hear any horse and rider approaching, nor her name being called from behind, but perhaps she simply couldn't hear due to the ocean below.

She peered over her shoulder. There was no one in sight. Only the mine's chimney was visible above the crests and turns of the cliffs she'd walked by. Thank goodness she'd escaped.

She slowed her footsteps and held a hand to her side, soothing the stitch that had formed beneath her ribcage from her hasty departure.

She was not used to the exertion after spending so long at the cottage with hardly any exercise. She would have to remedy that, so long as she didn't venture too far from

Lowena. She couldn't bear the thought of happening upon Mr. Hawkins again.

At the sound of herring gulls crying above, Sophia turned her eyes on the sea. The same light breeze the gulls glided on fluttered her bonnet's ribbons beneath her chin. The ocean had turned a deep blue as the sun moved to the center of the sky. The only breaks in the azure color were the white waves cresting across the water, like cream across a moist pudding.

Cream. That would go lovely with the strawberries. She would have to remember to tell Mrs. Cuff. If, of course, they could still afford cream.

The familiar feeling of misery she'd welcomed into her life the past few days crowded around her. There was no point denying it any longer. She was poor. Her family was poor. They would now have to suffer the fate that had befallen them.

If only she'd have lived her whole life destitute, like Gwynna. Then she'd be able to come to terms with the change.

Images swirled about her mind. Eight-year-old Gwynna as a bal maiden. Mr. Merrick coughing until his face turned purple. Children excited about the simple prospect of having a single strawberry.

Her brow pursed. She was glad to have had the life she did, *while* she did. She would be ungrateful if she didn't recognize the blessings she once had, and that her life was still far easier than Gwynna's.

Even if her path was gone.

Sophia stopped, her hands dropping to her sides. Her path, the pathway she'd been walking on, had literally disappeared into the rocky cliffside in front of her. She glanced behind her, wondering if she'd missed a turn, but the pathway led nowhere else but straight into the side of the cliff.

She released a frustrated sigh. She couldn't return along the mud-strewn pathway to the mine and risk seeing Mr.

Hawkins again. Dropping a hundred feet down the cliffside into the sea below certainly wasn't an option either.

But scaling the cliff to her left? She sized up the cliffside next to the vanished trail. From where she stood at the bottom, it was a fair ascent, the distance no more than twice her height. It wasn't a sheer drop, so if she fell, she would merely slide back down to the pathway with no risk of plummeting into the sea or breaking a limb. The rocks weren't so large either and appeared sturdy enough for her to grasp firmly.

Altogether, it wasn't a terrible idea. It certainly was better than humiliating herself in front of Mr. Hawkins again.

With swift determination, Sophia removed her gloves and tucked them up the side of her Spencer, having left home too quickly to have remembered her reticule. Then she approached the cliffside, reached high overhead, and gripped the top of the first rock with one hand.

She heaved herself up rock after rock, moving into a smooth rhythm. At least for the first few steps, before she realized how silly her idea had been. She continually had to kick out her skirts with her mud-caked boots before securing her footing on the next rock. The sunshine blared above her, so she couldn't keep her eyes up or the imprint of the sun's white light remained behind her eyelids.

Still, she refused to give up, even when her knees shook, and her fingers trembled. She had to be nearing the top now. Though, knowing her poor fortune, the cliff probably stretched out for half a mile.

She forced herself to fix her eyes on the tan rocks, having no desire to see how high she had climbed, nor how much farther she had to go. Finally, she clasped onto the last boulder, and her eyes landed on the grass at the top of the cliff.

Grass…and a pair of tall, black boots.

She gasped, her heart thudding in her ears. Her eyes trailed up long, lean legs, a red waistcoat, and a white, knotted cravat. Before she could reach the gentleman's face, the brightness of the sun caused her eyes to water, and she looked away.

She didn't need to see any more of him to know who stood above her. "Mr. Hawkins." Her voice squeaked. "You startled me."

She supposed she hadn't considered the fact that Mr. Hawkins could ride along the top of the cliff and meet up with her.

"My apologies," he began, his voice deep and smooth. "In my defense, you have startled me, as well. I was just walking by when I heard a grunting and thought it a feral animal struggling to climb the cliffside. Imagine my surprise when I discovered your own head popping up, instead of a wounded cat."

So much for not being humiliated in front of the man again. Sophia's whole face was aflame from exhaustion and sheer mortification.

"I really had no idea you could climb rocks so well," he continued. "If I did, I might have let you rescue yourself that day on the beach."

Was he smiling? It certainly sounded like he was. That charming, charismatic grin.

Her knees trembled, reminding her of the cliffside she stood upon. What a sight she must look. Bonnet askew, hair in ratted waves—and right in the middle of a completely unlady-like endeavor.

But she wasn't really a lady anymore.

"Well, I assure you," she said, speaking slowly to avoid sounding too fatigued, "I am perfectly capable of getting myself out of *this* predicament."

She had only said so to ward off further humiliation, but as she took another step up, her boot slipped, and she slid down the cliffside.

Or she *would* have, had Mr. Hawkins not reached out at

the last moment and grasped her hand with his. She sucked in her breath, scrambling before securing her feet on another rock.

"Are you all right?" Mr. Hawkins asked, all mirth gone.

She gaped at his strong fingers wrapped around her pale hand. Where were his gloves? Suddenly, her breathing hitched for a different reason. "Y-yes," she barely managed to stammer out.

"All right, up you go, then." He latched onto her other hand, and with a swift tug, he pulled her straight up the cliff and safely onto land.

But she wasn't safe at all. She launched straight toward him, her body falling against his. He released her hands and slid his fingers around her waist to steady her footing. Her head spun from the sudden movement and from their proximity. She couldn't help herself, she had to look up at him.

Where was that blasted sun now to prevent her view? His hat was gone, revealing his fair hair. His strong jaw twitched, the movement causing her pulse to race even harder. And when she looked to his lips, those perfectly smooth, angular lips, her mind strayed to places it shouldn't.

The last time they had been this close, he'd rescued her from the tide and from Mother's scolding. But this was different. They were no longer strangers. They had a history, a past. A short one, yes, but complicated, nonetheless. And she felt a pull to this man who had seen her in her most vulnerable of moments.

That reason alone would have caused any normal person to flee. That's why she had done so before. But now that she was in his arms, alone, secluded, she couldn't seem to pull away.

His warm hands seared through the fabric of her dress, heating her skin from front to back. He peered down at her. His eyes centered on her lips for a single, lasting moment before he took an abrupt step back. His hands dropped from her sides, cooling her skin in an instant.

"You nearly took quite the fall, Miss Rosewall. Are you well?"

He no longer met her eyes, his voice gruff.

She placed one boot slightly in front of the other, still attempting to gain her bearings. "Yes. Thank you for your assistance, Mr. Hawkins, yet again."

"Happy to be of service," he said.

He retrieved his hat from the top of his horse's saddle, the chestnut having been grazing nearby. "But perhaps you ought to stop putting yourself into dangerous situations. Otherwise it may appear that you are simply trying to do so for attention."

CHAPTER TWENTY-TWO

*M*iss Rosewall's mouth opened indignantly. Frederick was fairly certain he shouldn't be teasing her this way, especially with how seriously she was taking it. He had to do something to distract himself from looking at her lips again, wondering if they tasted like the strawberries she'd handed to the miners at Wheal Favour.

He blinked hard to dispel the image. He shouldn't be thinking such thoughts. At least, not about this woman. Not after all that had occurred between them.

"I would never seek injury simply to draw attention to myself," she protested, hands on her hips.

"I was only teasing, Miss Rosewall." He placed his hat on his head. "Besides, if you were truly in search of my attention, I'm quite certain you wouldn't have run away from me at the mine."

He quirked a knowing brow. She was clearly mortified, her eyes dropping to the grass beneath her feet. He hadn't noticed her gloves tucked into her jacket until then. Nor the stains on her skirts. Was that juice from strawberries, as well? Her kiss certainly would have tasted of the fruit if she'd been sampling them.

"You were at the mine?" she asked. Her right hand picked at the hem near her left shoulder.

When had she become such a terrible liar? Frederick was better at the sin than she was now. After all, she'd believed him when he said he'd just happened on her, rather than watching her leave and then purposefully taking the longer route above the cliffs simply to see her.

At the thought of adopting a trait straight from his father, Frederick could have shuddered. Instead, he pushed aside the memories of his past and directed his attention to the present.

"Yes, I was at the mine. Mr. Trevethan, the new owner, wished to show me Wheal Favour, along with the other investors." He paused, chewing the inside of his lower lip. "I saw you giving away the strawberries to the miners. That was very kind of you."

The slightest hint of pink lit her cheeks. Was this false humility, or sincere meekness? "I only brought them for a family who helped me the night of the...the-the other night. It was Gwynna Merrick who suggested we take them to the miners."

That was more plausible, for someone else to have suggested the kind act. Miss Rosewall couldn't have become selfless overnight.

Frederick had visited the Merricks to mend their roof before the rain had set in, so he knew the family was in need of any help they received. The Rosewalls must have felt obligated to bring their old tenants a basket, and Miss Rosewall was the chosen messenger.

"Were you on your way back to the cottage?" he asked.

She nodded.

"May I see you safely there?"

"I suppose. If you wish to."

A few days ago, Frederick couldn't wait to be rid of her presence. Now, he'd offered to walk her home, and this time, not to save the Madderns. As a gentleman, though, he really couldn't allow her to cross the countryside alone again. Especially as she was known to make terrible decisions whenever she was out of doors.

They took a few tentative steps forward, Frederick leading his horse behind him, Miss Rosewall at Frederick's side a healthy distance away.

The ocean's rushing waves and his horse's gentle nickering broke through their silence. The wildflowers next to them dipped in the breeze. They were red, like strawberries.

He cleared his throat. "I attempted to call on your family yesterday."

Miss Rosewall's brow rushed up in surprise.

"Your housekeeper said no one was well enough to come to the door." He hesitated. The woman had seemed earnest enough when he'd called, but seeing Miss Rosewall now made him believe otherwise. "I'm surprised to see you here only the day after, as healthy as ever."

"No, I was not unwell. But my energy was expended."

"Due to the ball?" There. He'd mentioned it. He wasn't going to, but he simply had to know what had caused that distraught look on her face before she'd disappeared.

She nodded. "Due to the ball."

"I didn't see you the rest of the evening. Did you leave early?"

"Yes, I was too tired to dance that night."

Another falsehood, as evident by her shifting eyes. Frederick ought to leave it alone, but he continued, nevertheless. "So your departing early had nothing to do with what anyone might have said to you?"

"You overheard their words then?" The pain from the ball reflected in her eyes.

He paused. "Whose words?"

She averted her gaze, her ever-perfect posture slumping. "Never mind. I left of my own accord, after I came to the realization that, as an impoverished female, my attendance is now futile at any future social gathering."

So the rumors *had* been the cause of her abrupt departure. He grimaced. That familiar guilt he'd felt ever since taking over Fynwary Hall gnawed again. How he wished he could be rid of it, to enjoy his time at his new home, rather than always thinking of what purchasing the house had done to the Rosewalls. He knew someone else could have acquired it, that Mr. Rosewall would have been in a worst state had Frederick not, but he couldn't bear it any longer. He had to say something.

He reached forward, placing a hand on her arm to stop her. "Miss Rosewall, please, wait a moment."

She stopped, staring at his hand until he withdrew it.

"Before we go on, I…" He removed his hat and raked his fingers through his hair. "I cannot allow us to continue in such a manner. I can see that being around me does you no good. If you no longer wish to socialize with me, I do not blame you, and I will, of course, respect your wishes. But before you make such a decision, please allow me to apologize for everything that has gone on between us."

He took a step toward her, his voice low, though no one was around to hear his words. "If I would have known that you and Mrs. Rosewall were not aware that I had purchased Fynwary Hall, I would never have remained there that evening. To have such a thing revealed, and to have me, the very man responsible for it, present while you received such news, I am terribly sorry. I only—"

"Please, stop." Miss Rosewall squeezed her eyes closed. "I cannot hear such an apology."

Frederick pulled back in disbelief. She was denying him the chance to apologize. When would he ever stop falling for her trickery? She was the same woman as before, the same woman she always would be. He reached up and tugged at his cravat. Worthless contraption. He could hardly breathe.

"I cannot hear you speak any more on this matter," Miss

Rosewall continued, "because it is not *you* who ought to apologize. It is I."

His finger froze beneath the white fabric.

She continued, looking out to the sea. "I have come to see how very wrong I was to accuse you of my family's misfortunes when it was my father who…" She shook her head. "At any rate, I beg your forgiveness for how I have treated you."

Frederick couldn't speak, his thoughts rolling forward with no end in sight. Could Miss Rosewall truly change? *Had* she truly changed?

The sincerity shining in her eyes, the shame pressing on her brow, whispered for him to believe her words. But if her circumstances *had* finally humbled her, how long would it last? If her wealth was renewed, would she not fall right back into seeking attention from everyone, losing all sincerity?

He needed to err on the side of caution, but a warmth spiraled from his heart and moved through the rest of his limbs. She had apologized, and that was a step in the right direction.

"Your apology is more than accepted, Miss Rosewall," he said, placing his hat atop his head and offering his arm. "Shall we continue as friends?"

She slowly slid her fingers around his jacket sleeve to rest her hand on his arm. He found himself wishing to remove his jacket to better feel the warmth of her touch.

He gently pulled at his horse's reins, his steed following behind him as they continued along the pathway. The silence Miss Rosewall maintained was peculiar. Since when had she learned she didn't need to chatter?

But surely friends could speak, and as they were friends now, he had no reason not to encourage conversation. "My reason for calling yesterday was to see what repairs I could help with at Lowena," he began, "and for one other reason."

"Oh?"

He fingered the reins in his hand. "Yes, you see, I'll be

hosting a picnic in a few days. We'll be traveling about an hour south of here in carriages. And I thought, perhaps, you and your parents might like to attend."

He glanced at her, the top of her head barely reaching his shoulder. She hardly looked pleased. Had he expected her to react differently?

"Thank you for the offer, Mr. Hawkins, but I believe I may safely decline for them both, and myself."

He nodded. Her response didn't surprise him. He knew she was still nursing her wounds after what had occurred at the ball. She ought not remain indoors forever, though. Not while there were still kind people who would accept her for who she was, despite her lack of fortune.

"I understand why you would not wish to come," he said, "but I hope you will change your mind. If it helps in your decision, I have only invited a few people. The Madderns, Summerfields, and Rennalls. It will be a small affair."

He'd enjoyed the company of each of the couples on his list. They were sure to be kind to Miss Rosewall. Even Miss Kinsey.

Miss Kinsey. Blast, he'd forgotten about her. He'd nearly missed the first dance with her at the Maddern's ball when he'd approached Miss Rosewall. Now he'd gone and invited Miss Rosewall to the picnic he'd specifically created to help him get to know Miss Kinsey.

He skirted the issue aside. What did it matter anyway? Miss Rosewall would not attend, and Miss Kinsey would not speak.

This picnic was shaping up to be a rather dull affair.

"Thank you, truly, for the invitation, sir," Miss Rosewall said. "But I do not think that I could bear it."

His heart sunk farther than he'd thought it would. "That is all right," he said, forcing himself to remain upbeat. "But should you change your mind, we will be meeting at Fynwary

Hall Friday morning. Then we will caravan to the location together. I do hope you will reconsider."

What was he doing, trying to talk her into it after the issue had been solved?

His thoughts ceased as Miss Rosewall abruptly slipped her hand away from him, walking sideways as she nodded her head.

"Yes, thank you, Mr. Hawkins. I see the cottage now, so I will be on my way. Thank you for accompanying me."

She curtsied as she attempted to walk, causing her to stumble across the grass.

He moved to help her, but she pulled out of his reach. "Good day, Mr. Hawkins." She spun around and scurried toward Lowena Cottage.

Frederick remained where he was, staring after the woman with a growing frown. Well, that settled it. He had pressed her too hard to join him at the picnic. Now he would have to spend the entire time with the silent Miss Kinsey.

He should be happy at the prospect. This was his plan all along. But instead of imagining how delightful the picnic would prove to be, all he could see was Miss Rosewall's swaying skirts as she walked away from him. And all he could think of was how much more entertaining the day would have been with *that* woman at his side.

CHAPTER TWENTY-THREE

*T*here was no reason for Sophia to accept Mr. Hawkins's proposal to attend a social gathering, even if it was something as simple as a country picnic.

Yet, there she was, standing at the open gates of Fynwary Hall, willing herself to move toward the house, *her* house. Her eyes caressed the beige stone piled three stories high in the center of the house as it reached a grey, turreted roof. Two-storied sections followed next on either side of the main edifice. The windows glinted in the sunlight, and the double doors stretched the height of the ground floor.

Her stomach churned.

This was all Father's doing. He was the one to blame for her accepting Mr. Hawkins's invitation, for her returning to her childhood home, for her raging nerves to be as on edge as they were days before, as she dangled from the cliffside.

She did have some fault in the matter. She was the one who had told her parents about the invitation. Though, she'd only mentioned it in passing.

"You saw Mr. Hawkins?" Mother had asked from her bed when Sophia had told her she'd returned home.

When Mother's nostrils had flared, Sophia was glad she

hadn't mentioned Gwynna and the mine. Mother obviously held a grudge against Mr. Hawkins, though she'd done her best to hide it until that moment. Who knew what she'd say about her daughter befriending a miner's child.

"And what did he have to say to you?" she'd asked next.

"He inquired after the family," Sophia had embellished, "and then he invited us all to a picnic."

Mother had barked out a derisive laugh. She had shown more emotion in that moment than Sophia could recall since they'd moved to Lowena.

"The nerve of the man," Mother had said. "He no doubt wishes to flaunt his wealth before us again. Will he never leave us alone?"

Sophia hadn't known what to say. She certainly wouldn't have told Mother that she'd apologized to him.

"I'm sorry you had to see him, Sophia," Mother continued, "but I will not force you to go to the picnic."

"Picnic?" They'd both turned to see Father entering the room, his eyebrows drawn together. "What picnic?"

Sophia explained Mr. Hawkins's proposal. Father had scratched at his chin before nodding. "I think you'd better go, Sophia."

"But, my dear," Mother had protested, "she will be without a chaperone. And Mr. Hawkins—"

"Is our landlord," Father had finished. "What if we cause offense to him and he chooses to retaliate? No, we would do well to do as he wishes. Besides, I'm certain the group will be large enough for them all to keep watch over our Sophia."

A panic had sparked within Sophia at her father's words. "Will you not come, though, Papa?" she'd asked, desperate for some ounce of comfort.

He'd firmly shaken his head. "No, I have matters to tend to here."

He'd had enough socializing at the ball and now wished to hide away like Mother. What did it matter if they sent their daughter out in the world to fend for herself, so long as their landlord was kept happy?

Sophia stifled a groan as she stood outside her old home. *Would* Mr. Hawkins be happy with her attending? And his guests? She recalled the names he'd listed to her, Madderns, Summerfields, Rennalls. They were all kind enough, but so were her friends, before they'd spoken so cruelly behind her back.

She didn't need reminding that she no longer belonged with such high society. Would they all think she was as selfish and deluded as Miss Ward and Mr. Chester had?

She shook the old acquaintances from her mind. She'd told herself not to linger on their unkindness, to dwell instead on Mr. Hawkins and the fact that he'd invited her to the picnic in the first place.

Then again, thinking of the man caused a whole new set of worries to flood her mind. He'd instantly accepted her apology, didn't seem to care about her inconsequential place in Society. In truth, he didn't seem to care at all what others thought, a novelty she'd never enjoyed.

He was too much for her. His gentlemanly behavior was too much for her. She couldn't spend the entire day in his company. She would simply tell Father that she'd attended the picnic and instead spend the day walking the cliffsides. Or better yet, she'd visit Gwynna.

She spun on her heel, anxious to get away, but after only a single step, the doors of Fynwary Hall clicked open. She paused. Short of darting into the bushes, a real temptation, Sophia could not be hidden from the guests. Attending the picnic was now inevitable.

With a wary heart, she turned around and headed back to the house, her boots crunching on the gravel.

"Miss Rosewall?"

Mr. Hawkins's delighted smile—was it due to her presence

or was it simply the excitement of the picnic?—eased her discomfort only slightly.

"There you are," he said, walking up to greet her. His guests filed out of the doors behind him, a few eyes lingering on her. "I received your letter of acceptance, but I was beginning to wonder if you'd changed your mind again about coming."

She swallowed. "Yes, I am sorry for arriving in an untimely manner."

"No, I didn't mean to complain. You have arrived at the perfect time, really. We were just about to leave."

She managed a nod in his direction before Mr. and Mrs. Summerfield approached her with warm eyes, followed by the others in the group.

"Miss Rosewall, we are so pleased to see you here," Mrs. Summerfield said.

Sophia nodded her gratitude. She wished the attention would shift elsewhere, especially as the Rennalls, the physician and his noticeably younger wife, gawked with such blatant pity, Sophia could have gagged.

"How are you faring, Miss Rosewall?" Mrs. Rennalls asked, her eyebrows drawn together so closely they created a wide depression in her forehead.

"I am more than well, Mrs. Rennalls."

"I trust your mother is in good health," Mr. Rennalls asked.

"She is, thank you," Sophia lied.

"We have not seen her in so very long," Mrs. Maddern said. "Do give her our best."

Mrs. Maddern certainly seemed happier to see Sophia than the last time she'd called at Benlett House. Was this because Sophia was no longer attempting to stay in the woman's home?

She looked away. "I will. Thank you, Mrs. Maddern."

Sophia glanced next to Mr. Maddern, who nodded in

greeting, then Miss Kinsey, who gave her a slight curtsy before her green eyes flitted toward Mr. Hawkins.

Sophia glanced between them. The two were certainly spending a great deal of time together, Mr. Hawkins calling on her at Benlett, their time together at the ball, now the picnic. Was there an understanding between them?

She ignored the unease creeping across her stomach at the thought.

Mr. Hawkins spoke, as if he knew her thoughts and wished to end them. "Well, now we have all arrived, I say let us begin our journey."

There was a murmur of agreement, and the group turned to the carriages lining the drive.

"Miss Rosewall, you may ride with me and the Madderns. Will that suffice?" Mr. Hawkins asked.

"Yes, thank you," Sophia responded, though she would have preferred riding alone.

They stopped at the side of the foremost carriage. Mr. Maddern helped his wife up, then moved to offer his niece the same courtesy, but Mr. Hawkins jumped in to help first with a smile for Miss Kinsey. Sophia pretended not to watch the exchange, then she allowed Mr. Maddern to assist her next.

When she entered the carriage, Mrs. Maddern on one side, her niece to the other, Sophia remained fixed to her spot.

If she sat in the middle or by the empty window on the same side as Miss Kinsey, Sophia would inevitably sit next to Mr. Hawkins. If she sat on the other side, however, she would have to face him for the entire ride. Surely Mrs. Maddern would want to sit beside her husband. But could Sophia bear sitting next to Mr. Hawkins for an entire hour?

She turned to Miss Kinsey. "Do you not wish to sit in the middle?" she asked, pointing to the smooth, brown leather.

"I'd prefer a window seat, thank you," Miss Kinsey replied.

"Having difficulty finding a place, Miss Rosewall?" came Mr. Maddern's voice from outside.

Sophia had forgotten he and Mr. Hawkins were still waiting to enter the carriage. Impulsively, she plopped down onto the middle seat.

Mr. Maddern entered first, moving beside his wife, then Mr. Hawkins, who took one look at the seat next to Sophia and sat down with only a slight flicker of his eyes toward her.

There was more than enough room for the three of them to sit comfortably together without touching, but Sophia knew the moment they pulled onto the road, they would surely bump against one another.

"Are we all comfortable?" Mr. Hawkins asked.

His deep voice sailed through her skipping heart.

She pulled in her arms, straightened her legs. One touch from him would be her undoing, she knew it.

And she was right.

The carriage pulled ahead, and instantly, her shoulder grazed against his. "Sorry," she mumbled, shifting closer to Miss Kinsey, who seemed none the wiser as she stared out of the window with somber eyes.

What was the matter with the girl? If she and Mr. Hawkins were close to an engagement, shouldn't *she* be seated next to him and not Sophia?

"We are sure to have fine weather today," Mr. Maddern said.

Sophia hadn't seen the man in weeks, due to his illness. Normally, she'd ask after his improving health, but now she didn't know her place.

"Indeed," his wife agreed. "Our niece does enjoy a country picnic. Do you not, Claire?"

"Yes, Aunt."

"She and her sisters would often picnic together," Mrs. Maddern continued. "And we all know Miss Rosewall enjoys a picnic herself."

Sophia's smile felt as strained as a rope ready to split in two.

As the ride continued, the majority of the conversation took place between Mrs. Maddern and Mr. Maddern. Miss Kinsey kept her eyes out of the window. Mr. Hawkins chirped in when the conversation allowed, but he was mostly silent, as well.

Sophia wondered if he was disappointed not being seated next to Miss Kinsey. He would not be conversing greatly with the voiceless woman anyway, even if he was closer to her.

But who was Sophia to talk? For as long as she had chided Miss Kinsey behind her back for remaining silent during social gatherings, Sophia was behaving the very same.

Then again, what could she say as a woman who no longer belonged in this social sphere? It was far better for her to keep her mouth shut. If only to avoid attention that would undoubtedly cause her further embarrassment, just like at the ball.

Sophia listened half-heartedly as the Madderns spoke of the picnic they'd shared together when they were courting.

"It rained the whole time," Mrs. Maddern said.

"And we were forced to eat in the carriage together," Mr. Maddern chimed in.

Mrs. Maddern linked her arm through her husband's. "Yes, it was all very romantic, though, wasn't it, Mr. Maddern?"

They shared a loving look, Mrs. Maddern's eyes sparkling.

When was the last time Mother and Father had looked at each other in the same way? Sophia had only seen the two of them speaking together once since their displacement to Lowena, and that had only been when talking of the picnic. She knew they loved each other, but the secrets Father had kept had put a strain on their relationship.

The corners of Sophia's mouth pulled down. Would her future husband keep secrets from her? Would she constantly have to put on an air of perfection in her marriage, as Mother had done until she lost everything? Or would her husband never even give Sophia a second thought?

A weakness came over her body. Her neck curved forward. She rested her leg on the wall beside her. There she was, worrying over the actions of her future husband when she wasn't even sure if she would ever marry.

Her leg warmed against the side of the carriage, strangely tingling until the wall shifted. She cocked her head. Walls didn't shift.

Legs did.

CHAPTER TWENTY-FOUR

*S*ophia jerked away. She was not seated at the side of the carriage. She had been resting her leg against Mr. Hawkins. No wonder the warming sensation had spread throughout her skin like a wildfire, the heat rising to her cheeks.

She stole a swift glance at him, but he hardly seemed aware of their touch. Why would he be when he was interested in Miss Kinsey?

As the ride progressed, with each bump in the road, each turn, each pull of the horses, she came into contact with Mr. Hawkins. She was grateful at least for her Spencer and his jacket to create some type of barrier between them, but that did nothing for her mind. She knew exactly who her arm grazed against each and every time.

After the agonizingly long carriage ride came to an end, Sophia nearly groaned with how stiff her legs and back had become. The Madderns exited, then Mr. Hawkins, who remained below the door of the carriage to extend his help to Sophia and Miss Kinsey.

Sophia moved forward first. She didn't look at him, but with her essentially numb legs, she hadn't noticed her boot becoming entangled in her skirts. She tumbled slightly forward, but Mr. Hawkins's hand tightened its grip around her own.

"Are you all right?" he asked softly.

She nodded, grateful his quiet tone brought no further attention to herself. She pulled her hand from his and smoothed her skirts down, attempting to calm her nerves in the process. She didn't know what was wrong with her. She was never clumsy. Except, of course, when Mr. Hawkins was nearby to witness it.

She moved off to the side as he helped Miss Kinsey down next. The woman scurried away from him and straight to her aunt's side. No look was shared between the two of them, no sparkling eyes like the Madderns'.

Sophia frowned. Perhaps there wasn't an understanding between them. Perhaps they were merely just friends. Or perhaps they were trying not to draw attention to their relationship due to Miss Kinsey's inhibitions.

Either way, she needed to stop concerning herself in their affairs.

"Shall we?" Mr. Hawkins said as the other carriages pulled up and the guests joined them.

They allowed the servants to go ahead of them, giving them time to set up the spread, all while the attendees enjoyed a leisurely stroll. Sophia tried not to notice the servants stealing glances at her as they walked by. She knew they recognized her, a few of them giving her subtle nods before going about their tasks.

She could only imagine their thoughts, the same she was sure Mrs. Rennalls had, with her constant solicitous eyes directed Sophia's way.

Poor Miss Rosewall. Fallen so far.

How does she manage without her servants' help?

She suffers from her own father's ineptitude.

"Miss Rosewall, are you coming?"

She blinked, looking to Mrs. Summerfield who watched her expectantly. The others had already begun to walk through the wooded area.

She scurried to catch up with them. The Summerfields had always been kind to her and her family, and as Sophia walked beside them, she was reminded again of their innate goodness.

"We've been meaning to invite you and your parents to Rudhek Manor for dinner," Mrs. Summerfield said. "But we wished to wait until you were more settled. Do let us know the moment you are available."

Sophia nodded but remained silent. She couldn't agree to go to dinner at the manor. The Summerfields were too fine a people for her family now.

The pathway through the trees narrowed and the bushes lining the trail thickened, forcing the guests to move along two-by-two. Mr. and Mrs. Summerfield, the eldest of the party, led the group to set the pace. The Madderns followed, then the Rennalls.

Mrs. Rennalls spoke constantly, whether she was listened to or not, about her "Dear Mr. Rennalls" and his ability to heal any sick or wounded beggar or king.

Mr. Hawkins escorted Miss Kinsey behind them. Bringing up the rear, Sophia walked by herself. That was what she preferred. She deserved to be without an escort. She was the odd woman out.

She was the imposter.

Mr. Hawkins occasionally glanced over his shoulder at her, performing his duty to ensure all his guests remained happy and comfortable. Sophia plastered a smile to her lips and eyed the greenery around them each time he looked back.

The trees were thick, the leaves nearly blocking out the sun entirely, apart from small veins between the foliage where light burst through in shining rays.

She'd always enjoyed a walk through the woods, but now

she longed for the sea. She'd found, as she'd grown accustomed to constantly hearing the waves crashing on the shores below the cottage, that the sound overpowered her ability to think of much else.

It was a welcome relief.

Here, with only the soft rustling leaves overhead, nothing prevented the guests' voices from drifting toward her, specifically Mr. Hawkins's.

He spoke to Miss Kinsey of his home in Bedfordshire, how Dawnridge was surrounded by fields of poppies that lit the countryside in blankets of bright red.

"It really is a breathtaking sight," he said.

Sophia's eyes wandered over his broad shoulders, trailed down his jacket's curved fit to the split tails reaching just to his knees. He walked with a slow, confident stride, his shoulders swinging slightly.

Sophia knew what was a breathtaking sight. And it certainly wasn't any field of poppies in Bedfordshire.

"Oh!"

A piercing pain stung her forehead, just below her hairline. She stopped walking, holding a hand to her head. What had struck her?

She glanced over her shoulder, seeing a bare branch eye-level, twanging in the air. That was the culprit. Wretched, blasted—

"Miss Rosewall, what happened? Are you well?"

She turned back around to see the whole party having stopped in front of her. She winced, then removed her hand and straightened her back.

"Oh, yes. I was merely caught by a low-hanging branch, but my bonnet managed to rescue me. I am well."

The guests exchanged looks. Did they think she was merely trying to draw attention to herself, being alone at the back? Perhaps there was a time she would have performed such an act, but now all she wanted was for them to leave so she might suffer alone in silence.

"Perhaps you ought to allow my husband to look after you," Mrs. Rennalls said, patting the physician's arm. Her eyes widened with an exaggerated look of concern.

Mr. Rennalls took a step forward. "Yes, you must wish to rest for a moment."

"No, I assure you," Sophia said. "I am perfectly well. I was merely caught by surprise."

Mr. Rennalls hesitated. Sophia looked between the guests, forcing her happiness to appear genuine, but Mr. Hawkins's studious gaze unnerved her.

"If Miss Rosewall says she is well, then she must be," he said, to her surprise. "Shall we continue?"

Her look of relief must have been apparent, for he gave her a subtle nod as the group continued.

Sophia waited, watching closely as they turned around and moved through the thick brush. Miss Kinsey pulled ahead, joining her uncle with Mrs. Maddern following closely behind. Mr. Hawkins was the last to disappear into the woods, and she waited until he was fully gone to groan with a wince.

The wound ached. She removed her bonnet and pressed a hand to where it hurt. She pulled it back, gasping at the blood that had appeared on the tip of her glove.

"You *are* hurt."

She looked up. Mr. Hawkins stood before her. The other guests had continued on, their quiet voices moving farther into the woods.

She hid her hands behind her back. "No, as I said before, I'm well." She motioned to the pathway. "You had better continue before you are left behind."

He stared at her forehead. Had he even heard a word she'd said? "How serious is the wound?"

"Not serious in the slightest. Truly, there is no need to make a fuss, Mr. Hawkins."

She attempted to move past him, but he reached his arm out to stay her. "Please, if you just allow me to see it, I will not mention it again unless Mr. Rennalls should see to you."

His voice was so soft, she couldn't say another word in protest. He took a step toward her, removing his right glove. Slowly, he brought his hand up, his fingers hovering just above her skin. She tried to maintain steady breaths, but the task was impossible as his eyes remained on hers.

Finally, he moved his attention to her wound. His finger-tips grazed her skin just above the scratch, brushing aside her hair. She closed her eyes.

"Did I hurt you?" he asked, pulling his fingers back.

She opened her eyes to see him staring down at her. "No." Only her heart. It was raging so painfully, she needed to escape before it burst through her chest.

Now that would be a wound to complain about.

He looked again to her brow. "You're bleeding," he voiced in a hoarse whisper.

She could only nod.

He reached into his jacket and produced a handkerchief, pressing it softly beneath her curls to soak in the blood. "It is only a small scratch, so I needn't tell Mr. Rennalls. I take it you do not wish to draw attention to yourself."

"No, I don't." Nor had she much to give the physician in return for his services.

He continued to dab softly at the wound, silence pulsing between them before he spoke again. "I am glad you have joined us today. May I ask what made you change your mind?"

"I simply fancied a day out of doors."

His eyes flickered to hers before he pulled his handkerchief down, folding the edges to hide the blood. "Keep this. I wouldn't wish for you to sully your own, should you need to dab at it again."

She accepted the handkerchief carefully to avoid touching him again.

He stared down at her. A bird chirped overhead. The trees rustled their leaves.

"Perhaps we ought to rejoin the others," she said softly.

He nodded, but he remained where he stood. "I think, first, that I ought to take a look at your wound, just one more time. To be sure that you are well."

His expression told her he was not interested in looking at her wound. He was interested in something far different, far more appealing.

Only moments before, Sophia had been convinced that he was falling for Miss Kinsey. Now, the way he looked at Sophia, his eyes sparkling brighter than she'd ever seen, any thought of Miss Kinsey vanished.

Her lungs compressed, though this was different than how she'd felt at the ball. This tightness was welcoming, gripping. Stirring.

Slowly, she nodded. "I think I should like you to do just that," she whispered.

He closed the distance between them with a careful step. She craned her neck to keep her eyes on him.

How could this be happening? Weeks before, she had despised the man, and she was fairly certain she had not been his preferred person either. They'd been enemies, practically strangers. But now? She couldn't make sense of it. She couldn't make sense of anything. Not with Mr. Hawkins's hand moving to her brow again, brushing back her curls.

This time, his eyes did not move to her wound. This time, they moved to her lips.

She swallowed. She'd never known her heart to race so fiercely. She'd never known such a powerful desire to share in affection with a gentleman. She stared at his own lips. They were parted, inviting her to enjoy their caress.

He leaned toward her. His breath was on her lips. She was awash in the musky scent of his cologne. His soft fingertips caressed the side of her face before resting beneath her jawline.

Slowly, softly, he urged her chin farther up, tipping his head to the side. She closed her eyes as his face blurred from his nearness. It was going to happen. His kiss would be on her lips at any moment.

Finally.

CHAPTER TWENTY-FIVE

"Mr. Hawkins? Miss Rosewall?"

Miss Rosewall gasped. Frederick dropped his hand and took a step back, blinking from the euphoria the woman had created around them.

Mrs. Maddern appeared around the trees. Her eyes sailed between the two of them. "Oh, there you are. Is everything all right?"

"Miss Rosewall was feeling faint." His voice cracked. He cleared his throat. "She needed to rest for a moment."

He flicked his eyes to Miss Rosewall. Her cheeks were as red as his forehead felt.

"Yes," she blurted out too forcefully. "Yes, that is what happened. I am recovered now. We were just on our way to join you again."

Mrs. Maddern raised her brow. "I'll alert the others that you've been found."

Her pensive look stayed on Miss Rosewall a moment longer before she nodded and backed away.

"We'll be right behind you," Frederick said to her departing figure.

When he was alone with Miss Rosewall once more, he

rubbed the back of his neck, blowing out a slow sigh. The silence between them was thicker than the doors of Fynwary Hall.

"I suppose we ought to return to them before they come looking for us again," he said.

Miss Rosewall nodded, rushing past him without a glance. He followed but not so swiftly. He needed to create some distance between them so he could think about what the devil he'd just done.

What he'd *nearly* just done. Their lips had not touched, thanks to Mrs. Maddern. He wanted to be angry with her interruption, but it was better this way. He'd been so pleased to have Miss Rosewall join him that day, but his craving to spend more time with her than Miss Kinsey created turmoil within his mind. Turmoil, guilt, and confusion.

This picnic was meant to bring him closer to Miss Kinsey, not Miss Rosewall. No wonder Mrs. Maddern had gone looking for them. He needed to remember his original intentions, and he needed to forget Miss Rosewall and their shared desire to make their kiss a reality. For it *was* a shared desire.

His stomach flipped pleasantly at the memory of her eager eyes and parted lips, but he pushed it aside. He wouldn't dwell any longer on what might have been. It was a mistake, pure and simple. Judging by the pace at which Miss Rosewall flew ahead of him, she wished to forget about it as greatly as he did.

He would do just that then, pretend it didn't happen. Move on. Force his mind away from how her soft skin had felt on his fingertips, and how her soft breath had tickled his lips.

Instead, he would attend to Miss Kinsey for the rest of the picnic. Just after he ensured once more that Miss Rosewall was well.

Mr. Hawkins came up behind her. Sophia tucked in her elbows to avoid any touch with him. Any *further* touch.

She could slap herself for being so stupid, so weak-willed. How could she have almost allowed a kiss to occur between them? What little improvement that had occurred in regard to their relationship was now damaged, made void by the awkwardness settling between them.

"Has your wound stopped bleeding?" Mr. Hawkins asked as he moved beside her.

She brought the handkerchief, *his* handkerchief, to her brow. The scent of his cologne wafted past her nose at the movement. She wanted to bring the fabric back to her nostrils and take a hearty sniff, but that would certainly draw his stares even more.

After a few dabs at the wound, she pulled it back to see only a lone dot of blood on the white cloth. "Nearly."

"Please let me know if you do feel faint. I should not like you to fall and harm yourself further."

The concern in his eyes set her heart flapping like her skirts in the breeze. But what did it mean? His concern, his near kiss, his attention toward her? This was more than being an attentive host.

Her mind continued to churn through his actions as they reached the others. The pathway opened up to a wide meadow speckled with orange and white wildflowers and surrounded by thickets of trees. A brooklet ran through the side of the meadow. Its trickling echoed around the area with a gentle lull.

The location was lovely. So lovely that Sophia's spirits lifted, despite the embarrassment still picking at her nerves.

They walked toward the spread the servants had prepared for them. White chairs were set out for those who wished for extra comfort, while blankets were laid down on the soft grass for the others. The food, all provided by Mr. Hawkins, was nothing overtly elaborate, but the selection was more than fine, including cheeses, fruits, various pastries, and lemonade for refreshment.

Sophia sat on the blanket next to Mrs. Summerfield's chair. "So nice, isn't it?" the woman twittered, and Sophia had to agree.

However, when she noticed Mr. Hawkins sitting down next to Miss Kinsey, her mood shattered like a glass dish falling on the floor.

She watched their interaction beneath her lashes. Mr. Hawkins barely looked at Miss Kinsey as he spoke with her. Miss Kinsey hardly responded. They did not appear to be enjoying themselves. There were no heavy glances, no sparkling eyes, nothing like what Sophia had experienced with him.

Heat flashed across her brow. She made to observe them further, but when she felt another set of eyes on her from the opposite side of the blanket, she turned and found Mrs. Maddern watching her with a calculating stare.

Sophia looked away, picking at the food on her plate.

Undoubtedly, Mrs. Maddern had already decided who she wished her niece to marry. Did the woman truly suppose that Sophia was capable of standing in Miss Kinsey and Mr. Hawkins's way?

First, Sophia would never wish to come between two people in love. If they were, indeed, in love. Second, Mrs. Maddern was as delusional as Sophia if she thought Mr. Hawkins would ever have Sophia. She was no longer the perfect match for any gentleman, especially one as honorable as Mr. Hawkins.

Even if he had almost kissed her.

Even if his eyes were now on her.

Sophia kept her head down at the realization, her heart pleasantly burning. She'd often caught gentlemen watching her from afar, but none of them had ever caused her mind to spin quite like Mr. Hawkins's eyes upon her did.

Perhaps his actions were merely a lapse in judgment though, a moment of weakness, like the near kiss. After all, he'd chosen to sit beside Miss Kinsey, not Sophia.

The thought caused her heart to sink as if she was sliding down an endless hill with no landing in sight.

She tried to grasp onto the conversation to distract herself, but as the women spoke of their growing ribbon collections, of decorating bonnets, and of purchasing new dresses, Sophia only fell farther. She could not join in with their discussion even if she wished to. Her life had changed too drastically for her to carry on as before.

"Mrs. Follett made my dress for your ball, Mrs. Maddern," Mrs. Rennalls said, referring to the modiste in St. Just. "We are so fortunate to have her talents with us."

Mrs. Maddern nodded. "Indeed. We certainly enjoy the special care Mrs. Follett shows with each dress she creates." She motioned to Miss Kinsey's pink muslin skirts. "This gown was made by her, as well."

"Of course it was," Mrs. Rennalls said with a twinkle in her eye. "One could see for miles how elegant the stitching is."

"And so becoming on my niece," Mrs. Maddern gushed. "Don't you agree, Mr. Hawkins?"

Sophia finally allowed herself to look at the gentleman. His eyes quickly pulled away from hers and turned to Mrs. Maddern with a blank stare. "Pardon? Oh, yes. Very becoming, indeed."

He gave a polite nod to Miss Kinsey, who stared at the blanket she sat on. She hardly looked pleased with his words.

"Miss Rosewall?"

Sophia turned to Mrs. Rennalls. "Yes?"

"You mustn't think we've not noticed your own lovely dress. Is it new, as well?"

"No, I purchased this quite some time ago."

Skirted glances and bright blushes spread throughout the party like an unforgiving disease. Sophia did not need to tell them why she was not wearing a new dress. They all knew her family's financial state.

"Well, it certainly is lovely," Mrs. Summerfield said. She sent an encouraging smile in Sophia's direction, but Sophia hardly noticed, too busy attempting to subdue her flushed face.

Mrs. Rennalls pumped her head up and down, attempting to gain her bearings after Sophia's words. "Oh, to be sure. At any rate, a woman does not need a lovely dress to attract a husband. In some instances, why, most that I know of, a lady's accomplishments are what ultimately attract a mate."

Sophia released a jeering sniff. All eyes fell to where she sat. She pulled in her bottom lip, chewing at it. She didn't mean to react in such a way, but Mrs. Rennalls's words were false. Ridiculous. Just as Sophia was ridiculous for coming to the picnic in the first place.

She stood up in an abrupt motion. "Excuse me. I should like to stretch my legs for a moment."

She only took two steps before Mrs. Summerfield called after her. "Oh, Miss Rosewall, you ought not go alone. Mr. Hawkins, see to her, won't you?"

CHAPTER TWENTY-SIX

*M*r. Hawkins rose to his feet without hesitation. "Of course."

Sophia debated running away to the carriage and demanding a ride home, but the idea of commanding her family's past servants prevented her.

Mr. Hawkins motioned her forward. She led the way with a fleeting glance at the group. They all watched her. Mrs. Maddern's lips were pulled inward with clear disappointment, and Miss Kinsey's shoulders had fallen forward. Was that due to disappointment or pure relief?

Sophia shook her head. What did it matter what any of them thought? She had too many troubles of her own to concern herself over a shy niece and her scheming aunt's opinions.

She moved away from the group, her pace swift, but Mr. Hawkins kept up easily with his long stride. Mrs. Rennalls's voice slowly drifted away as the trickling brook replaced her words.

Sophia tried to find peace with the soothing sound, but the task proved impossible as she found herself alone once more with Mr. Hawkins, though they were still in plain sight of the others.

Should she apologize for the kiss they'd almost shared, just to clear the awkward air between them? Heavens, no. Better to pretend it never happened. Better to pretend she still did not imagine how his lips would have felt on hers, how his intoxicating cologne would have nearly caused her to swoon, just as it did now.

"You did not come today because you wished to, did you, Miss Rosewall?"

Her thoughts ended, and Sophia looked toward him. Her eyes must have revealed the true answer to his question, for he nodded, unsurprised.

"Can you tell me why you *did* come then?"

She crossed her arm over her stomach.

"Because your parents wished for you to do so?"

Curse his astuteness. Apparently, she was unable to keep anything from the man. Did that mean he knew how greatly she'd desired his kiss, even now?

Heat crept up her neck. "Yes."

"Why did they wish for that?"

His voice was soft, his innocence tugging at her conscience. He deserved the truth, even if it caused her more embarrassment.

"My father," she began, "he fears you might remove us from the cottage. He bade me come so you would not be offended at our refusal."

She'd expected another look of discernment, another nod of understanding, but a flicker of hurt flashed over his features. "I suppose you would expect no less from me. After all, I have already forced you from one home."

She stopped walking, staring up in disbelief. This wasn't right. Mr. Hawkins shouldn't feel responsible for her family's circumstances. Since her parents wouldn't help him to see otherwise, the task was left to her.

"Sir," she began, her voice firm yet soft. "You did not force us from Fynwary. My father did. Furthermore, I must also clarify, though he may believe one thing, I know you would never intentionally evict anyone from their home. That includes even the Rosewalls of Lowena Cottage."

His brow smoothed, his countenance softening, and a warmth blossomed in his eyes. "Thank you, Miss Rosewall. That means a great deal to me."

Their stares mixed, lingering past propriety, but Sophia couldn't look away. Not with his eyes capturing hers so fully. Everything around them, even the very air, seemed to silence as she stared up at him. She wouldn't look at his lips. She refused to, those tempting, warm…

"Shall we continue?"

His smooth voice swirled around her heart like a silk ribbon. He motioned toward the brooklet, and they fell in step beside each other again.

"I'm sorry you couldn't come of your own accord," he said after a moment. "Enjoying a party is nearly impossible when one is forced to attend."

Sophia wasn't sure what to say. She *had* enjoyed herself in one regard. But she couldn't very well admit to herself or to Mr. Hawkins that her highlight of the picnic was spending time with him.

Before, she would not have hesitated to flirt with such words, if only to bring attention to herself. Now, it wasn't her place, or her right, to behave in such a way with a wealthy gentleman. But she couldn't let Mr. Hawkins think she was ungrateful for his invitation.

"Truthfully," she said, "I have enjoyed myself much more than I thought I would. I hope you know, my reasoning for not wishing to come didn't have to do with you. Rather…" She looked over her shoulder to where the group still conversed. Mrs. Maddern's attention was on Sophia and Mr. Hawkins before Mrs. Rennalls spoke with her. "But rather my lack of connection with those I once called my friends."

"Are they not still your friends?"

She turned away from the guests. "I suppose those here are kind enough to maintain the label. But I no longer share commonalities with them. I cannot participate in their conversations about matters that no longer concern me or concur with opinions with which I now disagree."

They reached the brooklet. The grass curved over their boots as they stood at the edge of the bank. Sophia's eyes followed the water trickling around the small rocks, moving with the curve of the land in soft, obedient movements.

She bent down and plucked a blade of grass from the edge of the water. Straightening, she absentmindedly brushed the grass across her fingers as she glowered at the submissive stream.

"Why do you scowl?"

Sophia struggled to find an appropriate response to Mr. Hawkins's question. Should she force a smile? Pretend all was well? Or would he see straight through her once again?

She pressed a hand to her pulsing temples. She was tired. Tired of the mask she wore, feigning everything was well. She couldn't hide, she couldn't pretend any longer.

The words slipped from her mouth, her weakened will no longer able to hold them back. "My entire life, I have been taught to control my emotions, to never reveal my true feelings about anything. 'Always smile, Sophia,' Mother said. 'It is unbecoming to wear one's emotions for all to see.' I dutifully followed her advice, but what good did it do?"

She stretched out her hand and allowed the grass to fall from her fingertips. It fluttered through the air and landed soundlessly in the water, following the small current along.

"I will tell you what my obedience did, Mr. Hawkins." She faced him squarely, her voice falling flat. "Nothing. It did nothing. Mother said my amicability and accomplishments would provide me with a wonderful husband. But what I stupidly didn't realize before was how very much money plays a part in a person's decision of whom to marry. After all, how can one live off of one's talents alone? It is all based on wealth already bestowed and status already conferred."

Once the words began, Sophia could not rein them in. Her exhaustion was replaced little by little with renewed energy, fueled by anger. Her complaints grew, the truths flowing out of her mouth like waves rolling endlessly up the sand.

"And my talents, the accomplishments I was tasked to perfect?" She fisted her hands, speaking through clenched teeth. "I despised playing the pianoforte. Every moment I sat before that forsaken instrument was agony. I felt the very same each time I was forced to draw or paint or read books Mother would choose for me to improve myself further. And the needlework. Oh, the needlework! I lost count of the number of times I'd prick my finger on that awful little point, bleeding over my fabric, forcing me to start again." She growled an exasperated sigh. "I have wasted away my life trying to attain perfection in all of the things I detest. And it was all for naught. For a woman is nothing without a dowry."

Her enraged words ended, her heart bound with regret for the life she'd wasted away.

Mr. Hawkins stared down at her. He hardly seemed surprised, but then, he wasn't responding either, undoubtedly stunned into silence.

Sophia looked back to the brooklet. She could only imagine the disapproving words he had for her outburst. How could she have lost control so easily? How could she have spoken such things, complaining to Mr. Hawkins that she would not be able to find a husband because she lacked the funds to do so?

Perhaps Mother was right. Sophia should be hiding her

emotions, if only to prevent further embarrassment, though she shouldn't care what Mr. Hawkins thought of her.

He was sure to know by now that Miss Kinsey was a far better choice in friend and wife than Sophia. Miss Kinsey, with her good breeding, an abundance of talents, a dowry. Better he discovered such a thing before he attempted to kiss Sophia again.

Again?

Sophia blinked rapidly, dismissing the idea. "Mr. Hawkins, forgive me. I do not know what has come over me. I've ruined your wonderful picnic with talk of such things. Let us return to the others. They will be missing you, I'm sure."

She made to walk away, but his hand lightly grasped her wrist. Despite their gloves preventing a more intimate touch, her heart still jumped.

"You have had your chance to speak, Miss Rosewall. Might you allow me the opportunity to respond?"

He released his hold of her as she faced him. "Of course. I did not think you could have anything to say after all of that."

"I do. But it is merely a question."

Sophia nodded, inwardly bracing herself as he continued.

"If you do not enjoy those pastimes, then what is it you *would* like to do?"

Sophia stared. He was not shaming her or shunning her for her distasteful words. He was asking her what she would like to do.

What would *she* like to do? What *would* she like to do?

The question caught her by such surprise, she had no answer. "I…I do not know, sir."

"Then I suggest you take time for yourself to discover the answer to this simple question. Perhaps then things will not appear so dismal for you. Should you need any help at all discovering your own desires, I am more than willing to offer my assistance."

The corner of his lip curved, and she returned the gesture with a smile of her own.

"Right now, however, I believe you are right. We must return. Even though the thought of sitting through one more discussion of ribbons pains me to my very core."

He winked, and her heart skipped. She could no longer prevent the smile spreading across her lips.

Together, they returned to the others. Sophia's mood drastically improved, even with Mrs. Maddern's brooding stare in her direction for the duration of the picnic. Mr. Hawkins's steady, encouraging smile was more than sufficient for Sophia to maintain a happier disposition.

That is, until the blankets, chairs, and food were gathered up by the servants and the guests made their way to the carriages.

Mrs. Summerfield linked her arm with Sophia's. "Miss Rosewall, why do you not ride home with us and the Rennalls? We are much closer to Lowena than Mr. Hawkins is."

Sophia glanced to Mr. Hawkins, but his eyes darted away before she could read them.

"Very well," she agreed, and she allowed Mrs. Summerfield to lead her toward the carriage, glancing over her shoulder for one last look at Mr. Hawkins.

Instead of his eyes on her, the last image she saw was Miss Kinsey smiling down at Mr. Hawkins as he helped her into their carriage.

And Mr. Hawkins smiled in return.

CHAPTER TWENTY-SEVEN

A slab of ice slid over the warmth that had enveloped Sophia's heart, freezing over her comfort. She entered her carriage, sitting down beside the Rennalls and across from the Summerfields. Her eyes remained on the passing landscape as the carriage finally rolled forward.

The sun had already begun its descent, an orange glow spreading across the countryside. The stone tors turned copper in the light, stacked tall near grazing sheep on the moors. The lambs' soft bleating for their mothers still sounded out above the carriage rattling on, the horses' steady steps, and Mrs. Rennalls's constant chattering.

Before long, the woman's words slowly faded away. Sophia glanced over to see her fast asleep, lying on her husband's shoulder, the physician resting, as well.

"I think she has finally tired herself out."

Sophia turned to Mrs. Summerfield, whose eyes shone with mirth. Mr. Summerfield rested his head against the back of the carriage next to his wife, his mouth slightly ajar as he breathed deeply in his own slumber.

"I think she has tired us *all* out," Sophia whispered in response. "I wonder it did not happen sooner."

They shared a smile.

"Did you enjoy yourself today, Miss Rosewall?"

Sophia nodded. She wasn't about to share her qualms with yet another person about attending the picnic that day. "I trust you did, as well?"

"Oh, yes. Mr. Hawkins certainly puts on a fine affair. That is so very much like him, though. He is a most generous man. My granddaughter has always spoken very highly of him."

Sophia recalled only then that Mrs. Causey, the Summerfield's granddaughter, had been acquainted with Mr. Hawkins in London before she married Mr. Causey.

"Were they close friends?" she asked, hoping to sound casual.

"I believe so," Mrs. Summerfield responded, stifling a yawn. "He was her closest friend in London. My Hannah has always said Mr. Hawkins would do anything for anyone."

That, Sophia could believe. She and her family had been witness enough to the fact.

Mrs. Summerfield continued. "He has a difficult time with his mother, though. From what I understand, she can be rather opinionated."

"Is that why he came to Cornwall, do you think? To put distance between them?"

"It certainly would not surprise me."

She said nothing further. Sophia clicked her teeth. Could she get away with asking more? "What was he like in London, do you know?"

Mrs. Summerfield watched her, but Sophia studied a wrinkle on her dress that had formed over the picnic.

"Oh, I imagine he was the same as he is now. Kind, sincere. Hannah says he gravitates to honest company. Apparently, he cannot abide falseness of character. He very much appreciates people who can be true to themselves, I believe."

Sophia's ears rang. She could no longer see the folds in her gown, nor the waning sun outside causing the grass to appear burnt orange. Her head spun as memories from the past weeks sailed through her mind.

Now it made sense. All of it made perfect sense.

Sophia had not hidden behind her smiles and flirtatious remarks for their first meeting on the beach. She'd been her true, gloveless, stocking-less self. But at the dinner party, she'd put on the same act she always had. That must have been why Mr. Hawkins wanted nothing more to do with her, because she'd been the perfect example of being false to one's self and to others.

Mr. Hawkins had then reached out to her again after the ball, when the fine dresses and the hair and the pompous smiles had been washed away. When Sophia had finally accepted her new circumstances and relinquished her sense of entitlement.

Did that mean Mr. Hawkins felt something for her? Something beyond compassion, beyond friendship? Or were his actions based solely on his own goodness of character?

Images of the gentleman approaching her, lowering his lips toward hers, flashed through her mind. Had he ever looked at Miss Kinsey in such a way?

"Mrs. Summerfield, do you know if…if Mr. Hawkins has formed an attachment to Miss Kinsey?"

No response came.

She glanced to Mrs. Summerfield, but the woman had fallen fast asleep like the rest of their companions.

Sophia sighed, turning her eyes once more to the window. She hoped to distract herself from her spiraling thoughts, though she knew nothing could pull her mind away from Mr. Frederick Hawkins and the growing attraction she felt for the man she had once despised.

Frederick stared out of the window, eying the orange landscape from the carriage. He was half-tempted to stop the driver so he might enjoy the sight from outside. With Miss Rosewall.

He stared more intently on the white, wispy clouds in the sky. He was thinking about the wrong woman. Miss Kinsey should be the one to occupy his thoughts. After all, she was seated right across from him, not riding in another carriage.

He glanced at the young woman, her head bobbing up and down as the wheels bounced along the dirt road. She was asleep, just like the others, just like Frederick should have been. But he couldn't rest, nor could he keep his mind from chasing after thoughts of Miss Rosewall, like an obsessive dog on a hunt.

What was wrong with him? Miss Kinsey was a perfectly amiable female. So why did his foolish mind continually seek after Miss Rosewall instead?

He rubbed his jaw. He already knew why. From their very first meeting, he'd felt that pull to her, that immediate attraction. He'd even felt it afterward at the dinner party, when she'd flirted with every gentleman she laid her beautiful eyes on.

Still, he'd managed to maintain a level head up until now, when she'd finally removed the mask she wore and revealed the person behind all the flirtatious smiles.

He never should have invited her to the picnic. There had been too many opportunities to draw closer to her. The more he had discovered about her, the more his mind remained on her, the more he wished to be near her. The more he wished to kiss her.

A soft whimper sounded across from him. He looked to Miss Kinsey, her eyebrows drawn together, clear pain etched on her face as she dreamed.

Frederick blanched. The look was gone in a flash, replaced by peaceful sleep once more, but the image continued to sting his conscience. It was as if she'd been pained by his own care-less thoughts. Thoughts he should not have had in the first place.

He couldn't dwell on Miss Rosewall when he was attempting to court another woman. That wasn't gentlemanly behavior. That was the behavior of his father.

Furthermore, what if Miss Rosewall changed again, reverted back to who she was before, pretentious with a weak mind and character?

No, he would be far better off with Miss Kinsey. If she rejected his pursuits, then he would go on to the next woman. And the next, and the next, until he found the one he wished to marry. He was sure any of them would do.

Any of them but Miss Sophia Rosewall.

CHAPTER TWENTY-EIGHT

*T*he birds woke Sophia again. The birds, and the sunshine peeping through her too small of curtains. Edith must have forgotten to sew the new ones again. She was probably too busy with her other chores to remember. It was just as well. Sophia would have woken up before long anyway. She couldn't remember the last time she'd slept past eight o'clock.

With a half-groan, half-sigh, she rolled out of her bed and stretched her hands high overhead. The mattress still left much to be desired in regard to comfort, but at least her body had grown used to the bumps the pad produced randomly throughout the night.

She walked across the floor, paying no heed to the cold wood against her bare feet as she admired the view of the ocean from her window. The sky was clear again, reflected brightly in the dark blue sea. Gentle waves rolled toward the shore. Sophia longed to walk across the sand again that morning, a pastime she'd grown quite used to since coming to Lowena, but she didn't have time right now.

She had wanted to see Gwynna ever since visiting with her at Wheal Favour, but Sophia's dread of the picnic prevented her from leaving the cottage at all. Now, however, with the picnic behind her by a few days, yet still troubling her mind, she needed a distraction. Gwynna always proved to be a fine one.

Sophia knew she needed to arrive early enough to catch her newfound friend before Gwynna could leave for the mine. Sophia couldn't bear the thought of joining her there and running into Mr. Hawkins again.

After dressing herself, a task she was becoming rather adept at, she bade Mrs. Cuff to tell Mother she was to go out walking, then left the cottage behind with swiftness.

Before long, she neared the Merricks' small house and spotted Gwynna standing outside, bent over a washboard and tub, scrubbing away at a sodden dress.

"Good morning, Gwynna."

Gwynna straightened from the tub, her face brightening. "Miss Rosewall, what brings ye out this way?"

"I merely thought to call upon you this morning, to see how you are faring."

"I be pleased ye thought of I, miss."

Gwynna's apron was soaked through with large splashes of water. Stringy strands of dark hair hung down past her cheeks, having come loose from the fabric holding back the rest of her locks. By the moisture on her brow, she must have been wrestling with the washing for quite some time.

"I'm sorry for interrupting your work," Sophia said, motioning to the tub of dark, murky water. "I can return another time if that suits you better."

"No, now be as good a time as any, miss. Ye can keep me company while I finish these dresses. Mama wishes them clean 'fore the rain sets in and we be required to dry them indoors."

Sophia nodded, and Gwynna took up scrubbing the dress along the washboard once more.

"You may call me Sophia, if you wish."

Gwynna arched her brows. "If it suits ye. How ye be farin' at Lowena…Sophia?"

She gave a little laugh after saying the name, as if she thought she was silly for speaking it. Sophia, however, was more than pleased to hear someone use her Christian name. It reminded her that she had a friend in this world.

"I'm adjusting well enough," she responded. "It is much more manageable now that I have accepted my circumstances. And I cannot complain living so near the sea."

"I'm sure ye didn't have much view of the sea from Fynwary Hall."

"No, I didn't."

Sophia's mind wandered to her old home. With no view of the sea, she had no desire to stare out of the window longingly apart from when she was forced to play the pianoforte or read aloud to Mother.

"Have ye been to Fynwary since ye left?"

Sophia nodded. "Only a few days ago, though not inside."

"Pardon me, miss, but——"

"Sophia," she corrected.

"Yes, Sophia. Beggin' your pardon, but I wonder what could have compelled ye to return? I wouldn't have had the courage to do the same."

"I didn't go of my own accord, I assure you. Mr. Hawkins invited my family to attend a picnic he was hosting. My parents didn't wish to accept, so they sent me in their stead to avoid Mr. Hawkins becoming cross."

Gwynna raised one eyebrow higher than the other. "Cross? Is Mr. Hawkins capable of bein' cross?"

Sophia pulled back. "Do you know the gentleman well?"

"Only as our landlord, miss—Sophia. But he's passed by here a time or two, helpin' folks mend fences and roofs and such."

Sophia stared at the water Gwynna splashed farther up her apron. Of course Mr. Hawkins would be more than happy tending to his tenants. That was just the sort of man he was. Always generous, never angry. Unless, of course, a person was behaving the opposite of her true character.

"Mr. Hawkins always be lively as he works, too," Gwynna continued. "And he's handsome. Don't ye agree?"

Gwynna's amber eyes shimmered in the sunshine.

"You are pressing me for information, Gwynna. Information I am unwilling to divulge."

Gwynna beamed, pleased with the information she *did* receive. "So did ye enjoy the picnic then? Even after your time at the ball?"

Sophia hesitated. "Well, I will simply say that Mr. Hawkins made it more bearable."

Gwynna's knowing smile was on Sophia again as she pulled the dress from the water and wrung out the fabric. "Well, I be glad it wasn't terrible for ye. Though, I still be wonderin' why ye'd attend a party ye don't enjoy. I'm sure 'tain't as fine as what we have for our parties on the beach either."

Sophia tilted her head. "Parties on the beach?"

Gwynna flapped the dress out, droplets of water sparkling in the sunshine as they flew through the air. "Ay. There be singin', dancin', horse racin', games. Good food and drink, 'course. The Causeys have parties often durin' the warmer months. They returned from London only a day or two ago and have already sent 'round invites for a gatherin' on Tregalwen Beach come Friday."

"That certainly sounds exciting," Sophia said. Far more exciting than sitting around listening to Mrs. Rennalls discuss ribbons with the ever-watchful Mrs. Maddern and the ever-silent Miss Kinsey.

Gwynna swung the dress over the line that hung from the house to a small tree.

"Ye ought to join us then," she said with a bright smile, wiping her hands on her wet apron.

"Oh. Thank you for the offer, but I couldn't."

Gwynna propped her hands on her hips. "If ye be worryin' over company, the Causeys are fine folk, as ye know. The Summerfields attend also, and a few other families. 'Tain't just upper class neither."

Sophia swallowed. "Yes, that is what I am more concerned about, the lower class."

Gwynna's head sunk low, but not before Sophia caught the hurt darkening her eyes.

"Oh, goodness, no," Sophia rushed forth. "No, forgive me. I did not mean it in that regard. I only meant that perhaps *I* would not be welcomed by *them*. When I went to the mine with you, I was, well, stared at."

Understanding replaced the pain in Gwynna's eyes. "That be because ye were a lady at a mine."

"No, it was more than that." Sophia looked away. "They seemed to be unhappy with me. As if for a specific reason."

Especially Gwynna's father.

"What do ye mean?"

"Well, I thought perhaps they didn't wish me to be there due to my lowered status, or because they blame my father for what happened at the mine."

Gwynna's eyes dimmed once more, but Sophia hardly noticed.

"From what I understand, he was not paying them proper wages," Sophia continued. "Of course they had every right to be displeased about that. However, I believe they blame him for the last incident that occurred, as do the investors. But how was Father to know a flooding would take place? He can hardly be blamed. At any rate, these collapses and floodings, they all occur rather frequently, do they not? It all seems rather inconsequential."

Gwynna didn't respond. Her face had paled apart from her ruddy cheeks.

Sophia paused. "Are you well, Gwynna?"

"Yes, miss, but ye must forgive me. I need to make ready for Wheal Favour. Papa will be waitin'."

She backed up toward her house.

"Oh, of course. Forgive me for causing you to be late."

Gwynna merely gave an awkward curtsy then turned on her heel and disappeared inside.

Sophia was left standing alone next to the tub. She glanced down at the clothing still submerged in the filthy water.

Gwynna had left before finishing her chore, and Sophia was certain the young woman didn't need to depart for the mine yet. That meant that Sophia's words had, for one reason or another, upset Gwynna enough to make her want to leave.

And now Sophia was alone once again.

With a sigh, she trudged away, leaving the Merrick's home behind, wondering how she had managed to offend the one friend she thought she'd finally attained.

CHAPTER TWENTY-NINE

The next few days passed slowly for Sophia. She had attempted to see Gwynna twice since their last visit, but her knock went unanswered each time. Sophia wondered if perhaps the Merricks were simply busier at the mine, or if they had taken ill. Deep down, however, she knew she was being avoided.

With a week having passed by since the picnic, and three days since seeing Gwynna, Sophia began to feel a mere shell of a person. Having had no contact with anyone, apart from her weakened mother and the ever-faithful Mrs. Cuff, she was anxious for company.

She wandered across the cliffsides and the beach near the cottage, hour after hour, hoping to come across Gwynna or Mr. Hawkins. Even a stranger would do. But no one appeared.

No one, until she spotted her father from afar, only now approaching the cottage.

Sophia narrowed her eyes as he walked across the land. He moved slowly, his head so low he couldn't see her.

She didn't know he had even left Lowena. To be fair, there was really no reason for her to know his whereabouts. She hadn't seen him for days. She wasn't exactly sure for how long, as he locked himself within his study so often, she never was sure if he was at home or away.

"Good morning, Father," she greeted as he approached.

His head lifted, his eyes falling flatly on hers. "Morning."

She refused to allow her spirits to sink at his less than enthusiastic response. He was tired, that was all.

"Where have you been this morning?" she asked lightly.

"St. Just."

He was in no mood to speak, but Sophia *was*. She needed to converse with someone, or she would go mad from the silence.

He continued toward the cottage, Sophia following closely at his side. "Were you calling on a friend? Or was it a matter of business, perhaps?"

By the look Father gave her, and the silence that followed, she knew he caught her inference. She was asking if he'd found work. And he was telling her that he had not.

Sophia couldn't understand it. As far as she was aware, apart from the meager funds he received from his small share in Wheal Favour, Father had yet to secure a way to fund their living at Lowena Cottage for much longer.

If it was up to Sophia, she'd take work herself to help her family, but Father would never allow her to do such a thing. Not to mention the pay they would offer her would be pittance compared to what was needed to support a family of three.

Whether he was working to solve their problem or not would have to be discovered later, as Sophia knew by her Father's firmly set lips and sullen brow that he was displeased with the conversation. If she wished to speak further, she needed to change the subject.

"Well, did you at least enjoy your time while in town?" she asked.

"Is one capable of enjoying anything when one is this poor?"

His words dripped with bitterness, his tone void of all hope. But his words weren't true. After all, Gwynna and her family were not wealthy, but they were happy. Were they not?

At the thought of the Merricks, Sophia's brow furrowed, and she wondered again what she'd said to upset Gwynna. She knew it had something to do with the incident at the mine. Was she upset that Sophia had taken Father's side? Did she blame Sophia and Father for the incident? Had a death occurred?

Her breath caught, a knot tying in her stomach. A death. She'd been so absorbed in her own sorrow over Gwynna ignoring her that she had not even considered such a possibility until now.

What if something had happened to one of Gwynna's friends or even a family member? To be honest, she couldn't recollect if there had been a death or not. Surely Father would remember.

He hardly looked approachable with his down-turned lips and hardened eyes. Then again, he hadn't looked cordial since before Lowena. She may as well speak with him now before he locked himself away again.

"Father," she began, carefully choosing her words, "do you recall the last time one of the shafts were flooded at Wheal Favour?"

His jaw twitched. "I do."

"Were there any casualties?"

He stopped walking, his sharp eyes on her in an instant. "Why?"

She pulled back. "I was merely curious."

He ran his tongue along his lower lip, his voice strained as he spoke. "Yes, there were deaths."

An uneasiness crept over her, a looming dread, like the

dark clouds creeping toward the shore that very moment. "How many suffered?"

"I don't recall."

Sophia knew he lied. But why did he? "Do you know the names of—"

"Good heavens, Sophia. Why would you need to know such a thing?" His eyes were hard, cold.

She sunk back. "No reason, Father. Forgive me."

His eye twitched, his mouth opening as if he wished to say something more, but he shook his head and plowed toward the house.

As the door slammed behind him, Sophia's bottom lip trembled, but she bit her tongue. She would not allow herself to cry. Not when she was determined to find the truth.

She remained out of doors until the rain set in, then she moved inside and took her dinner in her room. There was no reason to dine downstairs. Her parents hadn't eaten at the dinner table since Fynwary. They claimed there was no space. Sophia knew it was because they couldn't face the reality of their circumstances.

But Sophia could.

She waited patiently in her room as darkness fell, her view of the sea finally disappearing as night crossed the land. She prodded at the fire in her hearth to keep the embers warm then placed a few logs on the flames. There was no need to call Edith to tend to her fire any longer, as Sophia was perfectly capable of doing so on her own.

The fire crackled, and she stared, mesmerized by the dancing blaze until footsteps sounded, slogging up the stairs.

She jumped up from her spot in front of the fire and moved to listen at her door, holding her breath as Father's steps stopped nearby. A knock sounded on Mother's door.

There was no response.

His footsteps, slower than before, slid down the corridor

before entering the other room. When the latch sounded, Sophia knew Father had entered his room.

Still, she needed to be sure he was settled for the night. After waiting nearly a quarter of an hour, silence having fallen over the house, Sophia ventured from her room.

Slowly, she opened her door, pausing only when the creak echoed down the corridor. The light of her small candle flickered on the dark walls and across the wooden floor. When no responding sound came from her door's disturbance, she stepped into the corridor, closed her door behind her, and fled toward the stairs on her tiptoes, her dressing gown fluttering behind her.

She did not stop her progress until she reached Father's study downstairs and her hand hesitated on the latch. Was she truly going to enter? Invade his privacy? She didn't wish to betray his trust, but she needed to discover the truth about what had occurred at Wheal Favour. If he wasn't going to tell her, she hoped to find something that would.

With a resolute nod, she entered the study and pressed the door closed behind her.

Casting her eyes about the room, she blew out an unsteady breath, the only sound apart from the rain plinking against the small window. She'd not been inside until that moment. It was nothing like Father's old study—a quarter of the size, holding only one bookshelf, a small desk with thin legs, and an uncomfortable-looking chair with a wicker back. The walls were bare, and the floor was covered with scratch marks from the furniture.

How Father remained in such a depressing room for so long was beyond her. But now was not the time to wonder about such things. She needed to be about her business or risk the chance of being discovered.

Though, she had no idea for what she was looking. A letter, perhaps? A document mentioning Wheal Favour? Anything would do, so long as her questions were answered.

She moved straight to the desk and opened the three small drawers, thumbing through correspondences and spare pieces of paper. Yet, nothing stood out, not a single mention of the mine written anywhere.

Had Father disposed of all the old documents he had? Or had he simply transported them to the mine for Mr. Trevethan to keep when the man took over ownership of the mine?

She took a step back from the desk and placed her hands on her hips, sighing with disappointment. Whatever the answer, it was clear that her search was in vain. There was nothing of consequence in the study. She might as well leave before someone discovered her prying.

She turned to depart, but her eyes caught sight of a folded piece of paper peeking out from beneath a few books on top of the desk.

She settled the candle on the desk and leaned down toward the paper, sliding it out from under the books and eying the writing on top. It was a correspondence addressed to Father in a hand she did not recognize.

She glanced to the door, her heart tapping against her chest. Fold by fold, she opened the broken seal. Her eyes moved first to the signature at the bottom.

Mr. Peter Trevethan

Once one of Father's investors in Wheal Favour. Now the owner. With haste, she read his words.

Mr. Rosewall,

I trust this letter finds you well. My intention of writing you today is twofold, one of advisement, the other, business.

First, I understand you have been somewhat oppressed of late. Not only because of your reduced circumstances, but also because of the guilt you undoubtedly feel after the flooding at the mine. I must say, though we did advise the use of an extra surveyor, you could not have known further blasting would produce such an incident. Nor, I'm certain, would you have wished for one. Because of this, I suggest you attempt to forget the mishap and move forward with your life and with your family. You will feel all the better for it.

Sophia paused in her reading. She recalled that night many weeks before, when Father had revealed that he'd sold the mine. He'd told them that the investors had lost faith in him after the decisions he'd made. Was not using an extra surveyor one of those decisions? A surveyor that would have looked over the mine, found any weaknesses in the structure, and ensured its safety to be worked?

She'd not given Father's decisions a second thought before, too concerned with her own well-being. But now her stomach tossed with unease as she continued reading Mr. Trevethan's words.

Now I will move to the business portion of my correspondence. After reading over the papers you left with me, I discovered a discrepancy in the number of deaths caused by the flooding. I believe there were six, and yet, only four names are recorded.

A chill slid over Sophia, colder than any bitter draft in her room, icier than any freezing rain sliding down her back.

Six. Six deaths. Were they older fathers? Or younger brothers and sons? She knew mining was a dangerous occupation, but never before had she realized, never before had she truly considered the full scope of what had occurred.

Death. Death that could have been spared had her father followed the advice of others.

She pressed a hand to her mouth and continued reading, disparaging feelings swirling round her heart.

I have asked a few other gentlemen and miners if they recall the names of those who drowned, but I should like help from a few sources, to be certain the information is correct. As you know, I prefer a proper recording of the happenings here at Wheal Favour. As such, I would greatly appreciate your help in this regard. Names, as well as ages, would be most beneficial.

Thank you for your time, sir. And may God bless you in this, your time of need.

Mr. Peter Trevethan

Sophia lowered the letter, scanning the desk. A list of names. Had Father not written it yet, or had he already sent it to Mr. Trevethan?

Frantically, she pushed aside the books. A small scrap of paper rested on the desk beneath them, with three simple names scratched in black ink. She reached down with her free hand, her fingers shaking as she clasped the paper in her hand.

It was Father's writing, the rigid slant unmistakable. The paper was torn from the corner of a full piece, as if he'd been in a hurry.

Slowly, her eyes roved over the names.

Nicholas Hocking, 53
Robin Yeoman, 42
Jago Merrick, 17

Jago Merrick. *Merrick.*

"No," Sophia breathed.

It was a simple coincidence. He wasn't related to Gwynna. He couldn't be.

Her mind sped through moment after moment she'd spent with Gwynna for evidence of her relationship with the young man. The moment they'd met on the cliffside. Sharing straw-berries with the miners at Wheal Favour. Being wrapped in Gwynna's blanket in the Merrick's home.

But it wasn't Gwynna's blanket.

It was Jago's.

Her memory was clear, as if it had happened that very evening. Mrs. Merrick had asked Gwynna to retrieve a blanket from *Jago's* room. He must have died only a few weeks before, and they had wrapped his blanket around Sophia's shoulders.

He was their son. Gwynna's younger brother.

And Sophia had called his death inconsequential.

The door clicked. She looked up, refusing to move another inch. Welling tears blurred her vision, but she knew who stood before her.

"Father."

CHAPTER THIRTY

"*S*ophia? What are you…"

Father's eyes fell on the scrap of paper in Sophia's hand. She held the list of names and the correspondence in the air. There was no reason to hide them. "Father. Were you advised to use another surveyor?"

The candle he held caused shadows to lengthen his features, his eyes gaunt and cheeks sunken. He remained standing in the doorway. Gone was the angry man from that morning, the defensiveness in his eyes vanished. Any other moment, his tall figure would have filled the small doorframe, but now he shrunk before her very eyes.

His voice was no louder than a whisper when he finally responded. "They did advise me to, yes."

Her brow rose. "Why?"

She knew her questions were imposing, but she no longer cared. Nor, it appeared, did Father as he answered again in his somber tone. "Because they feared we were working the mine too far to the west. They wanted to pay for another survey of the land to ensure we were still a good distance away from the sea. But I refused."

Why, Father?"

"Because I wished to use the funds instead to continue blasting through."

Sophia's chin shook. "Had you not continued working the mine, the shaft would not have flooded. Lives could have been spared."

Father nodded, a barely discernible shift of his head. "Yes."

She closed her eyes, tears spilling from the corners and sliding down her cheeks.

Lives could have been spared. Gwynna's brother could have been spared.

A footstep creaked on the floor. Father's voice sounded nearer. "You must understand, Sophia. It was a risk. One I regret every day. But if we would have found copper, our financial woes might have ended. We—"

"Why did you not complete the list?"

"What?"

She opened her eyes but kept her head down. "Why are there only three names listed, instead of six?"

He paused, his voice faltering with emotion as he spoke. "Because I cannot remember the names of all those who drowned."

Sophia winced. More tears fell. Not from Father's ignorance, but her own. After all, she was the one who had not remembered that a single death had even occurred.

"Sophia, please. You must believe me. I was doing what I thought was best for our family. The money—"

"And what of the miners and their families? Had you once considered what was best for them?"

The words were spoken from the deepest part of her heart, a place she had never explored. A place she had never wished to, for it was tormented with agony and guilt. Guilt she tried to pass on to her father. But she couldn't do so any longer.

She raised her eyes to meet his own anguish. She could

not blame him for his actions. Had she not been so demanding of his money, had she not begged for new dresses and Seasons in London, perhaps then Father would not have gone into debt. Perhaps then he would not have felt the need to risk the lives of those miners, simply to support his spoiled daughter's selfishness.

How could the Merricks have even suffered her to be in their home? No wonder they could not bear to be near her any longer. No wonder the miners stared at her reproachfully. This, all of it, was no one's fault but her own.

"You must forgive me, Sophia," Father whispered, only proving to break her heart with more intensity. "I should have told you this before. I should have made better decisions financially."

Her hands began to quiver in time with her chin, contrasting with her barely beating heart.

"Sophia?"

She couldn't respond. Leaving her candle behind, she fled from the room, brushing past Father without another word. He called after her, but she did not stop until she reached her room, closing the door firmly behind her, though she knew he would not follow her.

He never did. No one ever did.

She leaned against the door, her forehead thumping against the cold wood as her shoulders shook from barely repressed sobs.

"Oh, Gwynna. I'm so sorry."

CHAPTER THIRTY-ONE

"*A* letter for you, sir."

Frederick set down his book and turned to the footman entering the library with a tray in hand.

"Thank you, Aaron," he said as he accepted the letter.

Frederick eyed the correspondence. It should have been from his steward with an update on Dawnridge. But one look at his name written with overly flowing letters told him this was definitely not from his steward, but from someone he'd rather hoped had forgotten about him. At least enough to not write to him for another month or so.

"Mother," he murmured.

"Pardon, sir?"

Frederick glanced to Aaron. He didn't realize the footman still stood at his side. "Oh, nothing. Was there something else?"

"Not a letter, sir, but callers. Mrs. Maddern and Miss Kinsey have arrived."

Frederick stifled a groan. "I'll be down in just a moment."

He waited for Aaron to leave before eying the letter again. He wasn't going to open it. Not now, at any rate. He wasn't in the right frame of mind to read what his mother had to say.

For she always had something to say.

He stood from his seat with a hefty sigh and placed his book on the sofa. Crossing the room, he stared out of the window as he retied his cravat he'd loosened earlier.

How nice his stay in Cornwall had been without Mother's constant prodding for him to marry. He didn't need help in finding a spouse, though she liked to believe otherwise.

It was his belief that he was doing perfectly fine on his own. He knew what he wished for in a wife. Just not who he wished for as a wife.

A set of sparkling blue eyes and shining black hair appeared in his mind's eye. The woman who possessed such striking features had not left his mind since the picnic. How could he not think of her? The honesty she'd shared with him, and her parted lips, so tempting, so inviting, flashed in every segment of his mind.

Living in Miss Rosewall's own blasted house certainly didn't help him forget her either. Every room he entered, every corridor he walked down, every window he peered without, thoughts of the woman occupied his attention.

Was this the room she played in as a child? Had she run down these corridors as a girl, or learned to walk them gracefully as she grew older? How often was she supposed to have been meandering through the gardens, where her mother thought her to be, when she was really walking on the beach instead?

And the question he asked more than anything—when would he have the chance to see her again?

He hardly thought he'd be welcomed at Lowena Cottage. Her mother no doubt despised him, and her father would only allow him to enter their home for fear of possible repercussions.

And Miss Rosewall? He couldn't be sure if she'd welcome his calling on her at all.

He stuck a finger between his cravat and neck. Why was

tying a noose around one's neck fashionable? Hanged be the person who created the style.

Though, perhaps that was not due to the cravat but his thoughts of Miss Rosewall instead. Thoughts that should be focused elsewhere.

He had two estates to run. A mine to support. Parties to attend. A wife to find. His mother's letter to ignore. Mrs. Maddern to visit. Miss Kinsey to remember.

And Miss Rosewall to forget.

Sophia didn't bother to call for Mrs. Cuff that evening. She'd already dressed herself hours ago in her simple, light blue gown. Her chemise was smoothed comfortably beneath her dress, and her stays were just snug enough for her to breathe easily. She'd managed to pin her natural curls back in a simple twist. It wasn't stylish by any means, but at least it wasn't falling chaotically from the side of her head. Besides, it didn't matter what her hair looked like. Not for where she was going.

She fastened her dark blue Spencer jacket, donned her silk bonnet, then pulled on her wrist-length gloves and left her room. She had not intended on telling either of her parents where she was going, but as she closed her door behind her, she came face-to-face with Mother. Sophia stood back with a gasp.

"I'm sorry, my dear," Mother said. "I thought you saw me."

Sophia pressed a hand to her middle. She couldn't remember the last time she'd seen Mother outside of her room. "No, I didn't. What are you doing about? Should you not be resting?"

"I needed to stretch my legs for a moment." Mother's eyes looked her up and down. "Are you going out?"

Sophia swallowed. "Yes, to a party. On Tregalwen Beach."

Mother's eyebrows rose. "The picnic must have been more pleasant than the Madderns' ball then, if you still wish to be seen in your social circles."

Sophia merely nodded. She had not told either of her parents much about the picnic, other than she'd had a pleasant time. She'd certainly not mentioned her moments with Mr. Hawkins. They didn't need to know about that, just like Mother didn't need to know that the gathering on Tregalwen was not to be within the Rosewalls' typical social sphere.

"Will there be someone there to watch over you at Tregalwen?" she asked. There she was again, ensuring someone else performed her duty as chaperone.

"Yes, the Summerfields will be in attendance." That was what Gwynna had said, hadn't she?

"You must implore them to see you safely home."

"I will," Sophia lied. She wouldn't need their help. She would be staying at the party no longer than it took her to apologize and flee.

"What of your friends, Miss Ward or Miss Kinsey? Will they be present, as well?"

Sophia could only pray for the contrary. "I am unsure. But I hope that one friend at least will be there." If Gwynna could ever consider her a friend again.

That was more of what Mother didn't need to know, that Sophia longed for companionship from a miner's daughter more than any friend she'd ever had before.

"Are you well, Sophia?" Mother propped her head to one side. The cap on her head remained in place, but her natural curls, like Sophia's, shifted. "You seem out of sorts."

Sophia clasped her hands in front of her. She didn't wish to answer any further questions. She wanted to leave. But Mother had not asked after her in weeks, and her resolve was threatened. Could she tell Mother all that had gone on, how Sophia must apologize to Gwynna, just as she had apologized to Mr. Hawkins, for her selfish, cruel ways?

No, she couldn't. Mother wouldn't understand. She would say that Mr. Hawkins was the one who needed to repent, and that Gwynna was not a person worthy of apologizing to.

Sophia stretched a smile across her lips and nodded. "I assure you, I am well. Merely anxious to depart."

"Very well. I will not keep you any longer. I am pleased you wish to go. A young lady ought not be alone as you have been made to be."

Sophia searched her mother's eyes, noting the sorrow within them. "And what about yourself, Mother? It is not good for you to be alone either."

"Oh, but I am not alone. Mrs. Cuff is a fine companion."

Sophia hesitated. "And Father?"

Mother blinked, taken aback. "Well, of course your father is wonderful company. Though, he has been somewhat preoccupied of late." She looked to his bedroom door.

Sophia knew her parents were drifting apart. She'd never once heard a complaint escape her mother's lips about Father, but moving to Lowena had pulled them away from one another. They were lonely. Both of them. Just as Sophia was.

"Mother, would you like to join me for the party?"

Mother's eyes widened. "Oh, I couldn't. No, I must stay here at Lowena, where I belong. And you must run along and enjoy your time with those who still accept you. That is where *you* belong, after all."

Her smile was strained, as if it took every last bit of energy to produce it. With a nod of her head, she turned to her room and closed the door behind her.

Sophia's shoulders fell, half from relief, half from disappointment. It was better that she had refused. She would not have enjoyed a party with multiple classes. Now Sophia could leave the beach as soon as she wished without explaining to Mother why the Rosewalls were unwelcome with the miners.

Still, the sorrow in her mother's eyes, and in her father's, was beginning to take a toll on her spirit.

With leaden footsteps, she quit the house. She didn't have to worry about making haste for fear of Father stopping her. He avoided her as greatly as Sophia avoided him. Neither of them wished to discuss the revelation from the night before.

Sophia secured the door of the cottage behind her and crossed the long grass of the garden, reaching the stone wall encircling Lowena.

She stood before the view, struggling to gain control of her nerves as she stared out at the ocean, her worries trembling in her mind like dried leaves on a dying tree.

Dark clouds billowed above the water, blurring the line between storm and sea as soft raindrops began to fall. A cool wind blew toward her, curling the ends of her ribbons and fluttering her dress and dark curls.

Would they cancel the party due to the approaching storm? Perhaps Sophia ought to remain at the cottage to avoid the risk of being caught in the rain.

Her shoulders sunk. She was simply creating excuses to pander to her own fears and selfishness. She was far better, far safer, at Lowena, like her mother and father, where there was a barrier between herself and the storms of other's thoughts and opinions.

The stone wall stood before her, insurmountable. She took a step back. She couldn't do it. She couldn't face Gwynna, her family, the other miners. She couldn't face the judgment, the possible rejection. The embarrassment of her own thoughtless words and actions. Yet, did she truly wish to live the rest of her life trapped within the cottage, within her own mind? Did she have a choice?

What is it you would like to do?

Mr. Hawkins's words broke through her muddled thoughts, growing stronger and brighter until they cast out the whirling storm within her altogether.

What is it she would like to do?

An image flashed in her mind of Gwynna standing next to the brother Sophia would never meet. Her heart contracted, yet her mind cleared. She knew what she wished to do. She wished to speak with Gwynna. Because Gwynna deserved an apology.

As she made her decision, a crack broke through the clouds, and the sun burst through the darkness of the storm. Light sparkled against the crests of the waves and the droplets of rain. Glowing, white mist sailed through the air on the wind, and a warmth filled her heart before the sun had even touched her.

She straightened, clasping her hands firmly before her and holding her chin level. With squared shoulders, she turned toward the gate.

She would speak with Gwynna. Even if she was rejected, ignored, set aside, she would speak with her. For this was what she wanted to do. With her own resolve and Heaven's help, she could do it.

Crossing the cliffside with determination, Sophia pushed aside any lingering fears that threatened to cripple her resolution to make things right with the woman she prayed would still be her friend.

The sun disappeared again as the clouds blew farther north, taking the rain with them. But when she reached Tregalwen Beach a half hour's walk south of Lowena, the sun shone once again, and the beach glowed in a golden light.

Sophia stood on top of the hill leading down to the sand. A single monolith stood tall in the shimmering sea. The wind had shifted, and the waves had calmed. But Sophia's anxious heart had not.

The group was already gathering on Tregalwen. A large fire roasted a haunch of meat turning over the flames. A few women laid out blankets on the sand with trays for food as children chased each other across the beach, their laughter drifting on the breeze toward Sophia.

She spotted Gwynna instantly with Mr. Merrick. They moved together across the sand, rolling logs toward the fire where a few large pieces of driftwood were already set up.

Sophia blew out a shaking breath, forcing Mr. Hawkins's words in her mind once more. His deep voice resounded in her memory, infusing her with confidence.

What is it you would like to do?

It was impossible to consider what she wished for long-term in her life with her selfish past weighing her down. But making things right with Gwynna would allow her to move forward, to change.

And she could be brave enough to do so.

She took one step after another. The tall, wispy grass lining the pathway brushed against her skirts until she reached the sand. She didn't have to move much closer before Gwynna caught sight of her. The young woman turned to her father. Words were exchanged, Mr. Merrick nodded, then Gwynna headed in Sophia's direction.

CHAPTER THIRTY-TWO

*S*ophia stopped in the sand a distance away from the others, allowing Gwynna to come to her. She didn't wish for their conversation to be overheard. This way, if Gwynna did not accept her apology, Sophia could make a quick escape.

"I thought ye'd decided not to come," Gwynna said, stopping a few paces away from her.

Sophia stared at the sand stretching far across the beach. "Forgive my sudden appearance. I was not planning to attend, and I will leave soon. If I may but speak with you for a moment." Gwynna motioned for her to continue. "I wished to apologize for my thoughtless words when last we spoke. I didn't know that you…that you had a brother."

Gwynna nodded, her tone somber, broken. "Yes, a younger brother. Jago. I was visitin' his grave the night I came upon ye at the cliffside."

The pain became even more acute within Sophia's breaking heart. "I only became aware of him last night, when I learned that my father…" She paused, emotion snagging her voice. "That my father was the cause of his death, as well as five others."

Gwynna's amber eyes glinted with tears. Her chin crumpled as she nodded. "Jago's death be the reason Father doesn't like me to work as a bal maiden anymore. He be afraid of losin' I, too."

Each breath Sophia drew only pained her heart further. All apprehension fled from her mind as she prayed she might make amends.

"Oh, Gwynna. I cannot begin to express how sorry I am, for my words *and* for my father's careless actions. I cannot imagine the pain you and your family must have suffered. The pain you must still suffer. I am so sorry my father and I have been the cause."

Tears spilled down her cheeks, and at once, Gwynna's arms were around her. Sophia returned her embrace.

"Miss," Gwynna said, her voice muffled in Sophia's ear, "ye must know, I don't hold no grudge against ye." She pulled back, swiping her hand at the moisture beneath her nose. "Though, I happily accept your apology."

The tension around Sophia's chest began to subside, though she still couldn't comprehend Gwynna's goodness. "You are a better woman than I, Gwynna."

They shared a smile before Gwynna rubbed the moisture from her eyes. "Come now. Let's be finished cryin' so we can enjoy the party. There be no tears allowed from this point forth."

She tossed her head toward the group, but Sophia held up her hands in protest. "Oh, no. I couldn't. The other families here will surely not be as forgiving as you have been. It will be better if I simply take my leave now."

"There be no one here who wouldn't be happy to see ye, I'm sure of it."

She nodded encouragingly, but Sophia glanced over Gwynna's shoulder with a wary eye. "Your father?"

Gwynna looked over her shoulder. Mr. Merrick stood a good

distance away, watching the both of them. She waved, and he returned the gesture. "Father be the one who told me to speak with ye tonight, miss. He ain't be holdin' no grudge either."

Sophia didn't believe her words, but when Gwynna looped her arm through hers and dragged her forward, she had little choice but to follow.

She kept her head low as they approached the gathering party, fearful of seeing unwelcome judgments in their stares. When they reached Gwynna's father, however, she dared a glance at his dark, steely eyes.

"Papa," Gwynna said, standing before him with Sophia at her side, "Miss Rosewall here be worryin' she ain't welcome here. But she is, wouldn't ye say?"

Sophia could hardly think with the man's intimidating eyes upon her. She wanted to express her sorrow and regret over her choices and her father's, just as she had with Gwynna, but her mouth refused to move.

They stood in silence, another moment passing by before Mr. Merrick's features softened. "My daughter is right, Miss Rosewall. Ye be most welcome here. And don't ye think otherwise."

Another stone from the weight around Sophia's shoulders was removed and tossed to the ground. She nodded with gratitude, and Mr. Merrick tipped his cap to her.

Gwynna proceeded to pull Sophia away and lead her around the fire, greeting people one by one and introducing Sophia to those she didn't know. Of course Gwynna and Mr. Merrick had been correct in their words. Sophia was welcomed and embraced with kindness by all in attendance. Though her nerves were still on edge, she found them lessening little by little as each smile broke down the fears encircling her heart.

After most of the introductions had been made, Gwynna, beckoned by her mother's call, moved toward the blanket of food. Sophia followed, pausing a moment to view the other guests in attendance.

The Summerfields had already greeted her with warm smiles and were now speaking with a group of children who giggled at Mr. Summerfield's teasing.

The Kendrickses of Golowduyn Lighthouse had also come that evening and chatted with Lieutenant Edmund Harris, a naval officer stationed on land as he recovered from an injured arm.

"Mrs. Kendricks is worrying over Mr. Oates this evening," Mr. Kendricks, who had recently retired from the navy, said to Lieutenant Harris. "You know she has a difficult time trusting anyone with Golowduyn. Even me."

Mrs. Kendricks raised her brow. "I learned to trust the both of you, haven't I? I'm sure I'll trust Mr. Oates soon enough."

Sophia's eyes traveled around the rest of the group, discovering the Causeys next as they approached her with broad smiles.

"Mrs. Causey, Mr. Causey," she greeted with a curtsy. "You have returned from London at last."

"Indeed, we have," Mrs. Causey said, "and what a pleasure it is to see you here with us."

Sophia laced her fingers together. "I hope I am not intruding. Gwynna Merrick invited me."

"No, of course you are more than welcome, Miss Rosewall." Mrs. Causey rested a hand on her swelling belly.

So she was expecting. With the couple as kind as even the Summerfields, they certainly deserved the happiness they exuded simply being near each other.

"Will your parents be joining us?" Mr. Causey asked, his arm encircling his wife's waist.

"No, they will remain at the cottage this evening."

"Oh, yes. My grandmother wrote to us to tell us that you now live at Lowena Cottage."

Sophia braced herself for the pity that always came after the mention of her new home. To her surprise, Mrs. Causey sighed with an airy smile. "It is such a lovely place. You must find the views of the sea incomparable."

Sophia nodded enthusiastically, grateful for the opportunity to speak of anything but how others wretchedly viewed her new existence. "Indeed. My bedroom window has the best."

Mrs. Causey sighed lightheartedly.

"I'm sure you recall my wife's obsession with the sea, Miss Rosewall," Mr. Causey said. "While in London, all she could speak of was the ocean. Now we have returned, one would think she could be happy with another topic of conversation."

Mrs. Causey swatted her husband playfully on the arm.

Sophia's mood lifted further just watching them. She'd known the two of them since they were all children. The couple seemed every bit in love now as they had been chasing each other around in the sand more than fifteen years ago.

"I certainly *can* speak of other things," Mrs. Causey said before turning to Sophia. "Miss Rosewall, have you—Why, Mr. Hawkins! There you are!"

Sophia's stomach lurched, as if a team of horses pulled her forward at a thunderous speed.

Slowly, she turned, facing the gentleman standing directly behind her. His black jacket fit perfectly over his purple waistcoat. He wore no hat, his fair hair being tossed about in the breeze. And his smile. His smile made Sophia's heart murmur and caused his blue eyes to shimmer, like a swallow's wing in the sunlight.

How could she have not thought he would be there? As friends with Mrs. Causey, Mr. Hawkins had more of a reason to be at the party that evening than Sophia had.

"It is wonderful to see you again, Mr. Hawkins," Mrs. Causey said, drawing Sophia's attention away from staring at him for longer.

Sophia took a step back, allowing their small circle to widen.

"And you, Mrs. Causey." Mr. Hawkins reached forth, placing a small kiss to her hand before turning to Mr. Causey. "Mr. Causey, a pleasure, as always."

A look was exchanged, a smile and a nod, but before Sophia could decipher what had passed between the gentlemen, the conversation shifted to her.

"You are acquainted with Miss Rosewall, I'm sure," Mrs. Causey said.

Mr. Hawkins's eyes turned to Sophia. "Indeed. What a pleasant surprise to see you here this evening, Miss Rosewall."

"And you, Mr. Hawkins," she managed to say without a quivering voice.

His eyes lingered on her, and Sophia fought to keep her mind from dwelling on the moment they'd shared at the picnic, secluded in the midst of the trees, his eyes on her lips, just like now.

"So tell me," Mr. Hawkins said, turning to the Causeys, "how did you find London? I am sorry to have missed you both when I was last there."

"Surely you recall Mrs. Causey's feelings for the city," Mr. Causey said. "This past month had to have been the longest of my life with her being so cross."

Mrs. Causey smiled sheepishly. "Yes, I fear my mother did not put me in the brightest of moods, either."

"Nothing has changed then?" Mr. Hawkins asked.

Mrs. Causey raised her hands helplessly in the air. "We have hope for the future. But for now, things have only slightly improved."

"Yes," Mr. Causey jumped in with a light tone, "my mother-in-law will speak with me now, when before she could not even look at me. That is an improvement, indeed."

"Which is more than I can say about your mother, Mr. Hawkins," Mrs. Causey said. "For reasons quite unbeknownst to me, the woman avoided me whenever we happened on each other."

Silence sounded before the three of them broke out into laughter. Sophia watched the exchange with amusement, unaware of what they found so humorous, nor understanding the comments about their seemingly overbearing mothers, but she didn't mind. She enjoyed the opportunity she had to observe Mr. Hawkins's smile without unabashedly staring.

"I must admit," he said with a sigh, "living somewhere besides the smoky streets of London, and away from Mother's clutches, has been quite refreshing."

"Is that the reason you chose to relocate to Cornwall?" Mrs. Causey asked.

Sophia's ears perked. She had wondered the very same. Though, she'd been too concerned with her own life to ever think to ask him the question herself.

"To be frank," Mr. Hawkins responded, "Cornwall was the one county Mother said she would never visit." More laughter ensued. "Truthfully, though, I recall you speaking of Cornwall and of the sea with such fondness, I had to see for myself what living here could do for me."

Mr. Causey turned to Sophia. "You see? My wife. Obsessed with the sea."

Sophia's lips curved with delight as Mrs. Causey swatted at him again, but Mr. Causey darted out of the way this time.

"I'm afraid I must agree with your wife, Mr. Causey," Mr. Hawkins said. "Cornwall is, indeed, the most beautiful of counties. She spoke of finding peace and love here, and I have certainly discovered the same for myself."

And suddenly, his eyes were on Sophia.

She stiffened. The Causeys exchanged glances. Mr. Hawkins seemed to be the only one unaware of his own words before pink brushed his brow.

"I have discovered a love for the land, I mean," he spurted

out, turning to the sea. "How could one not, with views such as this?"

"It is spectacular," Mrs. Causey said, though her curious eyes wandered to Sophia.

Sophia turned away, rubbing her forearm as heat flushed through her body.

"Sophia, would ye help me, please?"

Jumping at the chance to flee from the attention, Sophia quickly curtsied to the Causeys then sped toward Gwynna with only a fleeting look at Mr. Hawkins, though she felt his eyes on her long after she'd walked away.

CHAPTER THIRTY-THREE

*F*rederick could not keep himself from staring at Miss Rosewall for the better part of the evening, and not just because of her beauty. Something had changed within her. She was unsure of herself, hesitant. Humble.

Had this change occurred because she was living at the cottage? Or did it have to do with befriending the Merricks' daughter?

He watched the two of them together with great curiosity. He was sure Miss Rosewall would never have even considered speaking to a miner's daughter before. And yet, there she was, not only speaking, but—dare he think it—*enjoying* herself with her friend.

He continued to observe her as the evening progressed and throughout the meal. Her eyes frequently met his as they sat across the fire from each other. He longed to speak with her, but between his visiting with the Causeys, and Miss Rosewall conversing with Gwynna, no opportunity presented itself.

When dinner was cleaned, talk of games moved throughout the group.

"Shall we have another horse race, my dear?" Mr. Causey called out as a group moved toward the water's edge.

"No, I won last time more than fairly, Thomas. Besides, I shouldn't be racing in my condition, you know this."

Mr. Causey winked at his wife, who placed a hand on her stomach. Frederick was pleased to see how well Cornwall suited his old friend. He was happy for the both of them, having never seen a pair more aptly matched.

Now if he could but find such a match for himself.

Inadvertently, his eyes found their way to Miss Rosewall. She still sat on a log near the fire away from the others, her attention on the group gathering near the shoreline.

Frederick hesitated. He wanted to approach her, to invite her to join him with the others, but guilt lurked over his shoulder. When he'd discovered that Miss Rosewall was at the party, and Miss Kinsey was not, he'd felt nothing but relief. Now he had the chance to spend as much time with Miss Rosewall as his heart desired. But should he not be wishing for that opportunity with Miss Kinsey?

"Sophia, join us!" Gwynna called out from where she joined the others closer to the sea.

Miss Rosewall shook her head, though her eyes remained on them as she rested her chin on her palm, her gloves lying in her lap.

What was keeping her there? And what was keeping Frederick from enjoying her company? He was not so very attached to Miss Kinsey that he could not spend time with another friend. If anything, as a gentleman, he was obligated to ensure Miss Rosewall enjoyed herself that evening, as she evidently needed help to do.

Setting all other hesitations aside, Frederick took a step toward her. "May I convince you to join us, Miss Rosewall?"

She straightened, turning to face him. "Pardon? Oh, no. Thank you, but I do not know what game they are playing."

"Nor do I, but I'm sure it will be entertaining whichever they choose."

She pulled in her lips, still hesitant.

"Won't you join me?" he asked, offering his hand.

She stared at it with wary eyes, as if she were being asked to hurdle a great gap in the land to reach the safety on the other side.

Perhaps that was precisely what he was asking her to do.

Slowly, she set her gloves on the log next to her, then reached up, sliding her smooth fingers across his palm. Pleasant chills traveled up his arm.

"If I make a fool of myself, I shall never forgive you," she said, standing and withdrawing her hand as a smile tugged at her lips.

"That is more than fair," he responded. They walked together, bringing up the rear of the migrating group. "Has your forehead recovered?"

Confusion knitted her eyebrows together. "From what?"

He gestured to her brow. "Your quarrel with the tree branch. At the picnic."

Understanding lit her eyes. "Oh, yes. I am quite recovered, thank you."

They reached the others, a group of nearly fifteen, just as the Causeys began to explain the rules of the chosen game.

"One person will take a turn placing this"—Mrs. Causey waved a stick half the length and width of her arm in the air —"into the sand as the waves pull out. If you do not make it back to the dry sand before the water reaches you, you will be out of the game. And if the wave pulls out the stick you placed, you will also lose that round."

Mr. Causey continued. "Each person will be required to place the stick farther and farther into the sand. The person who places it the farthest without getting touched by the water or the stick washing away, wins. Shall we begin?"

Cheers sounded as the group lined up, the first person stepping forth for his turn, his arm in a sling.

"Go on, Lieutenant Harris!" a girl's voice shouted out above the others.

Lieutenant Harris looked over his shoulder. "With your encouragement, I'll be bound to win." He winked at someone in the crowd, no doubt the girl who'd cheered for him, but Frederick couldn't see who it was.

"If you take much longer, Harris, I'll disqualify you myself!" called out a man Frederick had been introduced to that day, Mr. Kendricks. He stood at the end of the line, draping an arm around his wife, a woman with a reserved smile and dark red hair.

"Oh, hush, Kendricks," Lieutenant Harris crowed. "You all must watch out for this old captain. At sea, he was known as Cunning Kendricks, because he'd win all the games *and* the girls!"

"Well he best not be known as that now he's married," quipped Mrs. Kendricks, her red hair flying out from her pins.

The crowd burst into laughter. Even Miss Rosewall's smile appeared, a fact Frederick was all too happy to notice.

"Go on, Lieutenant, or I'll put my sister before ye," a man near the front of the line called out. "She just turned sixteen, ye know, and would still be quicker than ye. Go on, Poppy. Show 'im." He nudged the girl next to him.

The girl, Poppy, shook her head. "No, Trevik."

"I don't doubt that she could win," Lieutenant Harris said with a smile in her direction. "If she's willing to go against me."

Poppy blushed.

Finally, Lieutenant Harris took off toward the retreating wave, running awkwardly with his arm in a sling. Frederick cheered with the others as the officer placed his stick with his good arm and returned to the shore without touching the sea.

"A prime example to you all," he joked with a wink in Poppy's direction.

Next, Trevik, Poppy's brother, ran toward the stick, but before he could even reach it, the waves returned and soaked his boots.

The crowd laughed, but Frederick wasn't interested in their reaction. He was too preoccupied with Sophia. His heart warmed to hear her delight again, those joyful bells chiming, filling his mind with memories of when he'd carried her across the tide.

How things had changed between them. How *Miss Rosewall* had changed.

Poppy took her turn next, picking up the stick and placing it a foot farther than Lieutenant Harris's placement before darting back up the sand without a hitch.

"Excellent," Lieutenant Harris said. She stood next to him now with her brother out of the game. "I certainly wouldn't mind losing to you."

Mr. Causey went next as Mrs. Causey cheered on her husband from the side, eventually greeting him with a kiss on the cheek when he was also caught in the water.

Frederick moved to the starting line. He removed his jacket, tossing it aside before loosening his cravat. The crowd cheered. He glanced back at Miss Rosewall, who grinned from ear to ear.

When the waves retreated, he took off down the shore, kicking up the sand behind him before reaching the stick. He managed to move it a mere few inches before fleeing back up the sand.

"You barely made it, sir," Miss Rosewall teased as he passed by her.

"Then let us see you do better," he returned, moving to the back of the line.

He watched with sheer delight as she raced down the beach, picking up her skirts to a modest level, retrieving the stick, and digging it into the sand a few steps forward.

"Two full paces!" the crowd cheered as she returned.

She stood next to Frederick. "How was that?" she said, breathing heavily.

"Wonderful," he responded.

Their eyes locked before the line moved, and they followed the others along the sand.

Miss Rosewall's placement of the stick forced three people to withdraw with wet boots, before Mrs. Kendricks managed to move it farther out.

Frederick found it increasingly more difficult to pay attention to the game when all he really wished to do was watch Miss Rosewall. He'd never seen her so carefree. So genuinely happy. Yes, she'd laughed and teased at that first dinner party at Fynwary Hall, but this time was different. This time, she was sincere.

Her rigid curls were no more. Now they were soft, framing her face in a way that only enhanced its slenderness. Her cheeks were rosy, not from the heat of too many bodies in a ballroom, but from the warmth of the evening sun and the exhilaration of running. Her eyes were not bright from the glow of a chandelier, but from the pleasure she experienced in the company of true friends. Her smiles were not put on to bring attention to herself, rather used to express her joy in sharing the attention equally.

Seeing her this way made Frederick question everything he thought he knew about her. Seeing her this way produced stirrings in his heart he'd tried to keep dormant. Now, he had no choice but to set those feelings free, to allow them to blossom in the sunshine that was Miss Rosewall.

The game progressed, and she and another younger girl were expelled. Soon after, Frederick joined them when a wave caught him straight up to his breeches.

"A good effort, Mr. Hawkins," Mr. Causey said. "Better than losing the first round."

Frederick laughed, chuckling as he moved to the back of the group, glancing around for Miss Rosewall.

His smile faded when his search came up empty. He looked to Gwynna, who stood watching him before she motioned up the beach.

"She said she needed to rest for a moment," she whispered.

Frederick's eyes followed a single trail of footprints up the sand to where Miss Rosewall sat on a rock near the tall grass.

"Does she wish to be alone?" he asked Gwynna.

She gave a helpless shrug before empathetic moans sounded around them. They turned their attention to Poppy, who approached the group with wet skirts.

"You were supposed to win for the both of us," Lieutenant Harris teased.

Poppy responded with a bright grin.

Frederick's eyes drifted once more to Miss Rosewall. He didn't want to impose if she truly did wish to be alone. But he had to be sure if she was all right.

More cheers erupted, and the Kendrickses embraced.

"Well done, my love," Mr. Kendricks said, kissing the top of her head.

The group again formed into a line, this time behind Mrs. Kendricks, but Frederick hesitated.

"Are you to join them, Mr. Hawkins?" Mrs. Causey asked.

He glanced over his shoulder. Miss Rosewall leaned over on the small rock as she traced her finger in the sand.

"I will for the next round," Frederick said. "For now, you must excuse me."

She nodded, her curious eyes on him until the game ensued. No doubt Mrs. Causey wondered if there was something between him and Miss Rosewall after Frederick's earlier mishap of words, when speaking of finding love in Cornwall, fool that he was.

But he was not thinking of such things now. He was thinking of no one but Miss Rosewall.

As he approached, she glanced up at him, straightening her posture again and placing her hands in her lap.

Frederick stopped a few paces away. "Were you leaving?"

"I thought so. Then I stopped here, realizing I had nothing else to go back to."

The tip of her nose was red. Had she been crying?

"Are your parents not at the cottage?"

"Of course they are. They are always there. Just as I ought to be."

"Why?" he questioned taking a step toward her. "Do you not wish to be here, with your friends?"

She watched the group still playing near the shoreline. The sunset's warmth reflected the moisture in her eyes. "No, I don't belong here. I don't belong anywhere." She scooped up a handful of sand. "Not anymore."

CHAPTER THIRTY-FOUR

*F*rederick's brow pursed. He couldn't make sense of the change that had come over Miss Rosewall, nor could he bear staring down at her any longer.

The rock she sat on was more than large enough for the both of them to sit together. He motioned toward it. "May I sit with you for a moment?"

She silently shifted to the edge of the rock. He sat beside her, their shoulders mere inches apart.

"Might you tell me why you feel that way?" he continued. "Why you no longer belong anywhere?"

"Because I don't," she replied simply. "I no longer belong with those of my old class. I tried to fit in with this group." She motioned to the others farther down the beach. "But being here with them, playing with them, I've come to realize that they are far superior to me in every way. They smile, and share, and help others, even amidst their own trials and heartaches. That is something I never do. As such, I cannot have a true place among them, not even as their friend."

Frederick stared at the setting sun, the waves rolling softly toward them. "Gwynna Merrick seems to consider you a friend."

Miss Rosewall sniffed. "I cannot imagine why. Nor how she has managed to forgive me after I..." She pulled her eyes away.

"After you what?"

She stared at the small amount of sand still left in her palm. "I called her brother's death inconsequential. I apologized, and I did not know at the time what I do now. That so many deaths occurred at the mine because of my father's poor choices. Still, I was too careless."

Frederick chewed the inside of his lip. He of course had heard of the flooding at the mine, and the resulting deaths, brought about by Mr. Rosewall's decision. Miss Rosewall's ignorance on the subject was not difficult to believe. After all, her father had waited until the last moment to reveal that she had lost her home and her dowry. Why would he speak further of his other failures?

He took a soothing breath to suppress his anger. It would not benefit either of them to recall his frustration over the man's cowardice. He needed to care for Miss Rosewall, something her own parents seemed incapable of doing.

"If you have apologized," he began, "and she has accepted it, I'm afraid I do not see what the issue is."

She pressed her lips in an unbending line before replying. "Had things not changed, had I still lived at Fynwary Hall, I would not feel this same sorrow for their loss. I would not—I *have* not—given a second thought for any miner, nor his or her family." She flicked away a rogue tear sliding down her cheek. "Does that not reveal my character most of all? That I am incapable of considering the feelings of others? I deserve my fate of loneliness and misery. As do my parents."

Frederick turned toward her. His knee bumped against hers, sending chutes of warmth up and down his leg before he pulled back. "I do not believe anyone deserves such a fate. Especially from a simple mistake."

"If I had only made a simple mistake, I would agree with

you. But it is much more than that. I am the cause of Jago Merrick's death, plus countless others who have suffered over the years. Their misery is my doing." Her back curved. Her expression drew low. "It is all my doing."

"In what way are you the cause?" he asked. "Did you flood the shaft? Encourage your father to push deeper into the mine?"

"No, but—"

"Had you known the lives at risk, what your father was deciding against, would you not have encouraged him to cease his work until a safer way could be discovered?"

"Of course, but I—"

"Then it is not your fault, Miss Rosewall."

He knew he interrupted, he knew he spoke forcefully, but he did not know until that moment that he *needed* her to see his viewpoint. For so long, he had wanted Miss Rosewall humbled. Now that he was witnessing it firsthand, regret for his own pride crushed his heart. This was not what he wanted, for her to be defeated, depressed. He needed to help her, to coax her to continue speaking in hopes that she might find the light once again.

"Father," she said, "his excessive blasting caused the flooding. He only continued to reach more copper, in order to fund the expenditures of his selfish wife and daughter. I cannot help but think, if I merely changed my ways, Gwynna's brother might have—"

"Don't," Frederick said softly. "Do not dwell on the 'might haves' of the past. Such thoughts only lead to misery. You must take my word for it."

Frederick had not meant to direct his thoughts, or their conversation, to the painful memories of his past. Yet, how could it be avoided with Miss Rosewall's feelings mirroring his from nearly ten years before?

"How do you know such a thing?" she asked, regarding him curiously.

He hesitated. He had not spoken aloud of his childhood for years. How could he now share such details with a woman he wasn't sure would flippantly disregard what he said?

As he met her eyes, however, he saw the humility, the change, within her. And he knew he could trust her.

With a deep sigh, he began his story. "Do you recall, that first dinner party at Fynwary Hall, when I mentioned that my father had died when I was a young man?"

Miss Rosewall nodded. "Yes. You were fourteen, if I recall correctly."

He stared at her. How had she remembered such a simple detail? "Yes, I was fourteen. We received many condolences when he finally went to the grave. Mother and I found them difficult to accept, as my father…" He rubbed the back of his head. "My father was abusive, physically and verbally, to both my mother and me."

Miss Rosewall pulled back, her eyebrows drawn low over her eyes. "How terrible. I am so sorry for you both."

"Thank you," he said, "but I did not tell you this for your pity, merely for you to understand. You see, in Society's eyes, he was perfection, always doing the right things, saying the right things. But in private, he was the worst kind of person. I hated the pretense, the lies. It was all to hide his own cowardice."

"Which is why you cannot abide any falseness of character now?" Her voice wasn't any louder than a whisper.

Frederick held his bottom lip between his teeth, nodding. "Yes, that is why. I used to think as a child that if I could simply change who I was, Father might not feel the need to treat me in such a way. But his behavior continued, and I, of course, blamed myself for it, as well as his treatment of my mother. I thought that if I could be a little taller, or a little braver, I might be able to stop him from harming her. When I could not, I blamed myself again."

Miss Rosewall grimaced. "But surely his baseness was not your doing."

"No, it wasn't. I did not understand that then, nor for years to come, even after his death. To assuage my guilt for being unable to help Mother before, I did everything within me to further her happiness once Father was gone. I even purchased her the townhome in London because it was the one place she wished to be, though Father never allowed her to visit Town when he was alive.

"While she finally lived comfortably and happily, I was still miserable, holding onto my guilt until finally, I was able to redirect that guilt to its rightful owner, my father."

Miss Rosewall leaned forward. "What made you finally do so?"

"A number of things. My mother's encouragement, the help of a few friends. A strong desire to no longer allow the man who was only my father by blood to control my life."

"So you have forgiven him then?"

Frederick shrugged. "As much as I am able to. There are days when I am reminded of his cruelty, and I feel that familiar guilt, that lie that I had caused his treatment of me. But I simply distract myself from the thoughts so they cannot house themselves within me for long."

Miss Rosewall retrieved another handful of sand. "May I ask what you do to set those thoughts aside?"

He leaned toward her with a knowing look. "I find that helping another is the surest way for one to forget about one's own troubles."

She stared up at him, a pensive light in her eyes.

"So please, Miss Rosewall," he said, lowering his voice, "do not allow a baseless guilt to plague your soul as it did mine for years. You do not deserve such a fate."

Her eyes, wide and pleading, peered into his own. "Not even for the mistakes I *have* made?"

"'To err is human,'" he said with a smile.

"'To forgive, divine,'" she finished. "So I suppose that makes me human and you divine."

He sniffed, amused. "I assure you, I am in no way divine. Not yet, at any rate."

A smile almost appeared on her lips at his comment. "Before Lowena Cottage, and Gwynna, and…you, I thought I was very nearly perfect. Now I see how far I am from that notion." She paused, releasing a heavy sigh. "You know, I quite dislike making mistakes."

"Everyone does." He stretched out his legs, crossing his boots at his ankles. Sand still clung to the wet leather. "But you are flawed, as we all are."

"Flawed?" She scrunched up her nose with disgust. "I don't like the sound of that."

"I'm afraid it cannot be helped."

She looked at him from the corner of her eye. "Are you not supposed to be encouraging me now, Mr. Hawkins?"

"I am. To recognize one's flaws is a wonderful thing. If I believed myself to be perfect, I would never change. But knowing I have flaws, then there is much I can do to begin improving myself. And should we not all be doing so? Bettering ourselves as individuals and helping others do the same?"

She stared at him, her eyes narrowing.

"What's the matter?" he asked.

"I merely wonder at your sanity, sir. No one can be as inherently good and willing to change as you are."

He smiled. "It is because I have seen the beauty that is brought on by trials, by flaws, and by change."

She leaned back, folding her arms. "That, or you are simply mad."

Sophia was glad to hear Mr. Hawkins chuckling at her comment. She hadn't meant to be rude, but honestly, how could this man be as good as he continually revealed himself to be? Especially with having such a past.

"Here," he said, leaning down toward the sand.

He shifted the granules back and forth before retrieving a shell from beneath the surface. He held it up between his thumb and forefinger at the bottom.

"Tell me what you see," he said.

"I see a shell."

He dropped his chin and quirked a brow. "What else?"

She smiled at her own joke before staring closer at the fan-shaped shell. Its ridges were spaced perfectly apart, and the colors—soft orange, light brown, ivory white—stretched out in a gradient before the highest portion of the shell revealed a dark orange, as if it had been dipped in a jar of paint.

"I see beauty," she said, her head leaning to the side. "And perfect uniformity. A fine array of colors. Altogether, a rather fine-looking shell."

He nodded. "I see the same."

"I passed your test then?"

He smiled, lowering the shell and holding out his free fingers toward her. "Allow me the use of your hand for a moment?"

Tentatively, she reached forth her hand. Softly, he turned it over so her palm was faced upward, and then, as she forced her breathing to remain unaffected, he placed the shell in the center of her hand.

"Oh," she said, her mouth parting in surprise.

It was the same shell as before, only his fingers no longer hid the large crack at the bottom of it, preventing the fan-shape to align perfectly on the bottom.

Sophia wasn't quite sure what to make of the revelation. "It's broken," she said, running a finger along the crack. The edging was smooth, made soft by the time spent rolling in the storms of the sea.

"I'm sure all you see now is the imperfection," Mr. Hawkins said. "But with it, this shell becomes uniquely different from all the ones in the sea. With this flaw, we discover the journey it has taken to become beautiful with its distinctive cracks."

He brushed his finger over the shell, caressing her palm in the process. "Unlike this shell, however, we have the ability to change and become as flawless as we wish to be."

Sophia's breathing faltered as his right hand slowly lifted to her face. His fingers hovered next to her jaw. Slowly, softly, they rested against her skin, gently turning her face toward his.

She stared into his blue eyes. His thumb stroked her jawline, and she struggled not to lean closer to him.

"But just because something is flawed," he whispered, "does not mean it is not worth keeping…or caring for…" His eyes found her mouth, his thumb trailing along her skin and brushing against her bottom lip. "Or cherishing."

Sophia swallowed. Her heart thrummed. How had she found herself in this situation again? So close to Mr. Hawkins that she could only formulate one coherent thought. What would it feel like to have his lips finally on hers?

He leaned toward her. His thumb sliding from her lips to rest at the hollow of her throat. Could he feel her feverish heart? Surely his heart was racing just as quickly. How could it not be with that look in his eyes, the clear desire shining forth?

In the next moment, however, his fingers trailed from her neck and down her shoulder before he pulled back and turned toward the fading sun.

Sophia blinked. Her mind reeled. What had happened? She knew he'd wanted to kiss her, as plainly as she had wished to. So why had he not?

"Let's return," he said. "They will be wondering what is keeping us."

Was that why he pulled away, fear of someone discovering them? Slowly, Sophia's reason returned. What on earth had she been thinking? It was hardly appropriate to kiss a gentleman in broad sight of others. Her reputation would surely have suffered. If, of course, her reputation still mattered.

"Will you join me?" he asked, standing and stretching out his hand toward her. "Or will you be returning to the cottage after all?"

She studied his hand for a moment, thinking over his words from earlier, the revelation of his father's choices, why Mr. Hawkins disliked false behavior. Slowly, she rested her fingers in his.

"No, I will join you." She allowed him to help her stand before her hands fell at her sides. "But before we return to the others, I must thank you for speaking with me. You have helped me more than you could ever know, Mr. Hawkins."

"It was my pleasure, Miss Rosewall."

With a shared smile, they walked together across the sand, the seashell pressing against Sophia's palm as she held it securely in her hand.

CHAPTER THIRTY-FIVE

The next morning, being trapped indoors with nowhere to go and no one to see, Sophia's mind inevitably drifted to her depressing situation. However, when she caught sight of the shell she'd placed on her windowsill the night before, she recalled her conversation with Mr. Hawkins.

"Helping another is the surest way to forget about one's troubles," she whispered to herself as she stood from her bed.

So that was precisely what she would do. Now who to help? Gwynna? Mother or Father? They hardly seemed in need of any help *she* could provide.

She pulled her lips to one side and paced about her room. She didn't make it two steps before her foot thudded against something on the floor.

Her dress.

She'd returned home so late and so exhausted from the party the evening before that she'd simply unfastened her clothing and left it on the floor.

Her mind drifted to Mr. Hawkins again, and the time they'd spent together after their conversation. He'd remained by her side nearly the whole of the evening as they played games and listened to songs near the fireside. He'd been so kind, so open and honest about the hardships of his past. She could hardly believe he'd overcome so much, but it gave her courage to press on with her comparably easier life.

She retrieved her gown from the floor and held it up in the air before her. The front was a wrinkled mess, the bottom still damp from the sea and covered in sand. It definitely needed a good washing, but Edith had completed the laundry only the day before.

Sophia clicked her teeth together. At Fynwary Hall, they'd had a room for the washing to be made easier for the servants. At the cottage, however, she'd seen the tub and washing board outside only yesterday. Would they still be out there? If so, Sophia could wash the dress herself and hang it up to dry before Edith and Mrs. Cuff made it back from market day that morning. That would surely help the girl, not asking her to restart on a chore she'd already finished.

With a determined step, Sophia found her apron she used for painting then tied it on as she marched out of doors.

The washing tub was still filled at the side of the cottage. Edith must not have had time to empty it. The water was cold but looked clean enough. Sophia was fairly certain it ought to be warmer, but she hardly knew how to boil water.

She pushed the dress into the tub then glanced around for the soap, though it was nowhere to be seen. She hesitated before setting aside her reservations. She would simply wash the dress without it. After all, soap was hardly needed to wash off a little sand.

Sand that was now swirling in the tub and covering the entirety of her dress, instead of just the bottom. Perhaps she ought to have removed most of the grit before submersing the dress.

Never mind. It was in the past. She would no longer worry over it, just as Mr. Hawkins had taught her.

She reached into the tub to find the bottom of the gown,

then set it on the washing board, rubbing it slowly up and down against the ridges. This wasn't so very hard. Not really.

Then she paused. When Gwynna had washed her own clothing, she'd bent over the tub with vigor. Perhaps Sophia wasn't doing it hard enough. She leaned closer to the washboard and scrubbed the fabric along the wood energetically. Not too hard, though. She did not wish to create a—

"Oh, dear."

The fabric caught on one of the ridges, and a muffled tearing reached her ears. She raised the dress from the water and disappointedly eyed the torn hem of her gown.

She sighed. This was not turning out at all how she had planned. But she would not give up. She could easily mend the hole herself, yet another task she could do to help Edith.

She returned the dress to the water and rubbed more delicately than before. Soon she smiled, oddly satisfied with the therapeutic action.

"Good morning."

Sophia gasped, her hands slipping on the washboard. Water flew into the air, across the side of her face, and over the front of her apron. In stunned silence, she looked up beyond the stone wall to see Mr. Hawkins sitting astride his horse, a smile playing about his lips.

Of course. *Of course* he would happen upon her in the middle of yet another embarrassing moment.

With a sigh, she wiped away the water from her cheek. "Good morning, Mr. Hawkins. To what do I owe the pleasure?"

His eyes shone with mirth as he dismounted and removed his hat. "I will tell you, just as soon as you tell me what it is *you* are about."

She held up her sopping dress, the water making it droop like a piece of water-logged seaweed. "Is it not obvious? I am doing what you told me to do."

He narrowed his eyes, his lips curving as he leaned against the wall. "I don't recall telling you to do the washing."

"No, but you said to help others. So I'm playing the part of the lady of the cottage and doing a little laundry." She looked at the hole more visible as the dress swung before her. "Though, I did tear it. I suppose I was a little too enthusiastic in my scrubbing. But I should be able to mend it well enough."

"That's a relief. It would be a shame if you could not wear it any longer. I quite liked that color on you."

Sophia pushed the dress back into the water to hide her growing smile. His compliment had been so sincere, so genuine. So very unlike the compliments Mr. Singleton and Mr. Chester had paid her those many weeks before.

"I have answered your question, Mr. Hawkins. Now might you answer mine?"

He blinked, straightening his stance. "Yes. I was going to ask a favor of you. Fortunately, I see I have come when you appear to be in quite a generous mood."

"Indeed, I am, sir. What is it you need?"

"I received a letter from my mother yesterday and only had the chance to read it this morning. She has written to tell me she will be here next week."

She stepped around the washing tub, wiping her hands on the only dry spot of her apron. "Oh? I thought you said she would never come to Cornwall?"

"So I had hoped." He pulled his gloves more securely on his hands. "I love my mother, but she can be very opinionated at times. And extremely overbearing. Still, I would like to make her visit as comfortable as possible."

His actions didn't surprise Sophia, especially after last night. The man thought only of other people.

"So what is it you would like me to do?" she asked, moving to stand before him. Only the stone wall separated them.

A sheepish smile appeared on his lips. "Well, I had hoped,

at some point during her visit, that you might call upon her at Fynwary Hall."

She blinked, trying to diffuse her surprise.

"I know such a task might be disagreeable," he rushed on, "and if you cannot accept my request, do not trouble yourself. But Mother would appreciate the acquaintance of many while here, and I know you would welcome her warmly. And I, well, I would like for her to meet you."

Sophia's mind swirled with unwelcome images. Stepping foot in her old home. Calling at a place she'd once received callers. Servants leading her through a house she knew all too well. Meeting his mother.

She paused. Mr. Hawkins wanted her to meet his mother? She looked up at him, his eyes hopeful. He looked very much like a young boy asking for an extra serving of dessert.

Her heart softened, and concern fled her mind. This man had done so much for her. He'd changed her very life. The least she could do was meet his mother, especially because he desired it.

"I would be more than happy to call upon her, Mr. Hawkins," she said. "So long as you will be there, as well."

He brightened. "I would not miss it."

Their eyes met before he took a step away, replacing his hat with a bow. "I will allow you now to get back to your washing. And I will see you Wednesday?"

Sophia nodded, and she watched him mount his chestnut horse before he cantered away.

She sighed. Wednesday. Why did it have to be so very far away?

CHAPTER THIRTY-SIX

S ophia stood in the entryway of Fynwary Hall, her eyes wandering across the cream walls, the black and white marble flooring, and the grand staircase curling around the room to the upper floor. The green curtains before the windows were pulled back, allowing the light to fill the room, and the chandelier sparkled in the sunshine.

Nothing had changed within the entryway. But everything had changed within Sophia.

"Are you well, Miss Rosewall?"

Sophia blinked, pulling herself from her reverie to face Aaron, the footman who had once served her family, who now served Mr. Hawkins. "Yes, thank you."

He nodded then motioned her forward. "This way, miss."

Her steps were slow as she followed him. It was a strange feeling, walking through her old home after being away for so long. A familiarity whispered from the paintings and tapestries hung on the walls, but an odd sense also spoke to her, telling her that this was now a foreign place. In a way, it *was* foreign. It no longer belonged to her.

Surprisingly, that knowledge sat better with her than she thought it would. In fact, she was not only fine walking through Fynwary Hall, but she actually found herself longing for Lowena Cottage—for her small, comfortable hearth, the warm gray walls, and the unrivaled sights, sounds, and smells of the sea.

She shook her head in amazement. So she had grown fond of her little home after all. Heaven help her.

Aaron stepped aside as they reached the drawing room, and Sophia's footsteps thumped softly across the floor as she entered within.

"I will alert Mr. Hawkins that you have arrived, miss," he said.

"There is no need," spoke a deep voice from outside the room. "He is already aware."

Sophia turned to the doorway. Mr. Hawkins entered the drawing room, his tall frame and broad shoulders commanding her attention, just like last time. Now, of course, the circumstances were far different.

"Miss Rosewall, lovely to see you again." Mr. Hawkins bowed, then faced her with a grin. "Aaron, you may tell Mrs. Hawkins that Miss Rosewall has arrived."

"Yes, sir," Aaron said, and with a quick glance between his new employer and old, the footman left the room.

Mr. Hawkins motioned to the sofa. "I trust you are well."

Sophia nodded, taking her seat as he stood near the warm, snapping fire. "And you?"

"I am as well as can be expected." He glanced precariously at the door before continuing in a whisper. "With my houseguest."

Sophia stifled a laugh. "How long does she plan to stay?"

"With any luck, only a week. But that is dependent on how well she likes Cornwall."

"Shall I make her dislike it more then, for your sake?"

His shoulders rose and fell with a quick laugh. "I will let you know." They shared a smile. "Thank you again for agreeing to meet with her. I know it cannot be easy, returning here."

Sophia considered the gilded frames and white cushions of the room. "I thought it might be difficult, but seeing how much of it has remained unchanged, and how you have taken care of it, puts my mind at ease. If it had to be sold, I'm glad it was to you."

His brow softened. "I have been more than happy looking after it." Their eyes met for an extended moment before he cleared his throat. "Did you tell your parents you were coming here?"

"No, they would not have taken kindly to the news. Father would have simply brushed me aside without hearing a word, and Mother, well, she would not have understood why I wished to come. I believe she misses Fynwary Hall too greatly to ever consider stepping foot on the property again."

Discomfort flickered across his brow. She changed the subject to avoid his unfounded guilt returning.

"And what of your mother? It has not been so very long, but does she miss her home in London?"

"I believe so. Though how one can long for such an awful place is beyond me."

The sullen tone of his words transported her right back to their time together playing whist in that very room, when Mr. Hawkins had accused Sophia of being as superficial as those in the city, concerned more over their hair and dress than the well-being of others.

How correct he had been.

"May I ask," she said, "is your dislike for London due to your father's behavior or someone else's?"

He closed an eye in a wince as he contemplated his answer. "He is part of the reason, yes. As well as a number of women who managed to taint my view when I was there last."

She looked away. "You fell in love."

"No, nothing ever so far as love."

A cool wind of relief instantly calmed her tossing stomach.

"I did pursue a few women while there," he continued, "but I found that all too easily, their attention would be redirected to wealthier gentlemen. They did not care for my own feelings. Only who could afford the next fashionable dress and when the next ball was. Everything was a façade to hide the truth of their characters. Frankly, I grew weary of it all very quickly."

Sophia couldn't meet his eyes. She'd behaved in that same abominable way to him, as well as to Mr. Singleton and Mr. Chester. She was a fool to have ever thought she wouldn't hurt anyone with her actions.

"But perhaps I am wrong," Mr. Hawkins continued. "Perhaps they chose another not because I was the poorer gentleman, but because I was the less attractive one."

Still distracted with her thoughts to realize he jested, Sophia scoffed. "I can assure you, that is certainly not the problem, sir."

He quirked a brow, a smirk cocking his lips. "Is that so?"

Her mouth parted. "I mean, well, they were in the wrong, not you," she managed to stammer out. "And as you told me, you ought not take the blame for someone else's mistakes."

"Right you are, Miss Rosewall. At any rate, my mother pressed most of the women toward me. At one point, she even convinced me to pursue Mrs. Causey before the woman had married. Fortunately for all parties involved, she is with the gentleman she truly loves."

Sophia toyed with a curl that had come undone from her pins at the back, attempting to appear unruffled at the thought of Mr. Hawkins marrying Mrs. Causey. "What about you? Are you happy with how things ended with Mrs. Causey and these other women in London, or are you disappointed?"

He peered down at her. "I am more than happy with how

my life has turned out. For otherwise, I would not have found myself here in Cornwall…with you."

Sophia thought he teased, but his stalwart eyes made her chest swell as if a ship had just unfurled its sails within her.

She looked around, anxious for a distraction. Otherwise she feared she'd jump to her feet and kiss the man soundly on those perfect lips of his.

Her eyes settled on the hearth, and a memory popped into her mind. "Do you know, I was rather badly behaved as a child."

A smile inched across his lips. "I must admit, I find that difficult to believe."

"No, it's true. I would often sneak out of doors and make my way to the sea instead of finishing my lessons."

"Well, that does not surprise me."

She hummed a laugh. "No, indeed. Other times, I would move around the garden, darting from tree to tree to hide from my governess. I once brought a pen knife with me outside and carved my initials into one of the trees at the edge of the property. When she found me, she told my parents that I had neglected my studies once again and then betrayed my carving. My parents forced me to double my practice of the pianoforte and increase my study of Latin."

"Which, I assume, you did not enjoy either?"

"Not in the least," she responded. "But I exacted my revenge in another way." His eyes followed her as she made her way toward the hearth, the opposite side from where he was situated. "Just here, I carved my initials into the floor."

He walked to where she stood as she pointed to the small, roughly curved letters in the wooden floor.

S. R.

He hunched down beside her, sliding his forefinger over the letters as he chuckled. "Ah, there they are."

Her eyes trailed across his wide shoulders. "I made them small enough so that no one could happen upon them unless they were specifically looking. But, oh, did I feel clever. So clever, in fact, that I took the pen knife to each room in the house and left my mark on bookshelves, tables, the backs of chairs, walls, hearths. Whatever I could think of, always with discretion."

"Were you ever discovered?" he asked, his eyes shining as he stood.

"Fortunately, no. I was silly enough not to realize, that had the carvings been seen, they would have known exactly who to come looking for—*S. R.*"

They shared a laugh as they stared again at the small initials.

"So they are in every room of this house, you say?"

"Yes, every one."

He scratched at his jaw. "Now I have to go looking for them."

"Well, I wish you luck, sir. I cannot remember the location of half of them. And if they are as difficult to discover as this one, you will be looking for half your life."

"Then perhaps one day, you might consider joining me here."

His smile faded, though the warmth remained in his eyes. Sophia's heart leapt. Did he mean…?

"Joining me here to help in the search," he finished. His voice was deep, throaty, as if there was something else he'd meant to say, but those words had been spoken instead.

"Of course," she muttered.

Silence followed, and Mr. Hawkins took a step back. "So what eventually helped you to become obedient to your parents?"

She looked at the initials in the wood to avoid staring at his strong jaw. "I suppose I changed to become more like my mother. She was always very elegant and well-liked, and her marriage was happy. I desired the same for myself, so when I came of age, I decided to be more like her, in hopes of obtaining the same things she had."

Sophia paused, staring across the room as she thought of Mother and who she used to be. "I learned much from her. Though, now I realize it would have been better to be more like myself rather than to be another Mary Rosewall."

Their eyes met once more. Before either of them could speak, footsteps patted on the floor outside, and Sophia took an abrupt step away from Mr. Hawkins.

A woman with hair a shade darker than Mr. Hawkins's, streaks of silver laced throughout, entered the room. Her posture was no doubt envied by Roman statues, and her demeanor was one of quiet regality.

She reminded Sophia of her mother, before she'd moved to Lowena.

"Mother," Mr. Hawkins said, crossing the room to greet her and motioning Sophia forward. "Allow me to introduce to you Miss Sophia Rosewall. Miss Rosewall, my mother, Mrs. Hawkins."

CHAPTER THIRTY-SEVEN

"*I*t is a pleasure, Mrs. Hawkins," Sophia greeted. Curtsies were exchanged before the women sat across from each other, Mr. Hawkins taking his place by the hearth.

"I trust you are enjoying your visit to Cornwall thus far," Sophia said. "We boast the finest views of the sea in the country, to be sure."

"Hmm. I disagree. I far prefer Devon. Its waters are more favorable for proper society."

Sophia glanced to Mr. Hawkins, but he closed his eyes. He'd said his mother was overbearing and opinionated. Now she knew he had not been exaggerating.

"Did you have a pleasant journey here?" Sophia tried next.

"It was too long, and the carriage uncomfortable."

Sophia nodded. "My mother finds it difficult to travel in discomfort, as well. She requires the finest of carriages to make any sort of journey."

Mrs. Hawkins raised her chin. "Where is your mother? Why has she not joined you, forcing you to make calls on your own?"

Sophia caught Mr. Hawkins's apologetic grimace before she replied. "She is home, indisposed."

"And pray tell, where is *home*? In relation to Fynwary Hall, mind you. I do not know this county well enough to have any other description be of use."

Mr. Hawkins had not told his mother where Sophia lived. Why would he? It's not as if he would speak about Sophia a great deal to anyone.

"My family and I have relocated to a small cottage above the sea. Just west of here."

"A cottage, you say?" Mrs. Hawkins's eyes moved to her son's, her nostrils flaring.

Sophia knew that look. It was one her mother had expressed often. Disgust.

If Mrs. Hawkins disapproved of Sophia living at the cottage, what did she think of Mr. Hawkins befriending the woman whose house he now owned?

Or had she no knowledge of that either?

"Tell me, Miss Rosewall, have you ever been to London?"

Sophia nodded. "My parents have taken me each year since I came out into Society."

"I wonder that our paths have never crossed. But I suppose we have our different social circles." Her pointed nose raised to the ceiling. "Where did you live before your little cottage by the sea?"

Despite Sophia expecting the question, tension slid up her neck. How was she to reply? Surely Mrs. Hawkins would wish to throw her from the house. Sophia's own mother would do the same. But Mr. Hawkins would not allow his mother to be so unkind, would he?

She glanced toward him. He opened his mouth as if to respond for Sophia, but the footman entered, preventing his words.

"Sir?"

"Yes, Aaron, what is it?" Mr. Hawkins asked.

"There is a matter that needs your attention, sir."

"This very moment?" Mr. Hawkins asked, his brow raised impatiently.

"I'm afraid so, sir."

Mr. Hawkins sighed. He turned to Sophia with an encouraging smile. "I shall be back in just a moment, Miss Rosewall. Mother, see to her comfort, will you?"

Was it just Sophia's imagination, or did Mr. Hawkins truly just send a warning look to his mother? Either way, he was gone in an instant, and Sophia was left alone in the room with Mrs. Hawkins and her elevated nose.

She watched Sophia as if she were spying a fly buzzing about her food. "Now, where did you call home before the cottage?"

Sophia swallowed. She had hoped the woman had forgotten the question.

"I lived with my family here, at Fynwary Hall," she said. Her voice, it strikingly resembled Miss Kinsey's timid tone.

Mrs. Hawkins's expression did not change, only the slightest narrowing of her eyes revealed she was displeased with the information. "I thought I recognized your name. You are of the Rosewalls who could not keep possession of their own home."

Sophia pulled back, surprised at the woman's candor. With a mother so rude and a father so offensive, from where had Mr. Hawkins's goodness come?

"Yes, I am the very daughter of those Rosewalls," she replied.

"What a pity. It is good of my son to still interact with you, despite your lowered circumstances."

That familiar feeling of insecurity, of worthlessness crept upon Sophia, her stomach tensing.

"Though," Mrs. Hawkins continued, "I do wonder how he has time for you when he is so very occupied with the other woman, the one he has spoken to me so much about."

Sophia's eyes snapped up. "Other woman?"

"Oh, don't you know?" A meaningful smile graced her lips. "My Freddy has told me he is very close to becoming engaged. I, for one, cannot wait to meet the woman. Apparently, she is as genteel as they come and has a great deal to offer. He is often with her and her family."

Sophia's head spun. Other woman. Genteel. A great deal to offer. That was not Sophia. That was any other woman *but* Sophia. Could Mrs. Hawkins be referring to...to Miss Kinsey?

Confusion pressed on her mind. If Mr. Hawkins was in love with Miss Kinsey, or another woman, why had he invited Sophia to meet his mother? Should he not have asked his intended instead? But Mr. Hawkins had said his mother would appreciate the acquaintance of many. Now *that* was Sophia. One of many.

Her heart ached, as if she'd been struck blow after blow. What a fool she had been for thinking she meant more to Mr. Hawkins. What a fool she must look to his mother, sitting there when her son was in love with another.

Unable to bear the humiliation, Sophia stood, pretending she did not see Mrs. Hawkins's arched, disapproving eyebrows.

"Are you leaving so soon?" the woman asked, though clearly unsurprised.

Sophia nodded. "Please tell your son I am needed elsewhere."

"Of course," Mrs. Hawkins said, sounding anything but disappointed. "Shall I call for a footman to show you out? Though, I assume you know the way, as this was *once* your home."

The words stung sharper than any knife. Sophia understood the woman's implication. Fynwary Hall wasn't Sophia's home, and it would never be again.

"That won't be necessary," Sophia managed to say. "Good day, Mrs. Hawkins."

With a short curtsy, she left the room. Mrs. Hawkins did not stand as Sophia departed. She didn't need to, her lack of respect for Sophia was already apparent.

As she moved down the corridor, Sophia's thoughts scattered in disarray, her feelings souring in her heart. She prayed Mrs. Hawkins was wrong in her assumption, that she might have misheard her son's words, or was perhaps telling a falsehood.

But when Sophia turned the corner and made for the entryway, her feet planted to the checkered, marble floor.

Mr. Hawkins was leaving the entryway to move down the opposite corridor from Sophia.

Next to him walked Miss Kinsey.

Sophia sucked in a sharp breath, pressing a hand to her mouth. The pair continued together, unaware of having been spotted. They stopped outside the study, Miss Kinsey entering first. Was his hand at the small of her back? Were they smiling? They secured the door behind them before Sophia could decipher.

Though, she already knew the truth. There was only one reason for two people to share a private audience together. An engagement was about to occur. In her old home. With her practically outside the door.

The realization sickened Sophia to her stomach and to her heart. Mrs. Hawkins had been telling the truth. Her son truly was in love with Miss Kinsey.

Sophia shook her head in disbelief. It was wrong, all of it was wrong. Mr. Hawkins was not supposed to love Miss Kinsey. He was supposed to love…

With a withered heart and quickened step, Sophia dashed across the entryway, leaving behind the house that held so many of her memories and the man she had hoped would one day hold her heart.

CHAPTER THIRTY-EIGHT

"*C*ould ye not be mistaken?"

"No. No, I saw them enter the room myself. And his mother's words were as clear as day. Mr. Hawkins is in love with Miss Kinsey."

Gwynna winced, her empathy clear. Sophia had met with her that morning for market day, a few days after Sophia had called at Fynwary. They now moved about the small town, completing Gwynna's various tasks as Sophia spoke.

"Do ye love him then?" Gwynna asked next.

"What does it matter now?" Sophia returned, though it still mattered very greatly to her. "My feelings are unimportant if the two of them are in love."

Gwynna's empathetic look nearly brought Sophia to tears, but such emotion would not do for the crowds brimming in St. Just.

She pasted on a smile and raised a shoulder. "I suppose I ought to be grateful. His marriage to Miss Kinsey has saved me from a lifetime of dealing with a dragon for a mother-in-law."

Their soft laughter brought the slightest form of relief to Sophia.

They continued up the street toward the stalls located near the modiste shop. As Sophia waited for Gwynna to purchase a few items for her mother, a bell rang out through the street.

Sophia recognized the sound at once. She had heard the bell ring almost weekly as she'd leave the modiste shop with newly purchased packages in hand. Her arms may have been full then with gowns and the most fashionable accessories, but her heart and mind had been empty. She far preferred her life now to be filled with the companionship she'd found with Gwynna, and once with Mr. Hawkins.

Absentmindedly, she glanced to the modiste to see who had exited. The last person she expected, the one person she wished to see, strode out of the shop.

She gasped. Mr. Hawkins's eyes caught hers in an instant, his warm smile filling her simultaneously with such sadness and joy, she could hardly remain upright.

"I'll wait for ye over here, Sophia," Gwynna whispered behind her.

Sophia sent a grateful smile to her considerate friend then turned to face Mr. Hawkins as he approached. Goodness, if he didn't grow more attractive by the day.

She dipped into a curtsy. "Mr. Hawkins, pleasure to see you this morning."

"And you, Miss Rosewall. I wanted to—"

"Miss Rosewall." Mrs. Hawkins appeared next to her son. Sophia hadn't noticed her until she'd spoken. "I didn't expect to see you again after your abrupt departure from my son's home."

Sophia was not ignorant to her pointed words. Still, she could not be cruel in return to Mr. Hawkins's mother. "Yes, well I am pleased to see you both again. Has Cornwall risen in your estimation?"

"Only in terms of its Society," Mrs. Hawkins responded. "I must say, I never expected such gentility. Though, I should not be surprised. My wonderful friend Lady Beatrice was raised here, and she is as elegant as any woman I have ever known."

Sophia glanced to Mr. Hawkins. He had yet to remove his eyes from her. Why did he stare? Where was his intended? And why was he *still* staring?

"My Freddy has such fine friends," Mrs. Hawkins continued, as if she were vying for the attention her son gave Sophia. "The Rennalls for one, and the Madderns. Benlett House is so very grand." She paused, resting a hand on Mr. Hawkins's arm. "Oh, and dear Miss Kinsey. Why, she is one young woman I have certainly loved getting to know better."

Sophia's throat narrowed, as if a rope had been cast around her neck and was now slowly constricting her breathing. Their engagement had to be official by now. Mr. Hawkins must have simply tasked his mother to keep quiet about the arrangement until he could share the blessed news himself.

Mrs. Hawkins continued. "Of course, Miss Rosewall, you would not know Miss Kinsey, as she is so very fine."

Insecurity niggled at Sophia's already weakened confidence. "No, I know the young woman, Mrs. Hawkins."

"Oh, I see. Yes, with how very genteel Miss Kinsey is, of course she would know you. Would you not agree she has many merits? A little quiet, perhaps, but that is to be preferred over a woman who cannot hold her tongue."

Mrs. Hawkins was certainly one to speak of such matters. Even her son was looking around the streets with uninterested eyes.

Or was he looking for Miss Kinsey? Was she there in St. Just? Sophia cringed. She could not stomach seeing the two of them together. She needed to leave before their loving glances tore Sophia apart.

"Yes, she is a fine woman," Mrs. Hawkins prattled on. "Any man would benefit from having her as a wife."

She gave Mr. Hawkins a knowing look, but Sophia didn't bother to note his response. She turned sideways, inching away from the mother and son. "Yes, I heartily agree. But I do apologize, as I must be about my business."

"Another hasty departure," Mrs. Hawkins muttered disapprovingly. "But we wouldn't wish to keep you. Your maid seems anxious to leave, as well."

"My maid?"

Mrs. Hawkins motioned behind Sophia, who turned to see Gwynna now standing just out of ear's reach. Her friend roved over the items in her basket, unaware of Mrs. Hawkins's mistake.

Mistake. Sophia could have scoffed. It was less of a mistake and more of an irritating, presumptuous inference. An inference that blinded Sophia to her inferiorities and tossed her insecurities to the cobbled streets of St. Just.

She turned, fully facing Mrs. Hawkins, her back straight and voice steady. "You are mistaken, Mrs. Hawkins. Gwynna is a miner's daughter, one who once worked at the mine my father sold to settle his debts. And she is not my maid. She is my very dear friend."

Mrs. Hawkins's eyes rounded, and satisfaction overcame Sophia, insomuch that she did not need to say another word. She curtsied, stealing a glance at Mr. Hawkins—was he smiling?—before turning around and returning to Gwynna's side. Sophia linked arms with her and continued with her down the street.

"What be that about then?" Gwynna asked, her brow wrinkled.

Sophia had no intention of reciting Mrs. Hawkins's assumption. "Oh, it was nothing. Did you need to—"

"Miss Rosewall?"

Shock jolted through her limbs. Mr. Hawkins. He'd followed her. She shot a quick glance to Gwynna before turning to watch him stride toward them. His mother was nowhere in sight.

"I be finished with my tasks, Sophia," Gwynna said in a hushed tone. "Perhaps we could meet later?"

Sophia nodded, sending a quick look of gratitude in her friend's direction before Gwynna left down the street. Sophia turned back to face Mr. Hawkins, who stopped a few paces from her.

"Mr. Hawkins, did you forget something?"

"No, I simply wished to speak with you alone for a moment." His eyes scanned the crowds before he motioned behind her. "If you are at liberty, would you mind very much walking somewhere a little quieter?"

"Very well."

Sophia's stomach churned, her hands growing damp and cold. Mr. Hawkins was sure to tell her now of Miss Kinsey. He would admit his love for her, his mother's pleasure over his choice. And Sophia would have to congratulate him and pretend that her heart was not crumpling to pieces.

They moved together to the quieter part of town, neither of them speaking until the crowds dispersed.

"Where is your mother?" Sophia asked.

"I left her with Mrs. Rennalls outside a ribbon stall. She will be sure to be entertained for hours."

A hint of a smile was on his voice. Sophia ought to be pleased with his happiness, but she could not find the strength within her to be so selfless.

"I'm sorry I didn't get to say goodbye to you at Fynwary Hall," he said, walking with his hands clasped behind his back. "My mother said you had other calls to carry out."

Sophia held her tongue.

"But, knowing you," he continued, "and knowing my mother, I'm sure I can safely surmise that you did not have other calls to pay. Unless, of course, it was to the Merricks."

She glanced up at him.

"Did my mother's behavior cause you to leave early from Fynwary?"

What could she do, lie to make him feel better, to pretend that she really did love his mother? But that was not who she was anymore. She would not hide behind a façade. She would be herself. "Truthfully, I did leave because of her, because of the things she said."

Mr. Hawkins released a heavy sigh. "I suspected as much. I'm sorry to have left you alone with her and for her treatment of you. I will have a word with her."

"There is no need. Fortunately, for both your sakes, your mother does not disapprove of Miss Kinsey as she does me."

"For both of our sakes?" he questioned.

A sigh deflated her shoulders. "I *know*, sir."

"What do you mean? You know what?"

She kept her mouth closed, unable to speak the words aloud.

"Miss Rosewall," he said, reaching out to stop her.

She pulled away from his touch, glancing around to be sure no one had seen. "Please, you mustn't reach out to me any longer. Even if we were to remain distant friends after your marriage, I hardly think your intended would appreciate you touching me."

"My marriage? Intended? Miss Rosewall, what are you speaking about?"

CHAPTER THIRTY-NINE

"**S**top, Mr. Hawkins," Sophia hissed, lowering her voice further as a couple walked by with curious eyes. "You must consider Miss Kinsey's feelings now."

She hardly thought she should be the one to correct the gentleman's conduct, especially considering how she had once behaved. But she respected Miss Kinsey enough to not allow their closeness to continue.

"Miss Kinsey?" he questioned.

"Yes, Miss Kinsey," she replied, eying his crumpled brow. "And you may cease your feigned puzzlement. I am well aware of the attachment the two of you have made."

His mouth parted, his look of utter disbelief increasing.

"Really, sir, you are doing yourself a disservice by continuing. I saw you that day, at Fynwary Hall. I heard your mother telling me that you have fallen in love with Miss Kinsey."

Mr. Hawkins squeezed his eyes shut, placing a hand to his brow. He was no doubt ashamed at his secrecy, and his lies. Perhaps even his behavior toward Sophia when he'd harbored love for Miss Kinsey all along. But she did not wish him pain.

"All is well, I assure you," she said, forcing her tone to

remain light. "And I must congratulate the two of you on your union. You will make a fine couple and—"

"No, Miss Rosewall, you misunderstand."

She stopped. "Pardon?"

He moved his hand from his head to his chest, his eyebrows drawn close together as he leaned toward her. "I am not engaged to Miss Kinsey."

"But I saw you with her."

"What you saw must have been the two of us entering my study to discuss…" He paused with a sigh. "She made me swear not to tell anyone, but I cannot allow you to believe one thing when…"

He looked around them. Without hesitancy, he grasped her hand and pulled her toward the side of a shop where no one could overhear them. They stood facing each other as he released her.

"It is true that Miss Kinsey called on me when you were visiting with my mother," he began. "However, we did not discuss our love for each other, but to discuss a love Miss Kinsey has for another man entirely. A man she knew before she even came to live with the Madderns."

As he spoke, hope threatened to burst from within her like a caged bird.

He continued. "Apparently, her parents did not approve of her choice, so they sent her to live with her aunt and uncle to forget her love and find another. But she cannot."

A wave of understanding rushed over her. Miss Kinsey's behavior, her timid nature and depressed state, all of it was due to being torn from her beloved and being forced to love another. How Sophia regretted her impatience with the woman, and her cruel treatment of her.

Mr. Hawkins continued. "She told me this because she feared I had grown an attachment to her, and she believed I deserved an explanation why she could never return my supposed affection." He paused, staring down at Sophia with a penetrating gaze. "So you see, there is no undertaking between us, and certainly no engagement."

The relief Sophia felt at Mr. Hawkins's words, the overwhelming joy she experienced—and the utter stupidity she suffered—prevented any word from leaving her mouth apart from a single, solitary, and nearly silent, "Oh."

A smile broke out on his lips. "I am sorry for all of this. I hope things are clearer for you now."

"Yes, they certainly are." What a fool she had been, again. Yet, she could not help but ask one more question. "So you were not disappointed by Miss Kinsey's revelation?"

His voice was deep and soft. "No. Because I do not love *her*." He took a step toward her. "Sophia, you must know that I…" His eyes flitted past her, and he frowned, shaking his head. "No, Mother will be finished soon. I must meet her, or she will wonder where I am."

Sophia nodded at once, willing her breathing to remain stable as the sound of her name on his lips caused a warmth to blanket her heart. "Of course, I understand."

And she did. Though that didn't mean she wasn't acutely disappointed to have not heard the rest of his words.

He leaned toward her with a determined look. "When Mother leaves, may I call on you?"

"Of course, sir," she said breathlessly.

He nodded with a curt tip of his head then turned and walked away without another word. Sophia stared after his departure. What had gotten into him, the fact that his mother might come in search of him, or that he had been about to share something so intimate, he did not wish to be interrupted?

She chewed on her lip, wandering through the town, distracted. His mother had said that Mr. Hawkins was close to becoming engaged. If she had been speaking the truth, and the woman he'd mentioned was not Miss Kinsey, then who was it?

Before she'd even asked the question, hope poured over her. But she couldn't voice it, not even in thought. Not yet. Not when it was too glorious and too wonderful a notion to dwell on for so long before she saw Mr. Hawkins again.

She determined to think no longer on it, but a smile had worked its way onto her lips long before she reached Lowena. She entered the cottage and closed the door behind her, so deep in thought that she'd made it all the way to the stairs before hearing a voice calling for her nearby.

"Sophia, there you are."

She jumped, turning to the source. "Mother?"

"We have been waiting for your return for an hour now."

Sophia stared. What was going on? Why was Mother out of her room with a smile lighting her face?

"My apologies," Sophia stammered, "I did not know you were waiting for me."

"Oh, all is well. Come, we have much to discuss with you."

"We?" She followed Mother into the sitting room, adjacent to the small entryway, to where Father stood near the fireplace.

"Good morning, Sophia," he greeted. "I trust you had a pleasant trip to St. Just?"

"I did." She had not said more than a few words to Father since that night in his study, and she had not seen her mother smile in such a way since before Lowena. What on earth was going on with the both of them?

"Come sit, my dear," Mother said, patting the chair near the fireplace as she sat down across from it. "Your father and I have wonderful news."

"Oh?" Sophia asked, her mind struggling to come to terms with the image before her. Had they not been seated in the minute sitting room of Lowena Cottage, Sophia would have thought they had somehow traveled to the past, her mother and father watching her with doting eyes, sitting before Fynwary's fireplace as they spoke about happy matters.

"Do you recall at the Madderns' ball when I'd mentioned that I had written to my aunt a few days before?" Father began.

Sophia noticed for the first time the letter he held in his hands. She swallowed. "Yes."

"Well, I am pleased to say that she has responded to my request for aid, in a way for which we could have only hoped."

Sophia waited, a strange dread filling her as the excitement in her parents' eyes grew. "And what way is that?"

"She wishes for us to come live with her at her grand estate in Yorkshire, Sophia," Mother said. Her hands were clasped in her lap as if she couldn't contain her joy. "Can you believe it?"

Sophia couldn't. She glanced between her parents. Her heart slipped from its rightful place and tumbled to the floor, preventing her from feeling happiness, peace, love.

The reason behind their joy was now clear. They finally had the chance to leave behind the life they so abhorred. The life Sophia had only now begun to love.

"But I thought Aunt June did not approve of us," she questioned, "that she despised us since Father took over Fynwary Hall?"

"Apparently, she has had a change of heart. Has she not, my dear?" Father placed a soft hand on Mother's shoulder.

Mother stared up at him with a warm smile. "It has been known to happen to us all."

Sophia stared at them, tears springing to her eyes. Weeks. It had been weeks since she'd seen her parents share such affection, when it used to be the daily standard. This was all due to their circumstances having changed, their wealth returned.

"Will it not be wonderful, Sophia?" Mother said, turning to her with hope-filled eyes. "To enjoy luxuries again, to afford dresses and shoes, even lady's maids?"

Sophia stared at the floor, trying to see what her mother

did. In truth, it *would* be fine to be able to afford such delicacies once more, to not worry if they could afford a ribbon or perhaps a new handkerchief. But moving to Yorkshire, leaving behind Cornwall, her home. Mr. Hawkins. How could she even consider such a thing?

"And Aunt has agreed to fund all of this? And to house us free of charge? Forgive me, but I don't understand why she would."

Her parents exchanged a look, and Father took a step forward. "She has agreed to spare no expense where we are concerned. We will be given a generous portion to live on yearly, and we will be allowed to remain at her estate in Yorkshire. But there is one small condition she has required."

Sophia stared. "And what is that? That we not speak of our past? That we quit Cornwall now?"

"No, it is in regard to you, Sophia." He unfolded the letter in his hand and held it up to read. "'I've had word that your daughter is a lovely creature,' she writes, 'as accomplished and charming as any woman in Town.'"

"Which certainly is true," Mother interrupted with an encouraging nod.

"Indeed," Father said before he continued. "'But I understand that she has not yet secured a husband. It just so happens that my dear friend, Mrs. Thompson, desperately desires a wealthy, amiable wife for her son. I believe your daughter may provide such a one.'"

Shock spread through Sophia's veins, her limbs growing numb.

"Is that not wonderful?" Mother asked. "Evidently, this Mr. Thompson is very handsome."

One thought crossed over the other, Sophia's mind a jumble of confusion. "But why would they wish for me to marry him when I have no dowry?"

"Oh, but Aunt June has agreed to secure that, as well, should we choose to live with her. Apparently, she is very close to this Mrs. Thompson and thinks the world of her and her son. They wish to join their families not only in friendship, but in marriage, as well. You should consider it a great honor that Aunt June has even thought of you to be a match for such a friend of hers."

Mother glowed. Father stared dotingly at his wife. But Sophia couldn't breathe. "And if I do not go to Yorkshire and marry this perfect stranger?"

"Then her invitation becomes void," Father replied.

Mother pulled back, her brow raised. "Why, Sophia. Are you truly considering refusing such an offer?"

Sophia hardly knew *what* to consider, only that her mind was on Mr. Hawkins, what he'd been about to say, and his request to call on her when his mother left.

"Sophia, my dear," Mother said softly, "I do not believe you are truly grasping the magnitude of what Aunt June is offering us. What she is offering *you*. It is a new life, a chance to start fresh, away from rumors and judgments. From those who once called us friends. Without her generous offer, the three of us will remain at this cottage for the rest of our lives, penniless and forgotten. But if you accept, we will have riches again. You will have a *dowry* again. A marriage. Think of it, Sophia. We knew finding a spouse for you was unlikely after moving here."

The words threatened to slice through Sophia's hope guarding her heart. She closed her eyes, willing the truth to fill her wounds. Mr. Hawkins had feelings for her, whether she had a fortune or not. Just as she had strong feelings for him. Knowing such a thing, how could she leave him behind, how could she leave her *heart* behind, and willingly marry another?

"Sophia?" Father spoke next, coming to sit beside her. His hand took Sophia's. "Do you think you might be able to do this for us? For our happiness?"

"For the happiness of us all?" Mother added.

The weight her parents placed on her pressed heavily on

her conscience. If Mr. Hawkins did propose to her, as a gentleman, he would provide for Sophia and for her parents. But Mother and Father would never be content to live on his charity, even if he was their son-in-law. Their pride wouldn't allow it. So would Sophia simply leave her parents behind to fend for themselves while she lived happily herself?

A memory pierced her heart. When Sophia had first moved to the cottage and hinted at the Madderns to help her escape Lowena, Mr. Hawkins had accused her of leaving her parents behind so she might live a life of leisure.

How could Sophia now, in good conscience, do the very same thing? How would Mr. Hawkins ever be able to look at her again if she chose to be selfish?

No, being selfish had no place within her now. She would be selfless. She would sacrifice her own joy, her own potential future with Mr. Hawkins, to secure the happiness of her parents.

"What is your decision then, Sophia?"

The hope lacing Mother's voice sapped what little was left within Sophia.

"Yes," she found herself saying aloud. "For you both, I will accept Aunt June's offer."

She hardly heard Mother's joyous clapping, nor saw Father leave the room to pen a response to his aunt. All she could hear was the ringing in her ears, and all she could feel was the empty beating of her hollow heart.

CHAPTER FORTY

"*I* do hope you haven't been too disappointed with your time here in Cornwall, Freddy."

Frederick quirked a brow at his mother. "As you have been disappointed?"

She pursed her lips, standing outside of her carriage. "You know I have enjoyed every moment I have spent with you."

"You'd just prefer if we were in London together," Frederick added.

"Precisely."

"That may happen yet, one day."

She sighed. "Well, I trust next time I see you, you will have found that elusive bride you so long for and hinted at. Heaven only knows how particular you are about your choice."

Frederick smiled. "I can only hope I have Heaven's help."

Mother patted his cheek. "I love you, son."

"I love *you*, Mother."

She stepped up into the carriage. "And don't give up on Miss Kinsey just yet. She really was a lovely young woman and would make you a fine wife."

Frederick shook his head. He'd just told his mother a mere ten minutes before that he would not be pursuing Miss Kinsey, that he had another woman in mind entirely. But he kept quiet on who that woman was. He didn't need his mother trying to convince him he'd made the wrong choice. He was decided on the matter, and nothing could convince him otherwise.

The morning Miss Kinsey had requested an audience with him, told him that she was in love with another, had been one of the most relieving moments of his life. He'd been worrying for so long that he'd shown too great of interest in Miss Kinsey to still honorably leave her behind to pursue another woman, namely Miss Rosewall. But at Miss Kinsey's revelation, the guilt he'd consistently felt had vanished. Best of all, he was now free to explore his feelings for Miss Rosewall.

"Goodbye, my dear," Mother said, leaning forward from her seat to peer out of the carriage door. "Write to me soon."

"I will."

He closed the door, and the carriage rolled away, his mother waving at him from the window.

A deep sigh of relief escaped his lips. She was gone. And now he would be leaving too, for Lowena Cottage.

He secured his top hat before accepting his horse the groom had brought forth. With a nod of thanks, he mounted the chestnut and trotted onward, but he didn't even make it out of Fynwary's grounds before he caught sight of a woman headed his way.

He fancied it was Miss Rosewall for a moment, but this woman's hair was lighter, and her fine dress and shimmering red reticule told him it was not Sophia, but the physician's wife, Mrs. Rennalls.

"Good day, Mr. Hawkins," she said with a curtsy as she neared. "I saw your mother departing in her carriage. I did not know she was leaving so soon."

Frederick dismounted. He itched to leave, but he didn't wish to appear rude. "Yes, she has had enough time away from London, I believe."

"What a shame. I had just thought to come over and offer her a sleeping draught from my husband."

"My apologies."

"Oh, it is no matter. Just so long as *you* will not be leaving us soon, as well."

"Not to worry, ma'am. I have every intention of remaining as long as possible in Cornwall."

"Oh, that is wonderful, for so many of us are coming and going. Your mother. The Stedmans. The Causeys have only now just returned, just as the Rosewalls are leaving. It truly is—"

"E-excuse me. The Rosewalls?"

"Why, yes. Don't tell me you haven't heard the latest in regard to their circumstances?"

An unsettling feeling upset his stomach, as if bees had swarmed his insides. "No, I haven't."

"Well, allow me to tell you."

Frederick hadn't known Mrs. Rennalls for long, but he already knew that she was an incorrigible gossip. She would do anything to spread information to others. He hated the fact that he was indulging the woman's base desires, but he couldn't help his curiosity.

Mrs. Rennalls leaned forward, lowering her voice to a conspiratorial tone. "I suppose you will have been too taken up with your mother to have not heard," Mrs. Rennalls continued, "but it has been the talk of St. Just. You see, Mr. Rosewall's estranged aunt has written to them and offered them a place to stay at their estate in Yorkshire. And the Rose-walls have accepted."

"Have they?" he asked, struggling to keep his voice steady.

"Indeed, I heard it from Mrs. Rosewall herself. The woman has stayed indoors for weeks, no sight nor sound from her since she moved to Lowena. Now that her situation has changed, she has not hesitated to share news of her good fortune with us all."

He looked away. "Have they all agreed to go to Yorkshire? Miss Rosewall, as well?"

"Oh, yes, Miss Rosewall especially. You see, she has been offered a substantial dowry if she marries a very wealthy friend of her great aunt's."

Frederick's jaw twitched, his hands fisting.

"Of course she readily accepted," Mrs. Rennalls said. "How could she not, with the promise of her life and her fortune changed forever?"

His voice fell flat. "Indeed, how could she not?"

"I believe they are to leave within a few days, but that is all I know."

He nodded, turning to his horse. "Well, thank you, Mrs. Rennalls, for the information. But right now, I fear I must excuse myself."

"Of course, sir. I am sorry to have kept you. Do enjoy your day." She sent him a pleasant smile, unaware of the turmoil inside him.

He mounted his horse and kicked him forward. Rage pulsed through his body as the hooves pounded across the countryside. What a fool he was, how idiotically he'd behaved. Falling for Miss Rosewall, believing she'd changed when he knew all along she would not. She would always seek wealth first, and the better gentleman.

How had he allowed his guard to fall? And how could she have betrayed him, after all he'd shared with her, all he'd done to help her?

He reached the cottage, flying off his horse and striding toward the house. He didn't bother with the gate, merely placed a hand on the stone wall and used it as leverage to hop over the barrier in a single leap. He pounded three times on the flimsy wood of the front door and awaited a reply.

When no one answered, he removed his hat and hit his fist against the door again.

This time, a plump woman appeared, the cap on her head

lopsided, a stunned expression on her round face.

"Mr. Hawkins to see Miss Rosewall," he stated before she had the chance to say a word.

"The ladies of the house ain't seein' callers, sir. But I'll tell them ye—"

"I must speak with Miss Rosewall."

The housekeeper raised her chin. "I be sorry, sir. But she—"

As anger took over his reason, he flattened his hand against the door and pushed it farther open.

"Sir!"

"Miss Rosewall?" he bellowed out, looking around the small entryway before his eyes fell on the stairs. Was she up there, packing away her finery for her new life? "Miss Rosewall!"

Finally, she appeared at the top of the stairs, eyes rounded, nose red. Her appearance twisted the dagger already in his back.

"Mr. Hawkins? What are you..." Her words faded away. She must have intended to leave Cornwall without a word to him.

Mrs. Rosewall appeared behind her with the same stunned expression. "Why, Mr. Hawkins, is that you? What in heaven's name are you doing here?"

"He be askin' to call upon Miss Rosewall, ma'am, though I told him ye were busy." The housekeeper turned to him with annoyance, her fists propped on her hips.

Mr. Rosewall appeared next, coming up to stand beside his wife. His eyes fixed on Frederick, though he said not a word.

"Well, Mr. Hawkins, I'm sure my daughter appreciates your calling," Mrs. Rosewall said. She did not lower her chin as she stared down at him. "But I do apologize. We have much to tend to at the moment. We hardly have time for a social visit. You see, we are to travel to—"

"I know," he said, his eyes remaining on Miss Rosewall. "And I should have expected it all along."

Even from the bottom of the stairs, Frederick could see the tears in her eyes. Her sadness was a ruse. She wasn't heartbroken to leave him. It was all just a game to get what she wanted.

Suddenly, he wondered why the devil he cared if the woman left. He ought to be glad. Now he would not have to spend another moment of heartache with her.

He shook his head, taking a few steps back before quitting the house without a word.

"Frederick, wait! Please!"

Mrs. Rosewall gasped, Miss Rosewall called again, but Frederick closed the door behind him, ignoring the way his heart throbbed at her use of his given name.

He had not moved halfway through the garden before the door opened and closed again.

"Please, you must allow me to explain," Miss Rosewall said, coming up fast behind him.

"Must I?" he questioned over his shoulder. "There is no need. I understand you perfectly, Miss Rosewall."

"No, you cannot know what has caused me to follow my parents to Yorkshire."

She was running to keep up with him, and when he abruptly turned, she nearly ran into him.

"I do know," he spat out. "I know all too well. You have not changed. You are the same as you have always been."

She recoiled. "How can you say such a thing? After what—"

"Because you are still the same, Miss Rosewall! Even after all this time. You are still choosing wealth, still choosing better circumstances over m—"

He stopped. He couldn't say it. He couldn't reveal the brunt of his pain, the very reason he was there now, so troubled with her choices. It was all just a blinder, placed over his eyes to prevent him from dwelling on the fact that she had chosen wealth and position over *him*.

"But I haven't chosen wealth. I only go to Yorkshire for—"

"Yourself," he finished for her, his voice cold, biting. "You go for yourself, to have the better life you so longed for. Never mind what I could have offered you and your family. Never mind the life we might have shared together."

She shook her head with ferocity, her voice faltering. "No, please. My decision was not made lightly."

Confusion and pain shrouded his heart. "No, but it was made by you, wasn't it? It was your decision to leave."

Her lips parted, sorrow turning her brow. "Yes, but not—"

The door opened behind them, and Mrs. Rosewall stepped over the threshold. "Sophia? Sophia, we mustn't delay. Aunt June and your intended will be awaiting our arrival, and there is still much to be done."

Miss Rosewall winced, turning back to Frederick with a look of pleading.

Her intended. Miss Rosewall's intended. It should've been him, but he wasn't enough for her. He was never enough.

"Please," Miss Rosewall whispered, taking a step toward him.

"Sophia?" her mother called out.

Frederick backed away. "Do enjoy yourself in Yorkshire, Miss Rosewall." His voice was calm as he replaced his hat. "I trust you will. For how could you not, being with people as empty as yourself?"

The words fell from his mouth before he could think better of them. He could not look at her again, knowing the pain he might see in her eyes after his harsh attack. He mounted his horse and rode away in a mad dash, leaving the cottage and Miss Rosewall behind. How he regretted going to her home, spending so much time with her, meeting the woman at all.

And how he regretted falling in love with her.

CHAPTER FORTY-ONE

A steady stream of tears fell from Sophia's eyes as Mr. Hawkins rode away from Lowena, from herself, and from her life.

With heavy footsteps, she returned to her mother who stood waiting for her in the doorway.

"Sophia, what in the world is going on?"

Her feigned jovial nature from before, put on for Mr. Hawkins's benefit, was now gone, replaced with shock.

But Sophia couldn't speak of the matter. The pain was too raw.

"Nothing, Mother," she said, walking by her to enter the house.

She moved past Mrs. Cuff's stunned expression and headed to the stairs. Father had disappeared.

"Nothing?" Mother spoke after her. "Mr. Hawkins has barged into our home, you have called him by his Christian name, then the two of you shout outside for all of Cornwall to hear. You tell me that is nothing?"

Sophia didn't respond as she walked up the steps, her hand sliding along the banister. She had always been afraid of picking up splinters by using the uneven wood of the handrail.

Now, any pain would be a welcome distraction from the agony within her heart.

"Sophia?" Mother called at the bottom of the stairs. "Do you…do you have a relationship with that man?"

Sophia paused, turning to stare down at her mother from the top step. "No. I do not."

Not anymore.

She moved to her room and closed the door behind her. Countless times, she had done the very same, hoping, praying one of her parents would follow her into her room.

Now, as her mother knocked and allowed herself into the privacy of Sophia's chamber, Sophia longed to be alone.

"Please, Mother. Not right now." She sat at the edge of her bed, her back facing the door.

"But, my dear," Mother said, coming to stand before her, "you must explain to me what has just occurred."

Sophia wiped the tears sliding down her cheeks. "I can't."

Mother sighed with a perplexed brow. She sat down on the bed beside Sophia. "Sophia, dear, do you have feelings for Mr. Hawkins?"

Sophia's brows pulled together. "I do."

Mother sat back, blinking in surprise. "Well, this is unexpected."

Sophia reached under her pillow for the handkerchief from Mr. Hawkins, the one she'd kept from the picnic, after he'd dabbed it on her brow. She could just imagine the musky scent it once held before she'd had the fabric washed, and a fresh wave of sorrow rendered her unable to formulate a single word.

Mother pursed her lips. "Can you explain to me how these feelings have come about? How you could have fallen in love with the very man who started the collapse of our family?"

Sophia's heart bent. "He has *saved* our family, Mother." She turned away, lowering her voice. "He has saved *me*."

"That is entirely untrue. Aunt June has saved us. She has

offered us wealth, improvements on our housing and connections. The chance to escape the rumors around our name. A new life. Mr. Hawkins has done nothing of the sort."

Sophia stared, dumbfounded at Mother's ignorance. "He purchased our home, saving Father from debtor's prison. He offered us the chance to live free of charge at Lowena before he even came to know us. He was the only gentleman who did not reject me when he saw my fall from grace." She paused, staring toward the window, the sound of the waves softly splashing beneath them. "And he offered me kindness and friendship, when no one else would give me the same."

Mother's nostrils flared. Of course she would take offense at Sophia's words. She was not used to hearing her daughter speak the truth. No one was. Except Mr. Hawkins.

Mother leaned forward, clutching Sophia's hand in her own. "My dear, you are not thinking clearly. You are not in love with Mr. Hawkins, only the *idea* of Mr. Hawkins. The idea of taking residence at Fynway Hall again, of having wealth and propriety once more associated with your name."

Slowly, she met Mother's eyes, her mouth agape. "How could you think so little of me to believe I would marry Mr. Hawkins for his wealth, to return to Fynwary Hall? I wish to marry for love, as you and Father did."

Mother raised her chin. "Love is all well and fine. But having a means to survive does wonders for the happiness of a relationship."

Sophia stared. Did Mother mean to say she was happy in her marriage only when wealth was involved? Of course that is what she meant. Sophia had seen the evidence the moment they left Fynwary Hall, and the moment they received word that their poor living conditions would end.

Sophia's brows pulled together in disgust. How could her parents live such a way? How could Sophia have ever considered living the same way?

Mother reached forward, trying to take her hand, but

Sophia pulled away, standing and crossing the room to stare out of the window.

Mother remained seated on the bed. "Sophia, please, try to see reason. In Yorkshire, your troubles would be forgotten. You could begin again, away from the gossip surrounding your name. In marrying Mr. Thompson, you would have twice the wealth and twice the reach in Society that Mr. Hawkins could ever offer you. That is, if he had ever truly considered you for a wife."

The words cut deeply. Mother would have her believe that Sophia was worth nothing without a dowry. But Mr. Hawkins had intended to marry Sophia. Had he not? Had love not shown for her in his eyes, despite the mistakes she'd made, despite her many flaws?

Her head drooped forward, her eyes sliding along the glass of the window as she leaned against the ledge. Her finger brushed against something cold and smooth.

The shell.

With her eyes, she caressed the perfect ridges, the smooth blend of colors. The large crack at the bottom.

Mistakes, flaws.

The words breathed back life into her heart, one thump, two. Faster and faster as her thoughts took flight.

Mr. Hawkins had said that flaws made a person unique, beautiful, because then one could change. Well, Sophia was more aware of her flaws than ever, and she could change. She *had* changed. She merely needed to remind Mr. Hawkins, and herself, how greatly she had.

Would he accept her, even after he believed that she was leaving him for a wealthier gentleman, harming him the way he'd been so harmed by others?

She ran a finger along the crack of the shell. Even if he did not accept her, she had to try. Now.

Whirling on her heel, Sophia made for the door.

"Where are you going?" Mother burst out.

"To find Mr. Hawkins."

Her fingers stretched toward the door, but Mother's soft words from behind made her hand freeze midair.

"And what about us?" she asked. "If you choose Mr. Hawkins, and he miraculously chooses you, then what happens to me and your father?"

Sophia spoke over her shoulder. "You will come live with us at Fynwary Hall. Or Mr. Hawkins could give you money to—"

"You and I both know your father would never accept such charity."

"But you will accept it from Aunt June?"

She could only imagine Mother's nostrils flaring at Sophia's impudence. "We are not happy here, Sophia. We cannot be, with so many of our old friends knowing so much of what has gone on."

She stood from the bed and approached Sophia. "When Aunt June's offer came, your father and I felt joy for the first time since coming to Lowena."

Sophia's back curved, the weight of her mother's words falling on her shoulders again.

"We were happy, my dear," Mother said, reaching out to wipe the tears falling from Sophia's eyes. "Your father and I discovered our love again, for each other and for you. If you choose to remain here and not go to Yorkshire, what if our love is never to be seen, never to be felt again?"

Sophia pulled away from Mother's touch. She couldn't think, so crippled she was between her duty to her parents and her love for Mr. Hawkins.

But she had to make a choice, and she knew what, and who, it would be.

"Mother, how is it fair for you to ask me to give up my love for the love you already have, but choose not to see?"

Mother's eyes hardened. "Sophia, you know nothing of—"

The door opened with a click, swinging wide until it

bounced softly against the wall. Father stood in the doorway. He ducked his head to enter the room beneath the low frame, then straightened to his full height.

"My dear," Mother said, raising her chin, "our daughter has—"

"I know," he said. "I heard what she has said." He turned to Sophia. "And I have heard enough."

The deep tone to his voice, the finality of his words caused a frenzy within Sophia. Would he force her to go to Yorkshire, to marry a man she did not love, forsaking the man she did?

"Father, please, I cannot—"

"No, Sophia. You have grown accustomed to doing your own bidding at Lowena. But now, you will do as I say."

He took a step toward her, but Sophia held her ground, staring at him headlong as she braced herself for the argument to come.

CHAPTER FORTY-TWO

*F*rederick ignored the call of the ocean. When once the soothing sound had calmed his heart, now it chafed his sullen mood. The constant waves sliding up the shore that evening, sending the sand into a frenzy, reminded him too greatly of the disarray of his own life. And the blue of the sea, the clearness of the water, reminded him all too well of the woman he could not forget.

Of course, standing at the gate of Lowena cottage did not help in that regard. But being there could not be avoided. He had to look over the house to ensure it was fit for tenants before he returned to Dawnridge tomorrow.

Dawnridge. He should be looking forward to returning home more than he was. After all, there he could live out his days in peace. He could forget his fanciful ideas of marriage, of finding a woman who could ever love him more than she loved herself, more than she loved her standing in Society. More than wealth.

For him, such a woman did not exist.

He rolled his neck, hoping to ease the tension that had been creeping in all day. The evening was not warm by any means, the clouds had already shrouded the sun, a light grey spreading over the sea and countryside. Yet, a heat rose within him, boiling his skin. He removed his jacket, gloves, and hat, laying them over his horse's saddle before trudging across the small grounds.

He tried to disregard the significance of returning to the cottage, to dispel the regret he felt blaring at every turn. But with each step he took, memories of his last moments there resurfaced. His wariness increased, making it harder to walk, as if an unseen rope was wrapped about his being, preventing him from the slightest progression. Just as it had been doing for three days.

Three days. She'd been gone three long days. Each moment, he'd expected it to get easier to forget the longing, the regret. The love. Yet, each day proved harder than the last. He'd kept inside his house, refused callers, meals, anything he could think of to keep his mind from the woman who had left him for another. Such a task proved impossible, when, in every direction he turned at Fynwary or on the cliffside, the memory of Sophia Rosewall blared back at him. Even the very door of the cottage spoke her name.

He hesitated before it. He was only holding a simple inspection. Just a few moments and he could leave his memories behind with Lowena. So why was entering inside so difficult?

With an unsteady hand, he tapped on the door, though he knew no one would answer. He hated himself for hoping Miss Rosewall herself would appear, flinging her arms around his neck and begging him to take her back.

But the cottage was empty as he opened the door. Silent, apart from the rushing waves on the shore below sounding around the bare walls.

He secured the door behind him, surveying the room with wary eyes. His first time within the home had been when he had confronted Miss Rosewall. He had not taken any notice then of the peeling paint or warped wood. He'd neglected his duty as their landlord. But he'd been distracted. By Miss Rosewall.

He took a quick look in each vacated room, making a mental note of the repairs his newly hired steward would need to see to, then moved up the stairs. The first two bedrooms he looked through appeared better managed, but the one at the end of the corridor, the smallest of the three, seemed the worse for wear.

A breeze blew past him as he opened the door. He glanced straightway to the open window, where the sea's muted waters reached his eye.

A view of the sea. That could only mean this was Miss Rosewall's room. *Had been* Miss Rosewall's room. His boots shuffled across the floor as he noted the state of the chipped paint, cobwebbed corners, and scratched flooring. The hearth was miniscule, not to mention filthy, and the bed hardly seemed large enough for a single body to fit length-wise on it.

He could only imagine what she had thought of such a room, after what she had been accustomed to at Fynwary Hall.

Facing the window, he tugged at the handle, but it didn't budge. He looked closer to discover it wasn't really open, only that the glass did not fit properly within its frame. The gap was so large, his fisted hand could fit through it.

How had the woman managed the undoubtedly large draft that must have seeped through the opening on cold evenings or rainy days? The fireplace must not have been any use to her either, what with the miniscule size of it.

Yet, had he ever heard her complain about the state of her living quarters? No. All she'd mentioned was her view of the sea.

He rubbed a hand to his chest to dispel the twinge in his heart. She must have found it unbelievably difficult to live in such circumstances. Though, toward the end, had she not considered Lowena her home? Was this not evidence that she had, indeed, changed?

He shook his head. He could not entertain such thoughts. She was still the same selfish woman. *That* was the truth. Being at the house and in her old room had merely warped his thoughts. He needed to leave, before even more dangerous notions threatened to change his mind about the woman.

He turned to depart, but his eyes dropped to the window ledge where a shell rested, its orange and white colors dimmed from the subdued light outside. A single crack marred its otherwise flawless surface.

She'd kept it. Miss Rosewall had kept the shell he'd given her at Tregalwen. The words he had spoken to her as she sat broken on the beach infiltrated the defenses protecting his mind, and the memory shook his weakening core.

Just because something is flawed, doesn't mean it is not worth cherishing.

He'd told her that no one was perfect, that she could come back from her mistakes, and he had meant it. Yet, when his own words had been tested, he'd lost his temper. He had called her "empty."

He retrieved the shell, eying the crack. Flashes of their time together sailed by. Sophia's admiring eyes, the attraction between them, the vulnerability and truths she'd shared with him and him alone—all of it was evidence, evidence of something he had denied for too long.

She loved him. Or was this shell she'd left behind evidence that she no longer did?

His thoughts spun, his mind a daze. If she *had* loved him, then why would she choose to leave him? Why would she marry another?

He tapped the shell softly against the wall. Mrs. Rennalls had told him that the Rosewalls' aunt would choose Miss Rosewall's intended, or her family would receive nothing.

Miss Rosewall herself had mentioned her parents when

he'd confronted her, but he had not allowed her to speak. By leaving, could she…could she have been acting on behalf of her parents, putting their welfare above her own, instead of doing so to improve her own standing with Society?

The truth struck him so fully, his legs weakened. He rested his hands on the window ledge to keep from falling. How could he have been so stupid? How could he have been so wrong?

He tried to swallow his shame, but his thick regret prevented him. He pulled at his cravat, untying it in a frenzy, his fingers fumbling over the knot until the white fabric trailed down his waistcoat.

It was not Miss Rosewall who had made an unforgivable mistake. It was not Miss Rosewall who was irrevocably flawed. It was he. If he wouldn't have ignored every thought of her, if he wouldn't have been so fiercely adamant of keeping hold of his own selfish desires, he might have come to the realization sooner. Perhaps then he would have listened to her explanation. Perhaps then he could have stopped her from leaving.

Now, it was too late. She was already gone.

How he regretted his mistake.

Unbuttoning his collar, he made his way out of the cottage with the shell in hand, facing the sea as he secured the outer door behind him.

The earth had turned a soft, rosy shade, matching the blossoming pink wildflowers scattered near the cottage, waving back and forth in the breeze. The sky stretched into a light purple before it fell into the steely blue sea. Placid waves kissed the smooth, white sand of the shore below. The world around him was calm, peaceful.

How it mocked him.

With a heavy step, he turned toward the stone wall of the cottage, heading for the gate. But when he glanced up to his horse tied nearby, his feet stopped.

No, it couldn't be. It was simply his imagination, his

thoughts from before conjuring a spright. She was not there at Lowena Cottage.

And yet, she was.

"Sophia," he breathed.

She watched him, her hand resting on his horse's forelock, her body half-hidden by the mount.

"Good evening," she said, as if her presence were the most natural thing in the world, as if she had not just assailed his heart with a fresh bout of emotions.

"You're here," was all he managed to say. His feet would not move. His mind would not function. All his senses centered on the woman before him.

His eyes followed the wave-like curls framing her face. The darkness of her locks, more visible due to her lack of bonnet, were nearly tinted pink in the light. She wore her blue gown again. Had she mended the hole her washing had created? He didn't have time to notice before her captivating eyes caught him in their grasp.

"What are you doing here?" he asked.

His horse nuzzled closer to the woman, taunting Frederick's distance from her.

"I happened to be walking by when I saw your horse," she replied in a soft tone, stroking the horse's nose. "He looked lonely, so I thought to wait out here for you with him."

He blinked, attempting to break the spell the woman had cast over him, causing him to forget what had occurred between them, what *now* needed to occur.

"What are you doing in Cornwall?" he asked next. "I thought you were going to Yorkshire, to be with your aunt and your intended."

Her eyes trailed down the bridge of the horse's nose. "I chose not to go, as I have finally discovered the answer."

He held his burgeoning hope down as he would a hound nipping at his coattail. He could not allow his senses to take leave. Not when he had so many questions to be answered, not when he had so much to say.

"You have found the answer to what?" he asked.

"Do you recall the question you asked me at your picnic?"

His mind traveled to when they had stood at the brook, after she'd shared with him how greatly she'd disliked so many of the pastimes she ought to enjoy. "I asked you what you wished to do."

"Yes." The breeze fluttered her curls. "I have finally found my answer."

"And what is that?"

She stroked the tip of the gelding's nose one last time before coming out from behind the horse. She took a few steps, then fully faced Frederick. "I wish to remain here."

He searched for a reply, trying to decipher her reasoning behind her desire. "Well, if you are to remain in Cornwall, you and your family are welcome to call Lowena your own for as long as you wish. I was to let it to another family before I left, but if you have need of it still—"

"You're leaving?"

The sight of her crestfallen face did more for his confidence than anything. She was upset about him leaving, and that knowledge set free his hopes, allowing them to sail higher than the pink clouds above the sea.

CHAPTER FORTY-THREE

"*I* was going to return to Bedfordshire tomorrow morning."

Sophia felt as if her heart had been wrung dry like a rag. Mr. Hawkins was leaving Cornwall? He couldn't. Not now.

She stared at him across the stone wall, love for the man standing before her once more filling her heart. She'd seen his jacket, gloves, and hat over his horse's saddle earlier. Now she couldn't help but stare at the state of his undress. His waistcoat was still buttoned, but his cravat hung loosely about his neck. His hair was tousled, as if the wind had taken a liking to it and couldn't help but fling it back and forth.

His disheveled appearance, the weary dimness to his eyes, made her wonder if the past few days had been as difficult for him as it had been for her.

"Thank you for the offer," she said, "but we will not be requiring Lowena Cottage any longer."

He narrowed his eyes. "May I ask why not?"

The white flaps of his loose collar lifted in the wind, tapping against his shoulders. His shirt draped open, allowing her to see the muscular curves of the top of his chest and angular lines of his throat.

She averted her gaze. "My father has accepted a job as a clerk in St. Austell. They have taken a home in the city."

His brow rose. "I see. Well, I wish them every happiness while living there." He looked out to the sea, the pink glow of the sunset cast across his skin. "And you, as well, of course."

"Thank you, but as I said before, I have chosen to remain here."

His eyes met hers. "But where are you to live then, if it is not with your parents or at Lowena?"

"I have been staying with Gwynna for the past few days." Her lips twitched at his perplexed brow. The fact that she was living with a miner's family had surprised her at first, as well. Though now it felt as natural as anything. "The Merricks were kind enough to offer me a room when I told them my parents were leaving and I wished to remain here. I am earning my keep, though, in every chore possible. Except for the laundry, for obvious reasons."

There it was, the curve of his lips she'd been longing to see. "Have you torn another dress?" he asked.

"I'm afraid so. This time it was Mrs. Merrick's. She has put me to better use scrubbing pots. Those I cannot break so easily."

The tension eased between them, if only slightly. "I'm surprised your parents have allowed you to remain in St. Just," he said. "After what your aunt promised them."

She tipped her head. "How did you learn of her proposal earlier, and that I was to leave?"

"Mrs. Rennalls."

He didn't need to say more. Sophia knew of the woman's love for gossip, but Mrs. Rennalls could hardly be blamed.

The day after Aunt June's letter had come, Mother had spent all day in St. Just, hoping to happen upon someone she could blather on to about her changed circumstances. That was yet another reason they'd chosen to relocate to St. Austell, to leave behind the gossip that surrounded them.

Sophia missed them. She had since leaving Fynwary Hall. She could only hope the distance between them would ease her parents' burden and allow them time to adjust to their new way of life, as Sophia had done.

"Your parents couldn't have been happy with your decision to remain here," Mr. Hawkins said next. "I'm surprised they even allowed you to do so."

Sophia took a step forward, resting her hands on the stone wall between them. "Mother was displeased. I thought my father would be adamantly opposed, as well, but he surprised me."

Her thoughts returned to days before when Father had entered her room after her argument with Mother. She'd expected him to command her to go to Yorkshire.

"You have grown accustomed to doing your own bidding at Lowena," he had said to her. "But now, you will do as I say. You will not go to Yorkshire. You will choose your own life."

Mother had stared, appalled, but Sophia had run straight to Father, embracing him as she fought off her tears.

Even now, at the mere memory of his words, she had to force aside her emotions. "My father said he no longer wished to make decisions that harmed others or changed the course of their lives. I suppose he has made enough mistakes for his liking." She looked away. "Very much like his daughter in that regard."

Mr. Hawkins's eyes were upon her, but he made no move to speak. Her heart raced. She needed to find the courage to say what she had been rehearsing for days, to share the words that had been keeping her at Gwynna's, instead of running straight to Fynwary Hall and confessing her love.

She would not cower again. She was finished hiding behind the masks of fear and falsehood that she'd created as Miss Rosewall of Fynwary Hall. Now it was time for her to hold her head high as simply Sophia.

"Sir," she began, standing just outside the open gate, "I

must apologize to you for what has occurred. For the misunderstanding. The mistake I made even considering going to Yorkshire was—"

"Mistake?" He ran his fingers through his hair. "Mistake," he muttered again with a shake of his head. "You were acting on behalf of your parents, Miss Rosewall. You made no mistake. I have."

He took a step toward her, sorrow pricking his eyes. "I have been a fool. Prideful and blind. I thought to teach you my ways, to humble you." He made a sniff of derision. "But it is you who have humbled me. I should have known, with your aunt's proposal, that you were behaving selflessly, but I was blinded by my anger. I am sorry for how I treated you. For not trusting you. For hurting you. I hope one day you might forgive me, though I would not blame you if you cannot."

Sophia's heart warmed despite the dimming light of the evening. She leaned her head to one side. "After all the times I have had to beg *your* forgiveness, with you readily bestowing it, I hardly think it fair if I do not accept your apology."

A look of understanding passed between them, a hesitant smile.

Mr. Hawkins walked toward her with an outstretched hand. "Here," he said.

She held out her hand at his bidding, and he placed the shell—her beautiful, broken shell—into her palm.

"I didn't know you had kept it that day on the beach," he said.

She stared at the ridges. "Yes, it was a good reminder for me."

"And yet, you did not take it with you when you left Lowena."

"No, I didn't."

"May I ask why?"

She stared up at him. "I feared I would not find the courage to come to Fynwary Hall and speak with you. So by leaving the shell here, I thought you might come to the cottage one day and happen upon it. I had hoped that it would remind you of me, the person who you have helped me to become."

He didn't speak, nor did he move closer to her, but his stance shifted. His back a little straighter, his shoulders more level.

His eyes softened as he stared down at her, spurring on Sophia's confidence. "My father regrets many of his choices," she continued. "And I believe my mother does, as well. But I have no desire to live in such a way, with such regrets. Before they left for St. Austell, and I for the Merrick's, Father told me whatever I chose to do, first and foremost, I ought to follow my heart." She raised her eyebrows, speaking ardently. "I wish you to know, Frederick, that I did. I followed my heart. And it has led me back here, to you."

Time stood still. His throat bobbed as he swallowed. The look in his eyes commanded her attention. In swift movements, he strode toward her with a determined stride, and her heart leapt. His hands cupped her face with a gentleness she hadn't expected. His shoulders raised as his fingers reached around to the nape of her neck, his thumbs resting at the sides of her face. His eyes moved between hers before dropping to her lips.

Her mouth parted, and she curved her neck back, watching him draw nearer, closer until she closed her eyes. She waited anxiously, impatiently, as his breath caressed her mouth before finally, his lips pressed against hers.

His kiss halted all thoughts, all worries within her mind, all the while heightening her senses. The sound of the ocean's waves mixed with his deep breaths. The scent of the sea mingled with his earthy cologne. The smooth wind blew her hair from her brow as his thumbs stroked her skin. But the taste of his mouth on hers as he shared his affection, shared his feelings...nothing could compare.

This was what she desired most of all. This was what she had been wishing for, longing for, all her life. To be held, to be protected, to be loved by the man who she loved in return.

For he did love her. It was evident in the way he kissed her, the way he held her tenderly, sweetly, as if she were the most precious person in the world.

Frederick's heart swelled. To have Miss Rosewall's lips—to have Sophia's lips—on his, to taste of her sweetness, her goodness, it was everything he had hoped it would be.

He tilted his head, softly urging her to do the same, and their kiss deepened. His hands slipped from her face, trailing down her shoulders and arms before holding her waist. He waited, gauging her response.

His breathing nearly stopped as her hands traveled the length of his chest. One hand curved around his neck. The other lingered where his shirt parted, her fingers resting against his skin. She was sure to feel the heavy thudding of his heart, but he did not give a care. He wanted her to feel the effect she had on him, to feel how he responded to her touch. He wanted her to see how his heart beat truly, solely for her.

He tightened his hold on her, fearing if he let go, she might evaporate into the very air he no longer wished to breathe, for it meant breathing in a moment less of Sophia.

How he had ever managed to live without her, he did not know. One thing was for certain, he would never do so again.

Slowly, he ended their kiss, resting his forehead on hers with a deep sigh. "I have wanted to kiss you for so long," he whispered.

"As have I," she said, a smile on her lips.

He pulled back, peering down into her eyes, her captivating, sea-blue eyes. "When I first came to Cornwall, I thought I knew what I wanted. I had my life planned out, who I would meet, with whom I would fall in love. Then I met you." He smiled, brushing away a curl that blew across her brow. "And I discovered that love is not always where we expect to find it. I am only grateful that you were able to push past my stubborn pride to help me see that what I have wished for all along is standing right before me."

Moisture gleamed in Sophia's eyes as tears brimmed in his own. "How I love you, my darling Sophia. How I long to hold you forevermore." He reached for her hands, pulling them up and holding them between their chests. He leaned forward, resting his brow on hers once more. "How I long to never be parted from you again. Will you allow me that, Sophia? Will you marry me?"

Her radiant face reflected his own joy. "Yes. Yes, Frederick. I will marry you."

And their lips met once more.

EPILOGUE

*I*t had been a wonderful dream, though Frederick could not recall what it was about. Something had tickled his brow, stirring him from the pleasant slumber. He sighed, and another tickle occurred, though this time on his lips.

He smiled. He knew that kiss anywhere, and the laugh that followed. He opened his eyes, squinting from the bright sun before he could see the blue sky above him. Or rather, eyes that resembled the sky. Eyes that were framed with dark lashes and shone with mirth.

"Sophia," he murmured sleepily. "What are you about?"

She grinned as she leaned over him. "Merely showing you the same courtesy you showed me when we first met."

His eyebrows raised. "I hardly recall kissing you then."

She swatted him on his leg, sitting upright on the blanket they'd laid out on the sand. "No, silly. I was waking you up before the tide reaches us."

He groaned as he sat up next to her, twisting out the knots in his back. "I'm sorry I fell asleep."

"That's all right. Shakespeare puts me to sleep, as well."

She winked at him, and his heart filled with love, as it always did when he looked upon his wife.

His wife.

It had only been two weeks since their marriage, and yet, the words still thrilled him. *His wife.* They'd had the banns read the Sunday after he'd proposed, neither of them seeing any reason to prolong what they both wished for.

It had been a simple affair, though the church was filled to its capacity. His mother had made the journey from London again, but Frederick was shocked to see her smiling face when she'd exited the carriage.

"My son! To be married at last! Oh, how thrilled I am."

She'd even gone so far as to embrace Sophia, welcoming her into the fold of the Hawkins family. "We Hawkinses are of a hearty breed," she'd said. "My son has told me how you've risen above the worst of it. You will fit right in with us, my dear."

She'd paused, whispering her next words in Sophia's ear. "I hope you will forgive my earlier treatment of you. My son's happiness is first and foremost what I desire, but he has been hurt by many in his life. I have since discovered, however, that you have chosen him above greater wealth and circumstances. I sincerely believe you will be the woman to finally provide him with the happiness he deserves."

They'd shared a warm smile, though Sophia had been fairly stunned into silence.

Another surprise occurred when Sophia's parents attended the wedding and the celebrations after. They were kind and polite to both Sophia and Frederick, and though they remained mostly in the background to avoid attracting more attention, they both shed tears of joy as the couple were pronounced husband and wife.

Frederick had been approached by Mr. Rosewall before they'd returned to St. Austell. "I want you to know, son, that I will be setting aside a monthly fund for Sophia's dowry."

Frederick had immediately protested, but Mr. Rosewall silenced him with a raised hand. "I know neither of you need it, but it is my duty as a father. You will understand one day."

Frederick knew refusing the money would only offend the man, so he graciously accepted the offer. Though, he was already creating ways to help his new parents-in-law with their finances later on. Still, the gesture proved to increase his respect for Mr. Rosewall, and that was more than welcome for both Frederick and Sophia.

A soft sigh broke into his thoughts, and he turned to Sophia. She stared out at the sea, her eyes soaking in the sights as a peaceful smile spread across her lips.

"I assume that is a sigh of happiness, and not one of boredom," he said.

She turned to him. "Oh, yes. A very happy sigh."

"Good."

That was what he wished, for his wife to be as happy as he was. For he *was* happy, happier than he ever thought possible. Happier than he'd ever dreamed of being. And it was all due to Sophia, and the blessing she was in his life.

Sophia glanced to Frederick. The deep contentment in his eyes that she had grown accustomed to seeing was still reflected in their depths.

"And are you happy, too, my dear husband?" she asked.

He leaned forward, kissing her temple as he wrapped his arm around her. "I am. Though, I cannot help but wonder if you truly are satisfied with not going on a wedding trip. It still isn't too late, you know. We could see the Lake District, Devon. Visit your Aunt June in Yorkshire." He winked. "I'd even go to London if you wished it."

She smiled, shaking her head as she leaned against his

shoulder. "No, there is no need. As I said before, this is all I desire."

He kissed her again, resting his head on hers. "So what do we have planned for tomorrow then?"

She raised her head from his shoulder. "We were to go horseback riding, I believe."

"Excellent. You are sure to enjoy that."

"Yes, I'm sure I shall."

Since the wedding trip was not to be, and they weren't planning to visit Dawnridge until winter, Frederick had insisted on taking Sophia on various outings each day since the wedding.

"This will help you discover what pastime you *do* enjoy," he'd said.

Sophia had kissed him in response, which, incidentally, was a pastime she was discovering to enjoy very much. Far more than playing the pianoforte or stitching.

Thus far, they had relaxed on the beach, visited old castles, attended a number of plays, and toured around the country-side. What Sophia was beginning to realize through it all was that she enjoyed things far better, no matter the pastime, when Frederick was by her side.

Unless they played whist. She could not play opposite his team, for he always seemed to win, and that she could not bear.

"What are you thinking about to make you smile so?"

She eyed him. "You."

"Is that so?" he asked, a mischievous glint to his eye. "And what is it that you are thinking about me?"

Typically, she would tease him right back, but as she stared up at him, her heart overflowing with love, she could not help but speak the truth.

"About how happy you make me. How you accept me, flaws and all. From the moment I met you, I knew I could be myself. It was as if my soul trusted you, as if it knew you before my mind even had the opportunity to decide."

He smiled down at her, placing a finger under her chin and tipping her head back to place a soft, lingering kiss to her lips. "So you did not marry me for my wealth, then?" he whispered, pulling back.

She gave him a stern look, and he chuckled. "No, sir. You know very well I did not."

"Not even for Fynwary Hall?" he asked, playfully narrowing his eyes.

"No, not even for Fynwary Hall," she repeated. "As I told you before, I did not need my old home to make me happy."

And she didn't. Of course, she enjoyed living at Fynwary Hall again, though it was strange returning as the lady of the house. But knowing her children, *their* children, would one day learn to walk, run, and jump through the very corridors she had as a child gave her more joy than she could comprehend.

"I only needed you," she continued. "I would have been happy remaining at Lowena Cottage if need be."

Frederick looked over his shoulder, and Sophia followed his eyes to where the newly thatched roof of the cottage stood up from the cliffside.

"Yes, but I would not have been happy," Frederick teased. "I have grown accustomed to certain comforts in my life. Windows that close, being one of them."

She quirked a brow. "You told me that was repaired."

He pursed his lips. "Very well. It has been. We may move in come tomorrow."

She leaned her head on his shoulder again. "Hmm. I quite like the idea of being the lady of Lowena. But worry not. I shall not make you live there, as much as I do miss my little cottage."

"I would live there for you, my love, if that is what you desired." His soft voice pulled her eyes to his again. "I would do anything for the lady of Lowena."

"I know you would," she whispered.

He bent down, placing a tender kiss upon her lips. As he pulled back and faced the sea, Sophia looped her arms around his. They watched the waves move back and forth along the shore, their hearts as intertwined as their arms.

She knew Frederick would do anything for her, for he had already done *everything* for her.

He had given her new life. New hope. New love. He had removed her mask and loved her for her flaws. He had taught her that perfection was not necessary.

For there was something more beautiful than perfection—and that was two people doing their best to change for the better, to forgive each other's mistakes, and to love unconditionally.

And that was perfect love, indeed.

THE END

AUTHOR'S NOTE

Ever since I wrote "On the Shores of Tregalwen," I've been longing to write Frederick Hawkins's story. That sweet man deserved a happily ever after, especially after all he's been through. Of course his happy ending didn't come easily, what with Sophia Rosewall being an enormous pain.

Can I share a little secret with you, though? Sophia's character has been my favorite to write so far out of all of my books. She was so fun to let loose as she flirted and flaunted. My favorite scene was when she blatantly hinted for the Madderns to open their home to her. It's so delightfully uncomfortable!

Along with these characters, I was thrilled to finally write about Lowena Cottage. Ever since I saw those little houses sparingly scattered along the Cornish cliffside, I knew I wanted to write a story about one. I can only imagine what it would be like to actually live in such a place like Lowena. I wouldn't even mind if the windows were crooked, so long as I had a view of the sea.

If you enjoyed "For the Lady of Lowena," please consider leaving a review. And if you'd like to receive the latest news about my future novels, sign up for my newsletter. I always share newly released and discounted clean romance novels, as well as fun polls, quotes, and giveaways. My newsletter subscribers are also the first to see sneak peeks and cover reveals!

Make sure to follow me on Facebook (for more clean romance deals) and Instagram (for photos of my travels to the UK and more).

I hope to connect with you soon!

Deborah

ACKNOWLEDGMENTS

After going to a writer's conference this past May, I came away renewed, refreshed, and ready to begin my writing journey anew. Before, my full-length novels would take me years to write with countless revisions and rewrites. "For the Lady of Lowena" took me four months. That's quite the difference! Of course, I owe this to the many people who have helped me along the way.

First, Jenny, my lovely editor. I can't tell you what your kind words and support for this book has done for me. Thank you, from the bottom of my heart.

Next, where would I be without my author friends? Especially the ones who helped me polish this book, Joanna Barker and Heidi Kimball. You are the best beta readers a girl could ever ask for. I will be forever grateful to you for sharing your time and talents with me.

A huge, written hug must also go to my sweet friend, Arlem Hawks. Your talent has encouraged me to push harder and do better with my own writing. Thank you for always being there for me and knowing when I need a care package, a listening ear, or a simple, supportive message. You're the best, my friend. The very best. Now hurry up and move closer to me.

Last, I need to thank my wonderful husband. Your kindness has made my life greater than I ever hoped it would be. You continually make my dreams come true. You are my perfect love! Let's go get that cottage in Cornwall.

ABOUT THE AUTHOR

 Deborah M. Hathaway graduated from Utah State University with a BA in English, Creative Writing. As a young girl, she devoured Jane Austen's novels while watching and re-watching every adaptation of Pride & Prejudice she could, entirely captured by all things Regency and romance.

Throughout her early life, she wrote many short stories, poems, and essays, but it was not until after her marriage that she was finally able to complete her first romance novel, attributing the completion to her courtship with, and love of, her charming, English husband. Deborah finds her inspiration for her novels in her everyday experiences with her husband and children and during her travels to the United Kingdom, where she draws on the beauty of the country in such places as Ireland, Yorkshire, and her beloved Cornwall.